Praise for *Riders of the Realm: Across the Dark Water*

"A story with both wings and heart, *Across the Dark Water* is a breathtaking ride into a rich and dangerous world. Animal lovers and thrill-seekers alike will cheer for Echofrost and Rahkki at each of the many twists and turns. Clever, epic, and wildly imaginative!"
—Kamilla Benko, author of *The Unicorn Quest*

"An epic adventure that moves at the speed of flight. Thrilling, compelling, and completely enchanting. I fell in love with the Storm Herd, and one particular winged steed that Pegasus himself would fall for!"
—Kate O'Hearn, author of the international bestselling Pegasus series

"Exhilarating! A well-woven tale full of loyalty, bravery, danger, and love. Readers will be delighted!"
—Lindsay Cummings, *New York Times* bestselling author of the Balance Keepers series

"A riveting, richly imagined epic tale of loyalty, bravery, and friendship that will make your heart (literally!) soar—a pulse-pounding adventure! Jennifer Lynn Alvarez is a true master of her craft."
—Kristen Kittscher, author of *The Wig in the Window* and *The Tiara on the Terrace*

"Getting swept up in Jennifer Lynn Alvarez's rich world of flying steeds, Landwalkers, giants, and spit dragons was the most fun I've had all year. It's like *How to Train Your Dragon* meets *Watership Down*. But with pegasi. A fantastic read!"
—John Kloepfer, author of the Zombie Chasers series and the Galaxy's Most Wanted series

"Honor and courage soar on every page of Jennifer Lynn Alvarez's books!"
—Jenn Reese, author of the Above World trilogy

"A beautiful tale of loyalty, adventure, and bravery. Readers will want to soar through the clouds with Echofrost and befriend kindhearted Rahkki. *Across the Dark Water* is a captivating opener to the Riders of the Realm trilogy."
—Jill Diamond, author of the Lou Lou and Pea series

"Gorgeously detailed and with heart-wrenching conflict,
Across the Dark Water is a breathtaking read sure to please new fans and old.
Jennifer Lynn Alvarez's fantasy world is richly developed with a cast
of characters readers will be sure to love, both winged and human.
I read it as fast as a pegasus can fly and am already longing for more."
—Mindee Arnett, critically acclaimed author of *Onyx & Ivory*

Praise for the Guardian Herd series

"From page one, Jennifer Lynn Alvarez weaves an epic tale
of a doomed black pegasus foal named Star, whose race against time
will lift the reader on the wings of danger and destiny, magic and hope.
It's a world I did not want to leave, and neither will you."
—Peter Lerangis, *New York Times* bestselling author
in the 39 Clues series and of the Seven Wonders series

"Perfect for fans of *Charlotte's Web* and the Guardians of Ga'Hoole series."
—ALA *Booklist*

"Chock-full of adventure and twists, making it difficult to put down.
Readers will be clamoring for the next book."
—*School Library Journal*

"Alvarez's world is lush with description and atmosphere."
—*Publishers Weekly*

"Will prove popular with both animal-lovers and fantasy fans.
A good choice for reluctant readers. The clever resolution will
get kids psyched for more tales from the Guardian Herd."
—ALA *Booklist*

"Filled with fantastical action, and rich with description.
A well-paced and engrossing story. Alvarez has created a series
that will be beloved by readers."
—*VOYA*

RIDERS
of the
REALM

2

THROUGH THE UNTAMED SKY

BY
JENNIFER LYNN ALVAREZ

HARPER
An Imprint of HarperCollinsPublishers

Also by Jennifer Lynn Alvarez

The Guardian Herd: Starfire

The Guardian Herd: Stormbound

The Guardian Herd: Landfall

The Guardian Herd: Windborn

Riders of the Realm 1: Across the Dark Water

Riders of the Realm: Through the Untamed Sky

Text copyright © 2019 by Jennifer Lynn Alvarez

Illustrations copyright © 2019 by David McClellan

All rights reserved. Printed in the United States of America.

No part of this book may be used or reproduced in any manner whatsoever without written permission except in the case of brief quotations embodied in critical articles and reviews. For information address HarperCollins Children's Books, a division of HarperCollins Publishers, 195 Broadway, New York, NY 10007.

www.harpercollinschildrens.com

ISBN 978-0-06-249443-6

Typography by Catherine San Juan

20 21 22 23   PC/BRR   10 9 8 7 6 5 4 3 2

❖

First paperback edition, 2019

FOR EVERY KID WHO WANTS TO FLY
(AND FOR THE ONE WHO DOESN'T),
WISHING YOU WINGS

TABLE OF CONTENTS

"Never dispute your own legend. Let it bloom."

—Brauk Stormrunner

⌒ SANDWEN CLANS ⌒

Humans

BRIM CARVER—animal doctor of the Fifth Clan

KOKO DALE—age fifteen; head groom of the Kihlari stable

MUT FINN—age fifteen; leader of the Sandwen teens, kids too old for games but too young for war

OSSI FINN—caretaker of Brauk Stormrunner. Sister to Mut Finn

WILLA GREEN—Daakuran merchant, operates a tent at the trading post

KASHIK HIGHTOWER—operates a food kiosk at the trading post. Mother to Tuni Hightower. Nickname: Kashi

TUNI HIGHTOWER—Headwind of Dusk Patrol, member of the Fifth Clan Sky Guard. Kihlara mount: Rizah

HARAK NIGHTSEER—Headwind of Day Patrol, member of the Fifth Clan Sky Guard. Kihlara mount: Ilan

JUL RANGER—age fourteen; Meela Swift's apprentice

BRAUK STORMRUNNER—Rahkki's brother, Headwind of Dawn Patrol, member of the Fifth Clan Sky Guard. Kihlara mount: Kol

UNCLE DARTHAN STORMRUNNER—rice farmer of the

Fifth Clan. Uncle to Brauk and Rahkki on their mother's side

RAHKKI STORMRUNNER—age twelve; Rider in the Sky Guard army. Kihlara mount: Sula

REYELLA STORMRUNNER—past queen of the Fifth Clan, supplanted by Lilliam Whitehall; mother of Rahkki and Brauk Stormrunner. Kihlara mount: Drael

MEELA SWIFT—provisional Headwind of Dawn Patrol. Kihlara mount: Jax

GENERAL AKMID TSUN—commander of the Land Guard army

PRINCESS I'LENNA WHITEHALL—age twelve; eldest daughter of Queen Lilliam and Crown Princess of the Fifth Clan. Kihlara mount: Firo

PRINCESS JOR WHITEHALL—age five; youngest daughter of Queen Lilliam

PRINCESS RAYNI WHITEHALL—age eight; middle daughter of Queen Lilliam

QUEEN LILLIAM WHITEHALL—leader of the Fifth Clan, prior princess of the Second Clan. Also referred to as *Queen of the Fifth*. Kihlara mount: Mahrsan

QUEEN TAVARA WHITEHALL—leader of the Second Clan, mother of Lilliam Whitehall

TAMBOR WOODSON—age fifteen; Mut Finn's best friend

Places

DAAKURAN EMPIRE—across the bay from the Sandwen
Realm is the empire, a highly populated land of commerce,
academics, and magic. Common language of the empire:
Talu

SANDWEN CLANS—seven clans of people founded by
the Seven Sisters, each ruled by a monarch queen. Clan
language: Sandwen

Sandwen Clan Divinities

GRANAK—"Father of Dragons," guardian mascot of the
Fifth Clan. Sixteen-foot-tall, thirty-three-foot-long
drooling lizard called a *spit dragon*

KAJI (sing.), **KAJIES** (pl.)—troublesome or playful spirits

THE SEVEN SISTERS—the royal founders of the seven
Sandwen clans

SULA—"Mother of Serpents," guardian mascot of the Second
Clan. Forty-two-foot jungle python

SUNCHASER—the moon

❦ KIHLARI ❦

(KEE-lar-ee) (pl.), Kihlara (sing.)
Translation: "Children of the Wind"

Tame pegasi of the Sandwen Clans

DRAEL—Queen Reyella's Chosen stallion. Small bay with black-tipped dark-amber feathers, fluffy black mane and tail, white muzzle, four white socks

ILAN—white stallion with black spots, black mane and tail, dark-silver wings edged in black

KOL—shiny chestnut stallion with bright-yellow feathers, yellow-streaked red mane and tail, white blaze, two white hind socks

MAHRSAN—Queen Lilliam's Chosen stallion. Blood-bay with sapphire-blue feathers edged in white, black mane and tail, jagged white blaze, four white socks

RIZAH—golden palomino pinto mare with dark-pink feathers edged in gold, white-and-gold mixed mane and tail

JAX—gold dun stallion, dark-orange wings at the mantle changing to midnight-blue toward the ends, black mane and tail, white snip on muzzle

⸎ STORM HERD ⸎

Wild pegasi from Anok

DEWBERRY—bay pinto mare with emerald feathers, black
   mane and tail, thin blaze on forehead, two white hind
   anklets

ECHOFROST—sleek silver mare with a mix of dark- and
   light-purple feathers, white mane and tail, one white sock

GRAYSTONE—white stallion with pale-yellow feathers each
   with a silver center, blue eyes, silver mane and tail

HAZELWIND—buckskin stallion with jade feathers, black
   mane and tail, big white blaze, two white hind socks

REDFIRE—tall copper chestnut stallion with dark-gold
   feathers, dark-red mane and tail, white star on forehead

SHYSONG—blue roan mare with dusty-blue feathers edged
   in black, ice-blue eyes, black mane and tail, jagged blaze,
   two hind socks

ᘓᕽ GORLAN HORDES ᕽᘓ

Giant Folk

Living in the mountains in three separate hordes—
Highland Horde, Fire Horde, and Great Cave Horde. They
stand from eleven to fourteen feet tall. All have red hair,
pale skin, and a double set of tusks. Language: Gorlish, a
form of sign language

RIDERS

of the

REALM

2

THROUGH THE UNTAMED SKY

SANDWEN

Darthan's Farm

Mill

Beach

Jungle

Barn

Rice Fields

Brim's Hut

Fallows

FIFTH CLAN

Ruk

Horse Pasture

Farmland

Horse Arena

Kihlari Training Yard

Supply Barn

Jungle

Fort Prowl

Kihlari Barn

Rain Forest

Leshi Creek

Sandwen Clan Travelways

FOURTH CLAN

SIXTH CLAN

River Tsallan

Lake

To the THIRD CLAN

Southern Mountains

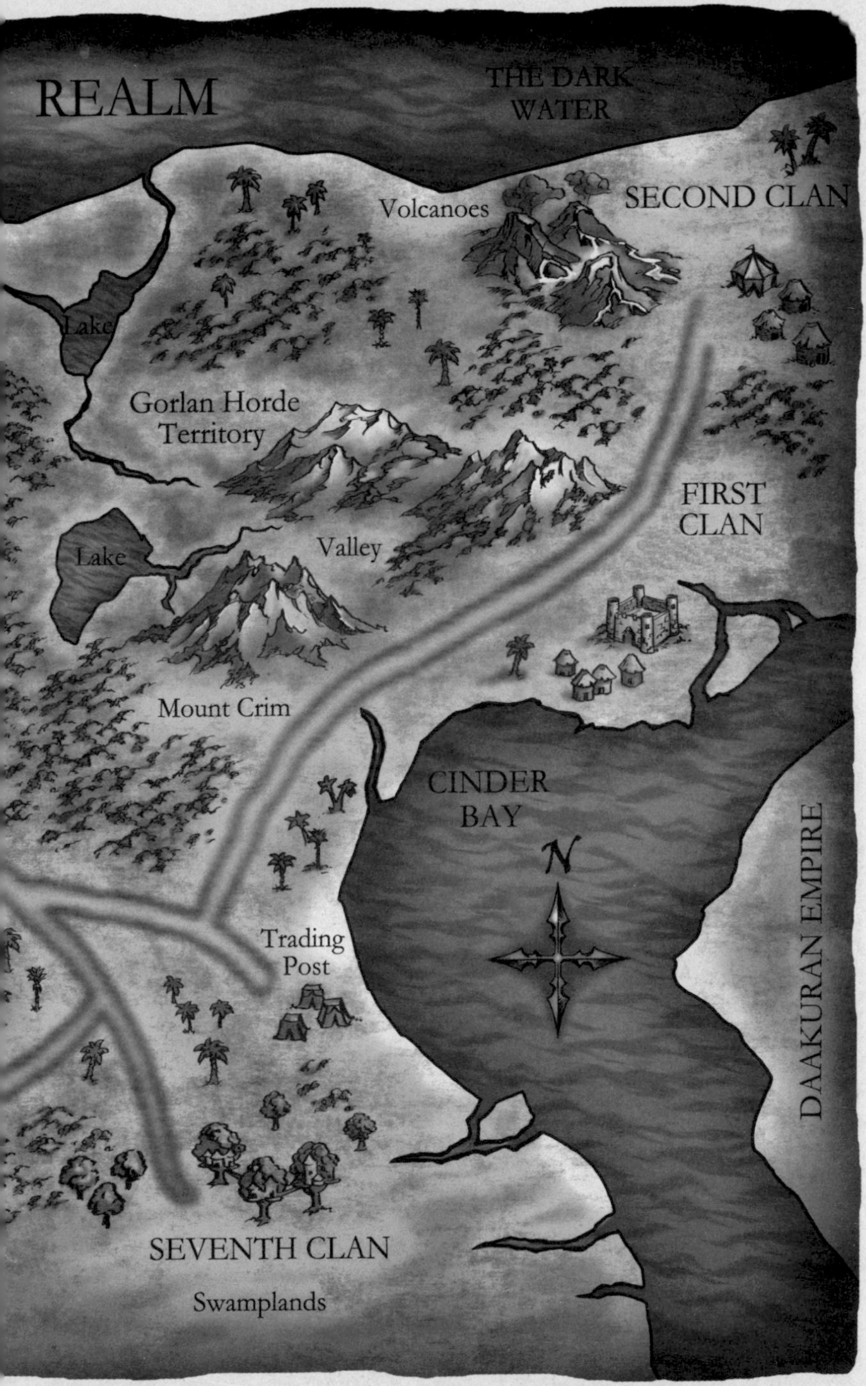

REALM

THE DARK WATER

Volcanoes

SECOND CLAN

Lake

Gorlan Horde
Territory

Lake

Valley

FIRST
CLAN

Mount Crim

CINDER
BAY

N

DAAKURAN EMPIRE

Trading
Post

SEVENTH CLAN

Swamplands

SNOW HERD

Two Lakes

Vein

Crabwing's Bay

Cave

The Drink

Cliffs

Sky Meadow

GREAT SEA

Big Sky
Lake

Grandmother
Tree

Coast of Anok

SUN HERD

Dawn Meadow

Northern
Nests

Vein

TERRITORY
of LANDWALKERS

Vein

JUNGLE
HERD

N

"Firemouth"
Volcano Swamps

Valley of
Tears

Wing River

Southern
Nests

Cave

Mavelyn

Road

Ice Lands

Hoofbeat Mountains

Ice Caves

The Trap

WESTERN ANOK

Blue Mountains

Black Lake

Wastelands

Canyon Meadow

Interior of Anok

MOUNTAIN HERD

Vein

Canyons

Vein

Tail River

Lower Grasslands

Valley Field

Feather Lake

DESERT HERD

Cloud Forest

Red Rock Mountains

Turtle Beach

SEA of RAIN

Vein

RIDERS
⌁ of the ⌁
REALM

⌁ 2 ⌁

THROUGH THE UNTAMED SKY

1

THE RETURN

ECHOFROST FOLDED HER WINGS AND PRANCED anxiously in the center of the horse arena. Steam curled off her sweat-soaked hide, a loose tether hung around her neck, and an unconscious boy lay at her hooves. She'd just landed from a flight, and Rahkki Stormrunner had slid off her back, jarred free by the hard touchdown. The silver mare arched her neck and braced herself as the Sandwen people stalked toward her.

"Is he dead?" asked one Rider to another.

"That mare's too wild. She should be put down," said another.

Echofrost flicked her ears, listening but unable to understand their language. Beyond the arena, a breeze whipped through the rain forest, causing the lush foliage to crash and sway.

As the Sandwens crept closer, Echofrost tucked in her end feathers, trying to appear smaller, less threatening. This clan had captured her a moon ago and tried to tame her. Yesterday she'd kicked one of them, and today she'd returned from a botched escape attempt with a Sandwen boy who now appeared dead. She didn't blame the Landwalkers for their mistrust. Her feathers rattled defiantly, and her jaw tightened. She had to remind herself that she'd *chosen* to return here. But for a good reason.

Harak Nightseer, a Headwind in the Sky Guard army, swooped down from the clouds upon his stallion, Ilan, and landed in the arena. He leaped off his mount, flung back his yellow hair, and prodded Rahkki's body with a branch-scarred boot. "Sula's killed the boy, yeah, just like she killed his brother." He threw a hot stare at Echofrost, whose Sandwen name was Sula.

Tuni Hightower, who was also a Headwind, shoved through the crowd and shouldered Harak out of the way. "Stop spreading rumors," she grumbled. "Brauk's not dead and neither is Rahkki."

"Not yet," the Rider spat back. "That mare is dangerous, yeah? She doesn't belong in the Sky Guard."

"Rahkki won her, and he'll train her," Tuni replied.

Harak snorted. "We'll see about that."

The boy in question groaned and opened his eyes, spitting sand. His people and the visiting Sandwen clans loomed closer still, and Echofrost flinched away from them.

"Give him space." Tuni waved off the people, squatted, and pressed the back of her hand to Rahkki's forehead. "Welcome back, Sunchaser," she said quietly.

"I won Sula?" Rahkki asked his friend.

"You flew her farther than you needed to, but yes, you won the contest." Tuni smiled, her brows pinched with worry.

Echofrost pricked her ears, wondering what they were saying. Rahkki rubbed his head and winced when his blood-striped hands touched his scalp. He'd held on to Echofrost's mane so tightly during their flight that her thick hairs had sliced into his palms, but still he'd fallen off her. She'd swooped down and caught him on her back; otherwise the boy would be dead.

"What happened?" he asked, rising to his knees. "Where's my tunic?"

A man leaned over Rahkki, and Echofrost recognized him as the auctioneer for the Clan Gathering winged-horse sale. "I don't know *how* you did it, but you completed the challenge," the man said. "Sula is yours. Congratulations."

Rahkki peered up at the man, then at the sky, and Echofrost followed his gaze. Queen Lilliam, the leader of Rahkki's clan, hovered above them on her stallion, Mahrsan. Her light robe hugged her pregnant belly, and her dark-blue eyes bored into Echofrost's, bright with fury. The queen had believed Rahkki would fail to ride her and that he'd lose the contest. Echofrost felt grim satisfaction to have spoiled those plans.

She inhaled a deep breath, still shocked that she'd returned to this place so soon after escaping. Echofrost and her friend Shysong had fled earlier today, but they had come back to the clan for a reason. A horde of giants had captured their waiting herd, and now they could not leave this continent and find a new home for Storm Herd until all the steeds were freed.

And since two pegasi could not battle more than six hundred giants alone, Echofrost was now counting on the Sandwens to rescue her friends. Pegasi were sacred to them, and over a hundred had been captured. They would help—they had to! They were Storm Herd's only chance.

Fresh sorrow drenched her heart at the memory of

Gorlan elephants dragging her best friend, Hazelwind, through the towering palms like an unruly dog. He'd bucked and strained against the rope around his throat, his neck flat, his jade-colored wings beating uselessly. She'd just forgiven him after a long and stupid fight that was all her fault, and now they were separated again.

And Dewberry, the pregnant battle mare, had also been leashed like an animal. Dewberry's belly had blossomed since arriving here, but the rest of her body had thinned from stress. Her unborn foal—the last living link to Echofrost's twin brother, Bumblewind—was in grave danger.

Echofrost nudged Rahkki with her muzzle. "Sula," he whispered, a weak grin on his face.

She pawed the sand, wondering what sort of Pair they would make in battle. They'd had their first flight together today, and it had terrified the cub, his fear of heights paralyzing him. She knew he didn't want to be a Rider, no more than she wanted to be a Flier, and she nickered, bemused. Perhaps *that* made them the perfect Pair.

Outside the horse arena, spectators began hollering at Rahkki. She recognized his name.

Rahkki Stormrunner, I knew he could tame her!

All he did was hang on! That mare's still wild.

Yeah? Then how'd he get her to fly back here?

Is he even twelve? I thought the contestants had to be twelve.

The yelling upset Echofrost, and she whinnied for her friend Shysong. The mare had been led away by her new owner, Princess I'Lenna. The girl had named the roan Firo and moved her to her bedroom, and Echofrost hated being separated from her. They'd fled their dangerous homeland a moon ago, hoping to settle Storm Herd on safer shores. But soon after arriving, the Fifth Clan Sky Guard had captured Shysong.

Echofrost had allowed them to capture her too, thinking she'd infiltrate the clan and free her friend—but the Sandwens had chopped off her flight feathers. The horror of it stabbed her anew. A full moon had passed before the cut feathers had grown long enough for her to fly again, and during that time she'd lived side by side with Shysong in the Kihlari barn.

Echofrost snorted. Her mission to live free in a new land had failed miserably. She shoved her muzzle toward Rahkki, feeling impatient.

"What's wrong?" he whispered, still collecting his bearings.

Echofrost pawed harder, digging holes in the sand.

She had flown Rahkki close enough to the giants for him to see that Storm Herd was captured. When was he going to tell his people?

The silver pegasus lifted her head, studying the Sandwen village, the fortress, the Kihlari training yard— all of it surrounded by the chaotic jungle. No, she hadn't failed, not yet. The Sandwens were as fierce as pegasi. They could fight the giants and free Storm Herd, and now she belonged to one of them. She swallowed her fears of being ridden, controlled, and tamed, and bent her head toward her future—the young boy at her hooves: Rahkki Stormrunner.

2

WINNER

RAHKKI REACHED FOR SULA'S REINS, CRINGING.
The silver mare didn't like to be controlled, but to his
surprise, she let him take the dangling leathers into his
palms.

The crowd began to disperse, shaking their heads. The
show was over, but Rahkki still felt disoriented. "I'Lenna?"
he called, looking around. The princess had been with him
on his wild flight through the jungle.

"She's okay, Rahkki," Tuni answered. "Just a bit
branch-torn, like you."

"But *where* is she?" he asked.

"The queen sent her and Firo back to Fort Prowl as

soon as the mares landed. Lilliam is not pleased. Where did you take her daughter?"

"The wild mares took *us*!" he sputtered. "We had no control over them." Rahkki remembered sliding off the mare and plummeting from the clouds, his cheeks flapping and the wind shoving down his throat.

"Shh," Tuni warned. "I wouldn't shout that too loudly. You're going to be a Rider in the Sky Guard now, a warrior. You don't want people thinking you can't pilot your Flier."

"But I *can't*." Rahkki brushed the dust off his worn leather trousers. "And I don't want to be a Rider. Uncle needs me on the farm." He groaned. "I wasn't thinking when I entered the contest." He eyed the silver mare he'd won, his gaze sweeping up her four strong legs to her muscled chest, long arched neck, and salt-white mane, and then coming to rest on her chiseled face. She flexed her wings, ruffling the deep-purple feathers that lightened toward her wingtips. "I just wanted to save Sula from the queen. If no one could ride her, Lilliam was going to feed her to the dragon."

Tuni frowned and lowered her voice even more. "I know you care for this wildling," she said. "But this isn't a game,

Rahkki. You won a Flier, not a pet. Sula was selected as a warrior, and you can't change that. You have to join the Sky Guard. You have no choice."

"But Uncle Darthan?"

"Ha!" Tuni laughed. "Your uncle bet the queen two full rounds—at odds of twenty to one—that you could fly that mare to the clouds and back, and you did it. He's just fleeced the queen out of a fortune."

Rahkki gulped. Now he knew why Queen Lilliam had been staring at his mare with such putrid anger. "But I didn't expect to win."

Tuni continued. "Doesn't matter. Your uncle can afford proper workers now, Rahkki. He doesn't need a halfhearted apprentice. Don't worry about Darthan."

"But—"

"It's done. Accept it. The Pairing ceremony is tomorrow."

Rahkki dropped his gaze to the sand floor of the arena. He didn't want to be a Rider. It wasn't that he was afraid of the Gorlan hordes—the merciless giants that raided his clan—and it wasn't that he was squeamish about war. It was the *flying*.

Sula had been quick and nimble in the sky; rising and turning so fast that Rahkki's gut had rolled like a marble on a rocking boat. Even now, the solid ground beneath him seemed to sway and whirl. Only his older brother, Brauk, knew the truth: Rahkki was afraid of heights.

"Let's get you into the shade," Tuni said, encouraging Rahkki and Sula to exit the arena.

"Wait!" Rahkki suddenly remembered why Sula had returned after first abandoning him in a huge tree nest— her wild herd had been captured by the Highland Horde. "I SAW GIANTS!" he shouted to his clanmates.

Everyone turned toward him at the mention of the giants; soldiers spat on the ground. "Where?" Tuni asked, her jaw tight. "Are you sure?"

Queen Lilliam also heard Rahkki's cry. She kicked her steed around and glided back to him. "Did you say *giants*?"

"Yes," he answered, suddenly breathless. It all came back to him now. "They were heading to Mount Crim, and they had her wild herd—over a hundred of them— tethered to elephants." He pointed at Sula. "Her friends are captured."

Lilliam called for the Fifth Clan Borla. He was not only the clan's healer, but also Lilliam's most trusted adviser. He oversaw the sacrifices to the clan mascot, read omens, and made predictions. When he emerged from his shade tent, she scolded him. "Your vision came true, except you said the giants would capture *our* trained Fliers. You didn't mention the wild Kihlari."

His body jolted; his mouth gaped open. "I—I saw winged steeds. I didn't—"

"If I'd known our Fliers were safe, I would have attacked the hordes and prevented the raid that destroyed our hay barn." Lilliam's blue eyes flickered dangerously. The Borla stared at his sandals, his face blazing red.

Disgusted, Lilliam turned back to Rahkki. "Did my daughter observe the captured steeds?"

"She did, my queen."

Lilliam paused, thinking. "I want to hear more." She glared at Sula. "Tomorrow, after you're Paired with that wilding, you will come to my command chamber and give a full report. This is your first assignment as a Sky Guard Rider. Do you understand?"

Rahkki nodded. "I understand, my queen."

She curled her lip. "And when you approach me, make certain you are clean."

Rahkki nodded again, acutely aware of his filthy, vomit-soaked clothing.

Lilliam, the clan Borla, and the Land Guard army left to feed the clan guardian, Granak, the Father of Dragons.

Each clan claimed a different mascot, and the queens fed their respective beasts live animals to keep them content, then stared at the gnawed bones as if their futures were written in them. A well-fed guardian brought good tidings and abundant harvests. A hungry or angry beast brought destruction, and Rahkki couldn't imagine how Queen Lilliam would handle an omen that adverse.

He turned to Sula. His mare whinnied, still anxious, and now Rahkki knew why. She was worried about her friends. "I want to free them too," he whispered as he led her to the Kihlari stable where the Sandwen winged Fliers lived. Tomorrow they would be Paired, and Rahkki's very short, and very boring, term as a rice farmer's apprentice would officially be over.

3

ECHOFROST

ECHOFROST TROTTED BEHIND RAHKKI AS HE LED
her from the horse arena to the Kihlari stable. The Landwalkers gawked, giving them a wide berth. The boy
walked unsteadily, and she slowed so as not to crowd him.

They passed the low hillside where most of Rahkki's
people had built their stone huts. White smoke puffed from
chimneys that jutted from thatched roofs, and the scent of
cooked meat filled the air, mixing with the tang of sea
brine that wafted from the ocean in the north. Goats, pigs,
chickens, and rabbits lived in small enclosures attached
to the huts; and freshly scraped animal hides dried in the
sun.

At the hillside's peak loomed Fort Prowl, the eight-sided

fortress that housed the Fifth Clan queen, her three princess daughters, the Borla, wealthy merchants, soldiers, and the elite Sky Guard Riders. Steps descended from the fortress toward the Kihlari stable and training yard. That's where Echofrost had lived for the last moon, and where Rahkki was taking her now.

Pastures, more animal pens, and the farmlands that the Fifth Clan and the Gorlan hordes had been battling over for a thousand years spread across the tree-cleared valley below the hill.

Echofrost drew a hard breath at the sight of it all. Living with Landwalkers was terrifying. They were weak, hairless, thin, and slow, so they harnessed beasts to become their muscles, legs, teeth, claws, and wings. Their ingenuity made them the most powerful creatures in the jungle, even giving them advantages over the Gorlan giants, who outstripped them in size and strength. But would their cleverness be enough to free Storm Herd? Echofrost hoped so.

They entered the Kihlari stable, where scores of tame pegasi lived in individual stalls. Several steeds nickered greetings to Echofrost. The rest ignored her.

Koko Dale, the head groom of the stable, ambled toward them. "Sun an' stars, Rahkki, yur a Rider now," she said, shaking her chin-length blond hair.

"Almost," he answered. "The Pairing is tomorrow."

A young groom caught Koko's attention. "No! That ain'
'ow yuh tie a knot." She plowed toward the girl without a
backward glance at Rahkki and Echofrost.

He continued on toward Echofrost's stall, and when
Rahkki opened the door, Echofrost entered automatically,
out of the habit instilled in her over the last moon of her
captivity.

"I know why you let me win you, Sula," Rahkki said.
"You need my help to save your friends. And I will help
you!"

The boy's skin was pale, and he shivered like an over-
shocked foal. *The fall off my back really affected him*, she
thought, and her heart beat faster remembering it: his
pleading eyes, his grasping hands and kicking legs. The
desire to save him had surprised her. This cub she'd once
vowed to kill—how had he wormed his way into her heart?
She stamped her hoof, frustrated but glad, because now
she needed him.

"I was going to free you, you know, if I won the contest."
His eyes shifted to her open stall door, and her standing
obediently inside it. "But I see you're here to stay, at least
for a while."

He removed her halter, exhaling softly, and his sweat-tinged scent wafted toward her. She flared her nostrils, drinking in his essence and memorizing it, as if he were her own foal. This cub had battled giants for her, stood up to the queen, and flown her into the sky despite his obvious fear of heights. She didn't know why he did these things (nor did he do them very well), but she trusted him as much as she could trust any Landwalker.

"See you tomorrow," he said, his golden eyes beaming. "The Pairing ceremony will be scary, Sula, but don't be afraid. I'll be with you."

She flicked her ears as he limped out of the stable and then glared at the four walls surrounding her. Old, dry hay lay at her hooves, and a bucket of stale water gathered mosquitoes in the corner. The stable ceiling blocked her view of the sky, and its walls blocked fresh wind from flowing through her mane and tail. Familiar repulsion filled Echofrost. She'd rather graze in the dangerous jungle than eat hay in the safety of a stall, but she was Sula of the Fifth Clan now. She had to accept that.

A mare nickered from the stall to her right. "Echofrost!"

"Shysong?" Echofrost flipped over her water bucket and stepped onto it with her front hooves. She spied her roan friend over the wall that divided them. "I thought you lived with the princess now."

Shysong angled her head to better see Echofrost. "I'Lenna brought me here so that Koko could treat my scratches."

"Were you badly hurt?" The two mares had led the Sky Guard on a fast chase through the woods after they took off with Rahkki and the princess, and scores of tree branches had ripped at their hides.

"Just a few scrapes," Shysong answered.

"Our friends are in worse shape," Echofrost nickered. "Graystone was bleeding, and Redfire lost a chunk of mane—but I only got a quick glimpse of them."

"It's Dewberry I'm worried about." Shysong batted at hungry mosquitoes with her tail. "She looks so tired and thin."

Echofrost's heart thumped. "Dewberry is strong. Bumblewind's foal could not have a better dam." Her twin brother had died in their homeland during the rebellion against Nightwing the Destroyer—the supernatural black pegasus stallion who had woken from sleep to enslave the five herds of Anok. And Bumblewind's unborn foal deserved the future he had fought to protect—a future where pegasi lived free.

A rustling noise disturbed their conversation, and then Kol, the shiny Kihlara stallion who lived in the stall next to Echofrost's, forced his head over the wall that divided them. "What are you doing here, Sula?" His eyes were swollen, his jaw hung slack. "Who won you?"

Echofrost recoiled. She'd severely injured Kol's Rider, Brauk Stormrunner, at the winged-horse auction, and Kol had hoped Echofrost would be sold to another clan, but that had not happened. "Rahkki won me," she answered.

The chestnut stamped his hoof. "One brother isn't enough. You have to kill the other too?"

"I didn't *kill* Brauk," she whinnied. But Echofrost had heard Brauk's spine crack and seen the pallor of his sun-tanned skin when she'd accidentally kicked him. Brauk could still die of his injuries or perhaps never fully recover from them, and Kol was furious. No, he was *devastated*. If Brauk failed to heal, Kol's life as a Kihlara Flier was over. He would be sent to the Ruk to sire foals. He would become a Half.

But she faced Kol because it *had* been an accident. Headwind Harak Nightseer had been striking her with a whip. He'd *deserved* the kick. It wasn't her fault Brauk had saved the man by intercepting the blow. "You know I didn't hurt Brauk on purpose," she nickered to the chestnut. "My target was Harak."

Kol flared his yellow wings and reared. "You don't kick people in the Fifth Clan, Sula. Not ever! For any reason!"

Echofrost pinned her ears. The Kihlari steeds adored the Landwalkers, and she didn't understand it. The clan kept the flying horses locked in barns and rode on their backs. Only Rahkki Stormrunner understood that she, Echofrost, did not want to be tamed.

As if reading her mind, Kol ruffled his feathers and said, "You don't deserve that boy."

Rizah, the golden pinto who belonged to Tuni Hightower, whinnied to Echofrost from across the barn aisle. "Is it true that the giants caught your friends?"

"Yes," Echofrost answered, welcoming the interruption. "They used those little dragons, the *burners*, to drive them into a trap. What's going to happen to them?"

"How many steeds are in your herd?" she asked.

"Over a hundred," Shysong answered.

Rizah considered this. "The giants can't eat that many Kihlari at once. It's possible they took your herd to bargain for the lowland valleys that our clan stole from them years ago."

"If that's true, then they won't hurt them," Echofrost said, hope blossoming.

Rizah snorted. "They're giants. Don't expect mercy."

Echofrost's heart tumbled. "The queen will send us to save them, right?"

"Ah, I see," Kol snapped. "You're using that boy to save your friends." He leaned against the wall. "Do you really think Rahkki Stormrunner is a fighter? Or a good pilot?" Kol tossed his sun-streaked red mane. "He's ridden on my back with his brother, so I know his secret. I can smell it. Rahkki's afraid of heights. And he can't fight. He won't survive a battle with giants. You might as well Pair with a monkey."

"I—"

"Don't say it," Kol rasped. "I already know that you haven't considered any of this. You think about yourself and your friends, that's it. The rest of us don't matter to you."

She closed her mouth and stared down at the straw. Kol was right. She hadn't given much thought to Rahkki. Not once. He'd risked his life to get her to fresh water and grass, fought giants, stood up to the queen, and tried to free her—but she hadn't considered the fact that he was safer *without* her.

Kol turned away, revolted.

Echofrost whinnied to Rizah. "What will happen at the Pairing?"

"It's best you just experience it," Rizah nickered back. "It . . . it's just easier that way."

Echofrost stomped her hoof. These Kihlari steeds lacked the straightforward speech of the pegasi in Anok.

"But after the ceremony, you'll be one of us, Sula—a Flier in the Sky Guard," Rizah continued. "When we're out there, fighting or flying, we watch out for one another. We're an army, a team—a *herd* if you like. You'll do *whatever* your Rider commands you to do, understand? And you *will* follow the Headwind of your patrol." Rizah flared her wings. "I know you think we're soft. You're wrong."

Echofrost watched Rizah's vein pulse down her throat. The way she pranced and rattled her feathers, she could have been a lead mare in Anok. "I hear you," Echofrost affirmed. But the ceremony meant nothing to her. The bond was a Sandwen commitment, and she only had to honor it until her friends were free, and then she'd break it.

But breaking it would leave Rahkki a Half.

The silver mare clamped down her tail. What happened to Rahkki after she left wasn't her problem.

Echofrost glanced around the stable. The Kihlari

steeds glittered in their stalls, glossed, polished, and brushed to gleaming perfection. Their manes and tails hung straight, free of burrs and as fine as spider silk, but these tame steeds put too much stock in looks. It was *heart* that made a pegasus shine—not hair and bones and pretty adornments.

The Kihlari didn't believe it yet, but Echofrost was sure they were the descendants of the lost Lake Herd pegasi. That herd had fled Anok during the first reign of Nightwing four hundred years earlier; but they hadn't passed down their legends, and most of their history had been lost. So their descendants, the tame Kihlari, did not know about Nightwing the Destroyer, and they couldn't remember what it felt like to live free.

Their culture had been absorbed and diluted by the Sandwen clans until it was gone. And worst of all, the Kihlari didn't care. They didn't miss being wild. Echofrost tossed her head. She had to free Storm Herd and get them off this blasted continent, and she'd take as many of these lost steeds with her as she could convince to come.

4

I'LENNA

UPON EXITING THE BARN, THE HOT SUN BLINDED Rahkki and scorched his bare skin. He needed to fetch a new tunic for himself, but first he stopped by Brim Carver's shed to visit his brother. When Rahkki arrived, the animal healer informed him Brauk was sleeping. "I can't risk moving him, not yet, so I'm giving him medicine to keep him asleep," Brim said. "Come back tomorrow."

"Is he any better?" Rahkki asked. "Will he walk again?"

Brim clasped her wrinkled hands. "It's much too early to know. If you want to help him, he could use some fresh clothing." Her kind blue eyes, bright as water, soothed Rahkki. The Stormrunner family trusted Brim, which was why they'd asked her to help Brauk. They did not trust Queen Lilliam's healer, the Borla. He'd once refused to treat Rahkki after Lilliam's guards had beaten him.

Pondering this, Rahkki promised Brim he'd return after the Pairing ceremony the following day. She packed him a calming tea and several packets of salve for his injured hands.

"I can't pay you," Rahkki said, flushing.

Brim hugged him and quickly let go. "I don't take payment for humans, remember?" Then she turned around and began dicing roots and herbs on her countertop, gently dismissing him.

Rahkki headed to the fortress to gather the extra clothes for Brauk. Picking up his pace, he passed the Ruk. Inside lived the Kihlari breeding stock, and he could hear the mares nickering to their new crop of foals. He longed to see the colts and fillies, but they were only allowed out once per day until they were weaned. Next, Rahkki came upon the Kihlari training yard.

On any given day, the yard was a thunderous hive of activity. Fliers crisscrossed the sky and trotted overland with their grooms. Riders filled the shade tables, betting on their fighting beetles, playing stones, or snacking on figs and dried meat. But today silence fell on the Riders as he strode past, and only the steady whirring of insect wings filled Rahkki's ears.

While the clan had loved Rahkki's mother, Reyella Stormrunner, the late queen of the Fifth Clan, no one knew how to treat her bloodborn sons. Their presence fanned the clan's guilt at failing to protect Reyella, their frustration with the new queen, and their fury that Clan Law had forced them to accept her. Over time, the orphan boys had become akin to Halves. Folks avoided them as if their bad luck were contagious, especially Rahkki, who was quiet and less outgoing than Brauk. And now he was to become a Rider, and he imagined that worried the warriors.

Rahkki bent his head and hurried toward the steps cut into the hillside that led to Fort Prowl. Upon reaching the top, he spoke his credentials to the guards. "Rahkki Stormrunner, here on behalf of Headwind Brauk Stormrunner."

The guards nodded and allowed him through the small gate. Rahkki traipsed across the courtyard to the northwest tower and climbed the circular staircase to the twelfth room, Brauk's quarters. He entered, locked the door, and fell onto his brother's cot. The small stone-carved room also held a dresser, a table, a window overlooking the courtyard, a larder for storing food, and a small hearth. Rahkki pulled on one of Brauk's old tunics, shut his eyes, and quickly fell asleep.

What seemed only a moment later, a scuffling noise awoke him. Rahkki jolted upright. "Hey!" He recognized Princess I'Lenna, standing near his hearth, a dagger strapped to her hip. "How did you get in here?"

I'Lenna's mother had assassinated Rahkki's mother in order to become the Queen of the Fifth, and Rahkki had avoided the Whitehall family for most of his life. But since their clan had captured the wild Kihlari steeds, he and the eldest princess had formed a fragile bond over their mutual love for the foreign brayas. Still, her sudden and unexpected appearance at his bedside worried him.

I'Lenna settled her wide dark-brown eyes on Rahkki, grinned, and flopped onto a chair. "Hello to you too, Stormrunner."

Rahkki relaxed his guard. He'd last spoken to I'Lenna this morning, during their flight on the wild mares. She'd been sweat-soaked and rumpled, her dress torn, one sandal lost. Now her long hair was coiled and shining, her scratches gleamed with a dressing of salve, her fine silk dress appeared brand-new, and she'd strapped gilded sandals around her neatly oiled feet. "Are you in trouble?"

Rahkki asked her. "Tuni told me your mom isn't pleased."

The princess scoffed and waved her hand. "I'm always in trouble." She pointed at Brauk's supply of pineapples and bananas. "That fruit's rotten, you know." Before Rahkki could comment, she added. "Are you all right? You landed hard on Sula's back."

He blinked, remembering the pain when his body had slammed into her spine. "I still can't believe she caught me," he said. "I guess it's because she needs me now."

"Ah, Rahkki, it's more than that. Sula *likes* you."

He shrugged. "Maybe, but she also needs me. She and Firo showed us the captured wild herd on purpose, so we'd save them."

I'Lenna grinned. "I know, and we will. They're too valuable to abandon."

"You mean too *sacred*."

I'Lenna shook her long, sun-streaked hair. "No, I mean valuable. My mom is already talking about selling them."

"Sell them! Why not set them free?"

I'Lenna swatted at the fruit flies swarming the table. "If I were the queen, I'd set them free." Then she snapped her eyes toward his. "Not that I want to be queen. I don't."

Rahkki grabbed a chair beside her, and without either of them wishing it, their awful past reared between them as it sometimes did, and tension stiffened their bodies. But as quickly as it arrived, the tension passed and morphed into a staring contest. I'Lenna's lips twitched into a smile and Rahkki tried not to laugh. When she made her eyes cross toward her nose, he finally blinked. "I win," she gloated.

"So how did you get in here?" Rahkki asked. "Did you use the fireplace?" He rose and examined the stone-work, the back wall, and the mantel. "I still can't find an opening!"

"Well, it's there," she replied, "and I can't exactly go through your *front* door now, can I? How else am I sup-posed to visit?" Under her breath she added, "My mother would kill me if she knew I was here."

"Then why come at all?" Rahkki asked. I'Lenna's mother didn't trust Rahkki and Brauk, the children of her slain predecessor, and Harak Nightseer had warned Rah-kki to stay away from the princess.

"Oh." I'Lenna blushed and stood up. "You want me to leave?"

"Sun and stars, no!" Rahkki grabbed her hand, and just as quickly let it go. "You're like . . . my only friend."

I'Lenna wiggled contentedly back into her chair. "You're my only friend too. You and Firo." Her eyes grew dreamy at the mention of her new pet.

Rahkki glanced at his fireplace. "Will you show me the tunnels?" he blurted.

I'Lenna narrowed her eyes. "Is this about your mother? Do you still think she escaped from my mother through a fireplace?"

"Yeah, but you don't have to help me search, just let me in there. Please." Although Rahkki's mind had blocked out most of that awful night when his mother died, a memory had recently surfaced. After he and his brother had escaped Lilliam aboard Drael, their mother's winged stallion, Rahkki remembered watching Reyella Stormrunner vanish into a fireplace. Brauk hadn't seen it, and, eight years later, he still didn't believe it, but Rahkki hoped his mother was alive.

I'Lenna considered Rahkki for a long while. "You know I shouldn't help you, not while my mother is queen."

"I know," he said. "I—I just have to look for myself, to know I'm not crazy. Please, I'Lenna, do it for me."

They locked eyes. Rahkki knew he shouldn't pressure I'Lenna, but he couldn't stop himself. Finally, she caved, shrugging one shoulder. "All right, I guess it can't hurt to look, but I don't know what you expect to find. The lower tunnels flood each monsoon season. Any evidence of your mom's escape will have been washed away by now. I've used the tunnels for years and haven't found any sign of your mom." I'Lenna stood. "Come on, let's go."

Rahkki's heart thudded. "Right now? Really?"

She smirked. "Does a Borla heal people?"

"Not our Borla."

"Does a dragon drool?"

"Not a dead dragon."

"Rahkki!"

He leaped up and hugged her. "Thank you."

She wrinkled her nose. "You need a bath."

He leaned back, elated. Perhaps he would finally learn something about his mother's disappearance. "Let me grab Brauk's things first." Rahkki rustled through Brauk's dresser, choosing a fresh tunic and trousers, undergarments, and Brauk's favorite nightdress, and then he packed them into his satchel.

"Close your eyes," I'Lenna said when he was finished. He did, and heard a soft click, a whoosh of air, and then silence. "You can open them now."

The back wall of his fireplace had hinged open, and Rahkki's heart clenched. *He wasn't crazy. It* was *possible his mother had disappeared into a fireplace. Maybe now his brother and uncle would believe him.*

5

THE TUNNELS

RAHKKI PEERED THROUGH THE SECRET FIREPLACE door. Beyond it, he spied a dark passageway that angled downward and smelled of mold.

"It's slippery," I'Lenna warned. "The rainwater leeches through the stone and makes everything wet."

She tugged on Rahkki's hand, pulling him into the tunnels. If she noticed that his palms were damp with sweat, she didn't care, and happiness filled Rahkki's body. Every moment he spent with I'Lenna was fun.

She pushed the fireplace door closed behind them, leaving them in darkness. "You have to feel your way since I didn't bring a candle or a lamp," she instructed. "Follow my voice and walk slowly. If we keep heading downward, we'll eventually reach an exit. There are three, and each ends in a drainage grate that leads out to the jungle."

"How many tunnels are there?"

"You can't count them," she said. "It's a maze. Easy to get lost."

"So can we travel anywhere in the fortress?"

"Almost," she replied. "Not every fireplace has a false door, so not every room is accessible."

"How did you find out about these tunnels? Why are they here?"

She paused, and Rahkki sensed reluctance, but then she answered. "In the case of a siege, the Fifth Clan queens use them to escape, that's why they're kept secret. I'm sure your mother knew about them, but since my mother was born to the Second Clan, she does not."

"But you know?"

"Yes, I learned about the tunnels while visiting a Sandwen museum in Daakur. My mother left me to explore and I discovered the plans to our fortress in the archives. The Daakurans built it, you know. So I studied them."

Rahkki nodded. He knew that his clan had hired the foreign builders to engineer a giant-proof fortress, but right now he felt a mixture of awe and envy. Before his mother died, he'd also enjoyed trips to the empire, which was full of shops, goods from all over the world, magickers who sold spells and charms, book lenders, schools, zoos, and museums.

It was also highly populated and a place where Sandwens went to hide. "I wonder if my mother is in the empire?"

I'Lenna's shoulders tensed, and Rahkki backtracked. If he found Reyella alive, then Lilliam Whitehall would be declared a false queen. I'Lenna's family would be banished or outright killed. The fact she was helping him at all was a gift. "I'm sorry. I'm just curious."

"You know what they say about curiosity?"

He sensed the smile behind her voice. "They say it calls the kajies," he answered. Kaji spirits harassed the seven clans, causing people to trip and slip and blunder where they were otherwise sure-footed and agile. Kajies came in flurries when Sandwens were either up to no good, full of pride, or curious about things that had nothing to do with them.

"Yep," I'Lenna said. "And we don't want kajies loose inside this dark, slippery tunnel. Do we?"

"Of course not."

They continued walking in silence. When they reached the lower tunnels, light began to pour in from the drainage grates, and they explored all three exits. I'Lenna was right—if his mother had left behind any evidence of her escape, the monsoon rains had long ago washed it away. He spied jungle rats, crumbling stone, rancid puddles, and bats. "There's nothing here," he said.

"Sorry," I'Lenna answered, adding a sympathetic hug.

Then Rahkki spotted a table and chairs hidden in the shadows. Parchments sat atop it and discarded fruit rinds surrounded it. "What's that?" he asked I'Lenna. "Do you eat down here?"

The princess scoffed and pulled him away from the table. "Why would I? Come on, let's go."

"But—"

"It's getting dark," she said.

By the graying light outside, Rahkki realized that the sun was going down and he'd better get to his uncle's farm before the dragons started hunting. Also, his belly was grumbling. He hadn't eaten since breakfast. "I need to get to my uncle's."

"Yes, I have to go too. You can leave through the storm drain." Masking her movements from him, I'Lenna unlocked the metal grate that led out into the jungle.

"Thanks for the tour," he said.

I'Lenna chewed her lip. "Rahkki, I don't think you're

asking the right question about your mother."

"What do you mean?"

"She either escaped or she didn't, what's done is done. But if she's alive, the real question is, why hasn't she come back?"

I'Lenna's words struck Rahkki like a hard slap, and her dark eyes rounded in apology. He caught his breath, slowly nodding. "Right, that makes sense." There was only one reason why Reyella wouldn't return—his mother was dead—and I'Lenna's words shone upon that sour truth like a lamp.

But then he shook his head. No, he wasn't going to give up. Reyella *had* escaped and gone somewhere, and he wanted to know where and why.

"Good luck at the Pairing tomorrow," I'Lenna said, and then she vanished into the bowels of the fortress.

Feeling exhausted, Rahkki began the long trek to his uncle's farm. Tomorrow he would become a Rider, and soon he'd help his mare rescue her friends. Sula would leave him when it was done, he knew that, but he no longer desired to *own* her. That had been the dream of a child. His new dream was to *help* her, and Sula wanted to live free.

6

THE PAIRING

AT DAWN THE NEXT DAY, THE SUN PEEKED OVER the eight-towered octagon that was Fort Prowl, and the morning bells rang across the Sandwen settlement. Rahkki approached the fallows, his heart racing. Uncle Darthan strode beside him, a sure hand on his nephew's shoulder. Rahkki had attended a dozen Pairing ceremonies, but never in a thousand seasons could he have guessed he'd be an Initiate.

Last night, he and Darthan had spent a long, quiet evening together, preparing for today. They'd gathered six buckets of water from the River Tsallan that bordered his uncle's rice farm. After boiling it, Rahkki scrubbed his body, trimmed his hair with a knife, and cleaned out his fingernails. The scent of soap and per-fumed oil lingered around him now, as foreign as it was pungent. Sula would hate the smell, he knew.

"Your mother would be proud of you," Darthan said.

Rahkki glanced up at his uncle's sun-crinkled face. "She never cared if I was a Rider or not. She wanted me to find my own path."

Uncle smiled. "That's true, but not what I meant. She'd be proud of you for saving that wild mare's life." He lowered his voice. "I know you don't like to fly, Rahkki, but you rode Sula anyway. If you hadn't, Queen Lilliam would have fed her to the dragon. It was the bravest—" Darthan's voice cracked, and his eyes glistened. "It was the bravest thing you ever did."

"But I was scared."

Darthan squeezed Rahkki's shoulder. "Bravery is about taking action in spite of fear, not in absence of it. You are your mother's boy."

Rahkki had informed Darthan about the tunnels and explained his theory about his mother, but Darthan had agreed with I'Lenna. The question wasn't where Rey-ella had gone, but why she hadn't returned. His uncle had said: *Queen Reyella Stormrunner was known as the Pantheress for a reason. If she were alive, nothing—no usurping queen, no jungle, no giant, no injury, no magic, not anything—could keep her away from her sons.*

In spite of his assessment, Darthan had agreed to help Rahkki search. "If she died in Daakur, I'll find out when and where," he'd said. "I'll bring her home." Darthan was referring to Reyella's bones, and Rahkki had shuddered that thought away. They'd agreed that Uncle would begin his search by riding the ferry across Cinder Bay and speaking to the workers on the docks. If an injured and pregnant Sandwen queen had dropped anchor there eight years ago, someone would remember. The trip would only take a day or two, and Darthan would be back in plenty of time for his upcoming harvest. He planned to leave as soon as his responsibilities to the rice farm allowed.

"We're here," said Uncle. They'd reached the fallows where hundreds of Sandwen clansfolk sprawled across the dormant farmland. Some were engaged in tests of strength on the grass; others rested in the shade or ate with their families. Kids roasted tarantulas and salted slugs over open fires, elders wove blankets, and grooms sold Kihlari charms to kids who would never earn enough coin to Pair with a Flier themselves.

Rahkki spotted the Initiates from the other clans waiting in the sun. He hugged his uncle and then joined them; but they edged away as he approached. Rahkki could guess why. He'd won his Intended Flier in a contest, while they'd each had to pay a small fortune for theirs.

An Initiate from the Fourth Clan rolled her eyes over Rahkki's ill-fitting attire and knife-shorn hair. "Have you or your mare had *any* training?" she asked.

"We've had enough," Rahkki lied.

The other Initiates giggled. They each wore expensive, custom-fitted clothing purchased in Daakur. With his handed-down clothes, his patchwork satchel, and his wild mare, Rahkki clearly didn't fit in.

"My stallion would never kick anyone," the girl added, referring to Sula's infamous attack on Brauk. She turned her shoulder, shutting off further conversation.

Rahkki exhaled, wishing his brother were here now and fiddling with the ceremonial garb he'd borrowed from Tuni: a bleached leather tunic and trousers that fit him like a small tent. She'd replaced his tattered footwear with clean, unmarred boots that she never wore because they hurt her feet. Sula's vibrant purple feathers dangled from each of his wrists.

The morning mist had vanished, leaving Rahkki and the other Initiates unsheltered from the sun. Sweat trailed down his forehead and into his golden eyes. Finally, a hush fell over the fallows as the Intended Kihlari appeared. Rahkki danced on his toes, hunting for Sula. When he spotted her, he caught his breath.

Flanked by six well-fed and pampered steeds, his wild mare stood out like a beam of moonlight. She high-stepped through the grass, swishing her glossy white tail, and her silver hide rippled over muscles that were hardened from living wild. Her glittering eyes swept the fallows, and her curved ears flicked round, not at bugs, but to catch every possible noise. She wasn't frightened—she was *aware*. The tame Kihlari plodded like water buffalo in comparison.

Rahkki's heart swelled with pride. "Sula," he whispered.

The Fourth Clan Initiate could not hide her surprise. "*That's* your Flier? Land to skies, I bet she's quick in the air."

Rahkki burst with pride and fear, remembering just how quick she was.

The procession halted in the center of the unplanted field. The hush lifted, and the clansfolk broke into loud whispers.

Is that the mare that kicked Brauk Stormrunner?

41

Yeah, his little brother won her at the auction. Got lucky.

If you call winning that man-killer lucky.

Across the field, Rahkki spied Queen Lilliam and her three daughters relaxing in their huge red shade tent. I'Lenna's sisters sat astride Firo's back, pretending they were flying while I'Lenna fed the roan mare treats. Blue wildflowers had been braided into Firo's lush black mane. Around the girls' mother, servants buzzed, refilling jugs, massaging bug-repelling oil into her skin, and fanning her with palm fronds. Familiar rage and grief rose within Rahkki at the sight of the queen.

Adjacent to Lilliam's tent were the shade structures of the other Sandwen clan queens. Each monarch reclined on a soft pallet to observe the ceremony. Off to the side of the field, a group of men tended a collection of hot coals. The First, Sixth, and Seventh Clans were absent. They'd been unable to travel safely to the Clan Gathering due to the raiding Gorlan hordes.

Suddenly, a buffalo horn rang out and brought Rahkki's attention back to the ceremony. The Fifth Clan Borla stepped out of his tent, and the spectators settled, waiting for the Pairing to begin.

"Initiates, you may approach your Intended," the Borla

announced. Rahkki's group strode across the grass, their eyes pinned to their mounts.

When Echofrost spied Rahkki approaching, she relaxed and folded her shimmering wings. He accepted her lead rope from Tuni, and the Headwind left the field.

"Hey," Rahkki greeted softly.

Echofrost huffed, still annoyed by the earlier ministrations of the grooms. They'd oiled her feathers, glossed her hide, and polished her hooves, completely washing away her natural scent. She dipped her muzzle toward Rahkki, noticing he smelled no better. Soap and Landwalker perfume had spoiled his familiar essence.

The Kihlari hadn't told Echofrost what to expect today, so she'd nervously waited. Her entire plan hinged on Pairing with Rahkki and infiltrating the Sky Guard, but her inability to communicate with the cub complicated everything. If the army didn't fly east soon, she—she would what? Leave the Sandwens and live by herself? Echofrost had no herd to return to. She tossed her mane—no! The clan loved all Kihlari—they would save Storm Herd and Bumblewind's unborn foal from the giants! She had to remain committed to the plan, however inconvenient.

The Fifth Clan Borla resumed speaking. Echofrost

watched Rahkki's heart thump faster, and her own nerves twitched beneath her hide.

"Welcome to the Ceremony of Pairs," the Borla shouted, and the crowd cheered. "Today you appear before your queens, seeking the highest honor in the Sandwen Realm: the position of Sky Guard Rider." He paused as the crowd murmured. Echofrost swiveled her ears, trying to understand.

"Your Intended steed stands beside you," the Borla continued. "These Kihlari have been selected for their ferocity of spirit and their skill in flight. They represent the highest-quality Kihlari stock in the seven clans." He cast a doubtful glance at Echofrost that sent snickers rippling through the crowd. Rahkki's jaw muscle fluttered angrily. "It will be your duty to serve and protect your Flier above yourself."

Rahkki mindlessly touched her chest, and Echofrost didn't pull away from him. He's my ally, she reminded herself.

"The bond you are about to form is second only to the fealty you owe your queen," the Borla said. "Do you understand that what is done today cannot be undone?"

The five prospective Riders answered in unison. "We do."

"Do you understand that only death can break a Pair?"

"We do."

"And do you understand that when a Rider or a Kihlara Flier passes to the next life, the other becomes a Half, and that a Half can never Pair again with another?"

"We understand," Rahkki answered with the others.

"Now for the Pairing," the Borla said. "In the presence of your monarch, answer your truth." He raised his voice higher. "Is this the Kihlara Flier you have chosen of your own free will?"

"Yes," the Riders agreed in unison. Echofrost felt tension swelling within the crowd. She sensed that the ceremony was almost over.

"Name your Flier."

Rahkki shouted, "Sula of the Fifth Clan!" Then he reached for her again, but this time Echofrost scooted sideways, her nerves jangling.

"Do you promise your lifeblood to protect your Flier from harm?"

"Yes," the Landwalkers answered.

"Do you promise to care for your Flier until death parts you?"

"We do."

"Do you promise to feed your Flier before you are fed?"

"We will."

"And do you promise to outfit your Flier in full Daak-uran armor for each and every battle?"

"Always!" Rahkki shouted with the others, but he cast a worried glance at his mare.

Echofrost neighed to Shysong. "Why is everyone shouting?"

The roan pranced inside the queen's shade tent, scattering servants. "I don't know. I don't like it."

The Borla raised his hand and addressed each Rider and Flier individually. He ended with Rahkki. "By your monarch, Queen Lilliam Whitehall, who is present here today, by the witnesses gathered, by the flesh sacrifice you are about to give, and by my own hand—I Pair you, Rahkki Stormrunner, with your Kihlara mare, Sula of the Fifth Clan."

The Borla shut his mouth with finality. Before she or Rahkki could react, ten men swarmed Echofrost and knocked her down.

Shysong reared. Her head slammed into her tent's ceiling, causing it to collapse. "Fly away!" she whinnied. The two princesses slid down her back and into I'Lenna's quick embrace.

Echofrost struggled but the men held strong.

She watched as they lifted Rahkki off his feet and tossed him onto his side.

The spectators whooped and hollered.

"It's okay! Don't fight," Rahkki cried. He was trying to calm her, and Echofrost realized this attack must be part of the ceremony.

A huge man, the blacksmith himself, yanked a metal rod out of the smoking coals. Heat shimmered around its molten end. He strutted toward Rahkki and Echofrost, and then she understood what was happening—she and Rahkki were about to receive matching brands.

She froze, her heart thudding.

The blacksmith was swift, and as quickly as it had begun, the branding was over, leaving each Rider and Flier with identical marks.

Echofrost rolled to her hooves, shaking. It was done. She and Rahkki were Paired. Her new Rider composed himself and joined her, and the two walked off the field to the cheers of all four clans. Their first task as a unit was over. They were in the Fifth Clan militia now, and one step closer to saving Storm Herd from the giants.

7

BRAUK

WHEN THE PAIRING CEREMONY ENDED, THE other branded Riders had rushed to their clan Borlas for help, but Rahkki and Sula stumbled across the field as he led her toward Brim Carver's animal clinic. He'd ask her to treat their wounds, visit Brauk, and drop off the clothing he'd gathered yesterday.

Rahkki glanced toward Lilliam's shade tent. When the blacksmith's men had knocked Sula down, Firo had reared and collapsed the entire structure onto the queen's head. Now Lilliam screamed at her servants to resurrect it and clean up the overturned trays of food. She pointed at her eldest daughter. "If you can't handle your winged pony, I'Lenna, I will send her to the Ruk."

"Yes, Mother." I'Lenna clucked to Firo, who was prancing and shaking her braided mane. "Shh," she soothed, and led her new pet toward the fortress. Rahkki felt bad for I'Lenna. Most Sandwen queens cherished their children, but Lilliam never had. Instead of viewing her female heirs as blessings, she perceived them as threats, especially her crown princess.

Rahkki returned his attention to Sula. Her eyes bulged and her breath came in rapid bursts as she absorbed the pain of the branding. Rahkki's body had gone numb except for his throbbing shoulder. He couldn't believe he was a Rider now, like Brauk. *No*—not like Brauk. His brother couldn't walk, or ride, or fight. He might be paralyzed, forever.

A voice broke into his thoughts. "How'd you do it, Stormrunner?"

Mut Finn, the leader of the Sandwen teens, intercepted him. Mut's best friend, Tam Woodson, stood beside him.

"How'd I do what?" Rahkki asked.

"Tame her?" Mut nodded at Sula. "You a Meld or something?" Mut and Tam burst into laughter. People thought animal speakers were crazy, but Rahkki was neither a Meld nor crazy.

"She chose me," Rahkki answered, shrugging casually.

49

Mut's mood instantly blackened. When he'd tried to win Sula, she'd bucked him off. "Sula's an animal, Rahkki, she didn't *choose* you." Then something caught Mut's eye, a group of girls from the visiting clans. He tagged Tam's shoulder, and the two boys slunk toward them. Now that the Pairing was over, the clans were packing to return home, and these girls would soon be gone.

Grateful for the reprieve, Rahkki arrived at Brim's small medical hut and knocked on the door.

"There you are," Brim said, as if expecting him. She stepped aside to allow Rahkki and his Flier inside the animal clinic. Sula folded her purple wings as she entered.

Shelves full of Daakuran medical books, jars of herbs, gleaming instruments, and stacks of parchment lined the walls. The room also contained three open exam tables, several teakwood chairs, and low cabinets. A huge canvas painting hung on the back wall, the scene depicting a muscular Kihlara steed battling a spit dragon.

"Is Brauk awake?" Rahkki asked.

"He's still sleeping." Brim nodded toward a closed horse stall.

"During the day?" Rahkki stared at the door. Brauk was always training, flying, fighting, teasing—he didn't lie still. "Is he getting better, you think?"

"Now, now," Brim soothed. "If I left it to Brauk, you know he'd never rest. It's the medication that's making him sleep." She showed Rahkki a vial of liquid and explained how she made the drug. Sula recoiled at its tangy scent.

"You fed my brother dragon drool? But that's poisonous!" Rahkki cried.

"You know I'd never harm your brother." Brim clucked. "Boiling the venom removes all the toxins but leaves the anesthetic properties intact."

"The what?"

Brim replaced the medicine, laughing. "It makes him sleep, and it's safe," she promised. "Just a drop does the trick, but it wears off fast, only lasts about an hour at a time."

Her eyes darted to several timekeepers stacked on a side table. The largest was the hourglass, and its white sand spilled slowly from the top of the glass, through the thin center, and piled into a conical shape at the bottom. She pointed at it. "Now is a good time to visit. See, that says his medicine is almost done, but let me look at your shoulder first. Would you like a song?"

Rahkki just stared at her, barely understanding the last thing she said. Around him, Brim's shed seemed to pulse in unison with his throbbing wound. The ceiling of her hut rose and fell. The lighting went from bright to dim.

"Oh! No, no. Don't pass out on me," Brim chirped. She broke into a clan lullaby while treating the matching brands on Rahkki and Sula.

"Sula's mine now," the boy said, a smile creeping across his face.

The skin around Brim's eyes crinkled. "She was yours before you won her, you know. Everyone saw it. She'd not balk at stomping any one of us, but you—she likes you."

Tension settled between them at the mention of Sula stomping people. Rahkki glanced at the closed stall door again, and a hard lump filled his throat. His brother was on the other side, helpless. His brother who battled giants alone, who flew Kol bareback, who had the grip of a python, who had cared for Rahkki since their mother died—he was lying inside that stall. Alone. "Hurry," he urged.

"Of course." Brim spread a cooling mud across his brand. "This will stop the burning and numb the pain," she said. He flinched with each touch of her spatula, and each time he flinched, Brim yelped as if she were the injured one. Soon Rahkki was grinning. Next she bandaged the wound in clean cloth. "All right," she said. "You may visit Brauk while I finish with the mare. But come back tomorrow for a bandage change." She reached for a salve and turned to Sula.

Rahkki nodded and pushed open the stall door. Reed mats covered the dirt floor, and a cot stood along the side-wall. The table next to it held a mug of hot liquid, probably tea, a bowl of water, and packets of medicine. On the floor rested an empty bowl that smelled of urine. Brauk slept on the cot beneath a wool blanket, looking pale.

Rahkki set down the extra clothes he'd gathered and eased next to him, staring at his brother's legs. When he stretched out his arm to touch them, Brauk snapped, "Don't do that." His eyes had opened, as bright as stars.

"Hel-hello," Rahkki stammered.

Brauk gazed at his brother's ceremonial clothing, his jaw ticking, and then he grabbed the bleached leather in his fist, grimacing as he did so. "What's this?"

Rahkki opened his mouth. No words came out.

"You didn't," Brauk rasped. "You didn't Pair with that viper Sula, did you?" He let go of Rahkki's tunic and shook his head. "No, you couldn't have bought her. You don't have a dramal to your name."

Brauk didn't know about the contest. Rahkki scooted out of his brother's striking range, knowing it was best to confess, and confess fast. "I didn't buy her; I won her in a contest. I Paired with Sula today."

Brauk gaped at him.

Brim poked her head into the stall. "Everything all right in here, boys?"

"Get out!" Brauk snatched up his urine bowl, and he tossed it at the opposite wall, where it struck and then fell with a clattering ring. Brim shut the door.

Rahkki leaped to his feet. "Don't yell at her!"

"Bloody rain." Brauk spat on the floor. "I'm sorry, Brim, but my brother's an idiot!" He glared at Rahkki. "Tell me you're lying. Please tell me you didn't do it." His voice lowered to a soft growl.

"I'm not lying." Rahkki cast his gaze to the floor. "She's mine."

His brother shut his eyelids for a long moment. His chest rose and fell in controlled breaths. "How?" Brauk asked. "What contest?"

"No one would pay more than a few dramals for her at the auction. Not after she hurt you . . ." Rahkki trailed off. "So the queen said that whoever could ride her to the clouds and back could keep her, and she let the merchants bet on the contestants."

"And *you* flew her?" Brauk snorted in disbelief.

"I did."

"I don't believe it. You're afraid of heights. If you were any taller, you'd be afraid of yourself."

Rahkki's eyes stung, and his cheeks flamed. "I rode her, and I won her. I'm a Rider now, like you."

"Like me?" Brauk clenched into a hard, bitter laugh and pointed at his legs. "With that mare beneath you, I have no doubt you'll soon be *exactly* like me, Rahkki. Now listen and listen close, because I won't repeat myself: *That wild* braya *will kill you.* She's nothing like our tame Kihlari. *Nothing.* And when I get out of here, I'm going to strangle that vicious silver filly with my bare hands. Now go away." He closed his eyes, cursing in Talu. "*Sa jin,* you're dumber than you look."

Rahkki inhaled sharply. "Brauk—"

"Go!"

Rahkki left the horse stall and closed the door. He faced Brim, his body shaking. "He hates me."

Brim threw her soft arms around Rahkki, smelling of tree sap and melons. "You know that's not true."

He drew a long breath and peered up at her. "You have to heal him, Brim." Rahkki pointed at the stall door and

55

whispered, "That's not my brother in there."

"No, you're wrong," she said, taking his hand. "That *is* your brother. You and he must accept what has happened. Of course I'll try my best to heal him, and perhaps he'll walk again, but that's not a promise I can make. You and Brauk must focus on the path in front of you. Don't bend your eyes toward what *should* be or you will stumble."

"You sound like my uncle."

She grinned, her tan skin crinkling around her eyes and mouth. "Thank you. He's a wise man."

"How long will Brauk stay in that stall?" Rahkki asked.

"I'm working on moving him to your uncle's farm, but first I need the swelling in his spine to settle." Brim opened the front door of her clinic. "Let me worry about Brauk. You've got a Kihlara Flier to care for."

Rahkki peered at Sula who stood awkwardly in the hut, waiting. Her breathing had calmed, and she was no longer shaking. He imagined all her needs—quality hay, expensive grain, her battle armor, a saddle, and a grooming kit—and he blanched. Mut Finn had stolen the last of his money, a mere eight jints, and Brauk had long ago gambled away their inheritance. Now Rahkki was flat broke, and he didn't have a wealthy family to sponsor him.

He also had to fund his brother's flying horse, and Kol required enormous amounts of hay and grain. Then his uncle's face flashed in his mind. In all the excitement, Rahkki had forgotten Darthan's wager—and the fact that Uncle was rich!

"I have to talk to Darthan," Rahkki mumbled. But first he needed to give his report to the queen. Lilliam met with her advisers each day just before *se-vu*, the clan's resting hour. She heard complaints and reports, and lunched with clan leaders. Rahkki glanced at the sun, not wanting to be late. He clucked to his mare and she expectantly followed him back toward Fort Prowl.

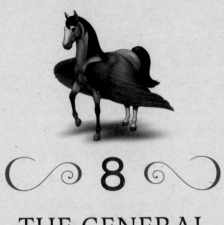

8

THE GENERAL

ON HIS WAY TO THE FORTRESS, GENERAL TSUN, the commander of the Land Guard army, intercepted the new Pair. "Stormrunner," he grunted.

Rahkki paused, surprised. This man had spoken a handful of words to him in as many years. "Yes, General?"

"A word, please?" He didn't wait for Rahkki to answer; he took hold of the boy's elbow and guided him toward the jungle. Alarmed, Sula flared her wings as she trotted beside them.

The general halted within a dense thicket, and Rahkki squinted through the leaves, his pulse thrumming. Why were they standing within the borderlands of Granak's hunting territory? He swallowed, nervous and alert for any sign of the black-scaled, drooling dragon. Overhead, the forest canopy rustled in the breeze, and Sula rattled her feathers.

General Tsun nodded to Rahkki's mare as if to pacify her and took a long breath. "I hear Queen Lilliam ordered some of my soldiers to attack you after the giants raided us. Is that true?"

"What?" Rahkki cringed, his panic rising. It was true that soldiers had beaten him as punishment for trying to free Sula, but he'd told no one about that, or had he told Tuni—he couldn't remember. Either way, he answered, "I didn't tell anyone."

The general's hard, sun-lined face softened. "I know you didn't, son. Word got out in the barracks, but it's true, isn't it?"

Rahkki felt frozen by the man's flint-blue eyes. He slowly nodded.

The general sighed. "I'm going to spit this out, boy. There's no other way to tell you. Queen Lilliam's birth clan didn't educate her about anything: war strategy, handling a treasury, raising heirs. Why would they? She was tenth in line to their throne, but now she's our problem." He glanced east. "The giant hordes are escalating toward war, and the queen is afraid of them. We need a new monarch, one who can handle this kind of trouble. Some of your clanmates are planning an uprising against Lilliam."

"I'm not!" Rahkki had spent the last eight years staying *out* of Lilliam's way, just trying to survive. And now he was a Rider, but he was *not* a traitor. Lilliam was queen. He may not like it, but that was final.

Unless my mother's still alive, a small voice whispered inside his head.

General Tsun studied Rahkki's face. "You don't believe Queen Lilliam is good for the clan, do you?"

Rahkki felt trapped, and he set his jaw. Was the general going to report his answer to Lilliam or was he a rebel too? *Leave me alone,* Rahkki thought.

"Your mother was a good queen," the general continued. "The clan loved her."

Rahkki's eyes shifted toward the village, his feet flexed. Should he run for it? He didn't want to talk to this man about the uprising. The only way to dethrone Lilliam was to kill her, or convince her to renounce the crown on her own—and she'd never do that.

"Rahkki," the general pressed. "We could use your name, the Stormrunner name, to rally the entire clan against her. Will you speak to your family about joining us?"

"Us?" Rahkki reeled away from the general. "You're *one of them*?" Land to skies, Rahkki was meeting with a traitor in the jungle! If anyone saw . . .

"Your family's dislike for the queen is no secret," the general stated. He made a fist and then opened it, pointing all four fingers down, a studied gesture or signal that Rahkki didn't understand.

"I—I won't join you. I won't do that to I'Lenna," Rahkki stuttered, his eyes rolling toward the distant fortress on the hill. "Don't—don't tell me any more about it. Come on, Sula." He clucked to his mare, and they bolted out of the tree line, away from General Tsun.

The man's voice trailed after him. "Choose a side, Rahkki, before it's too late."

After a few lengths, Rahkki slowed, trying to walk like he wasn't on fire. Since it was almost se-vu, the fallows were deserted. Rahkki and Sula traveled beneath the naked sky, his heart racing, his brow sweating. His mare nickered and lipped at his tunic. Absently, he murmured soft words to her.

The general was one of Lilliam's top advisers. Rahkki

had heard whisperings about an uprising, but he hadn't imagined it was this serious. And whether the Stormrunners joined it or not, Lilliam would assume they had. No usurping queen trusted the children of her predecessor. Anger seethed within him. This wasn't his fight. *Yes it is*, said a voice in his head. *Lilliam killed your mother.*

Rahkki tugged on his short hair, feeling confused.

For a clan to rise up against their sworn monarch, well, that upset the order of Clan Law. Only a princess could usurp a queen! What the general was plotting could rile the neighboring clans against the Fifth. It also meant that I'Lenna would inherit a clan she could never trust— unless the rebels planned to destroy the entire Whitehall family! I'Lenna had told Rahkki she didn't want the throne, at least not yet, but that wouldn't matter if she were dead.

His breath rushed from his chest. Did I'Lenna understand how much danger she was in? Rahkki mulled this as he jogged toward Fort Prowl.

9

REPORT

HEADWIND HARAK NIGHTSEER MET RAHKKI AT the base of the fortress steps, his expression screwed tight. *What now?* Rahkki wondered.

Sula snorted at the man and tossed her head. Rahkki sensed her impatience. He could imagine her thoughts— *when are you going to rescue my friends?*

"Hey, little Rider," Harak said, his green eyes cold. He and Brauk had never gotten along, and Harak's animosity had overflowed onto Rahkki long ago. "We start drills tomorrow, yeah. Think you can keep that beast in formation?"

"I'll try, Headwind Nightseer."

"Come on then, it's time to tell the queen what you saw

out there." Harak slapped the back of Rahkki's head, too hard to feel playful.

Rahkki let out his breath. "After you."

The Headwind shot Sula a dark look and turned, springing off the balls of his feet. Rahkki tugged gently on Sula's lead rope and the trio climbed the wide steps cut into the hillside. The day sweltered, as if the vast sky were sweating moisture. A light wind met them at the top, and Rahkki glimpsed the flat ocean shimmering in the north. Harak had tied his stallion's black-and-silver feathers to his wrists, and they fluttered in the salty breeze.

When they reached the smaller of the two fortress gates, Harak yanked Rahkki through and whispered into his ear. "You can't trust the guards. Some of them are against the queen."

Rahkki absorbed this, noting what it meant—that Harak must be *for* the queen, which was no surprise. Lilliam favored him above the other Headwinds. Rahkki stared at the guards, wondering if everyone knew about this uprising.

"Tie your braya there until you're done with the queen. The one place Sula's not allowed is in the command chamber, yeah."

"Come on, girl," Rahkki said, urging Sula toward the wooden post.

She lowered her head and sniffed the structure.

Harak squinted at the mare. "I don't agree with this wildling joining the Sky Guard. She's dangerous, yeah? She doesn't know our ways."

"She's just different; she was born wild," Rahkki said.

"You see?" Harak bumped Rahkki's shoulder. "That's exactly what I don't like about her."

Rahkki tied a slipknot so that he could quickly free her, and Sula dug at the spongy soil with her sharp front hoof.

"Wait here," he pleaded.

The silver mare stared at him for a long moment, violence churning in her gaze.

"Please," he said.

Sula seemed to read his pleading tone and ceased pawing.

"I'll be right back."

As Rahkki entered the royal command chamber, he passed Jul Ranger, Meela Swift's wealthy young apprentice. It was Jul's duty to be available to the Headwinds for errands and other services. But right now he was digging into his nostrils and flinging the contents to the floor. When he saw Rahkki, he stood taller and blushed. "Greetings."

"Greetings," Rahkki answered.

Inside the chamber sat Queen Lilliam, General Tsun, and the three Headwinds of the Sky Guard: Harak, Tuni, and Meela Swift. Meela had been chosen to replace Brauk until he healed, *if* he healed. Also in attendance were the three princesses—I'Lenna, Rayni, and Jor—and the Fifth Clan treasurer. Attendants flocked to the table behind the throne, replenishing bowls of soup and stew, adding fresh cooked fish, pouring steaming pots of tea, chopping pine-apple, and whisking away empty skins of rice wine and adding new ones.

"We're ready to hear your findings, Stormrunner," said Queen Lilliam, leaning back against the throne that had once been his mother's. Her iron crown, a replica of Reye-lla's lost one, encircled her head. "Princess I'Lenna, take the floor with our new Rider as witness to the report."

I'Lenna rose and walked to Rahkki's side. She didn't meet his eyes but stood next to him as they each faced her mother. Lilliam's advisers, who were stuffing sauced meat and dripping fruit into their mouths, paused to wipe their fingers across their trousers.

Rahkki and I'Lenna took turns explaining what they'd seen the day before when the mares had flown off with them.

"You saw six hundred giants?" General Tsun asked. Nothing about his tone or posture betrayed his earlier conversation with Rahkki, and Rahkki wondered if the queen had any idea he was plotting against her.

"It's my best guess, General," Rahkki replied.

"Six hundred is a big number," Harak interjected. "Can you even count that high?"

"It's an estimate," Rahkki answered. *But yes, I can count that high*, he thought.

I'Lenna spoke up. "I verify it."

Queen Lilliam lifted her hand and asked, "What was the condition of the winged herd?"

"Captured, but good," Rahkki answered, remembering that he'd noticed little blood on the giants or on the wild Kihlari.

The queen turned to a lithe woman dressed in clothing from Daakur. "What are they worth?" Lilliam asked her.

The Fifth Clan treasurer consulted a parchment.

"Each steed is valued between eighty dramals to a full round," she answered. "But to the Daakurans across the bay, they're worth up to five rounds apiece. Depending on how many steeds we rescue, the wild herd could fetch between five hundred to seven hundred rounds in total. In our coin, that's five hundred to seven hundred thousand dramals."

Silence filled the chamber as each person considered her assessment. The sum was unbelievable. If all seven Sandwen clans combined their treasuries, the total would be less than seven hundred thousand dramals! But to get those coins, they'd have to sell the wild herd to the Daakuran Empire.

I'Lenna glanced at Rahkki, her look saying: *I told you she'd sell them.*

But no Kihlari had ever been sold to the people across Cinder Bay, and the Daakuran Empire protected the sacred steeds from illegal sale and theft, ensuring that the winged horses remained in the Sandwen Realm. Lilliam wouldn't break that tradition, would she?

The general's thoughts matched Rahkki's. "Are you suggesting we *sell* the wild steeds, my queen?"

"I'm suggesting that as an option, yes."

General Tsun's mouth snapped shut.

Rahkki felt sick, as though they were discussing something criminal.

Tuni rose from her seat, struggling to control the harsh tone of her voice. "Queen Lilliam, the Kihlari steeds don't belong in Daakur."

"The other clans won't agree to sell them," Headwind Meela added.

Lilliam smiled, showing her small white teeth. "Do you think you are educating me?" Her dark-blue eyes shifted from one Headwind to the other.

They shook their heads.

Lilliam paused to touch her rounded belly and then continued. "The wild herd has not enjoyed hundreds of years of domestication like our prized animals. They are thin and needlessly aggressive." She pointed at Rahkki. "You saw what this boy's Flier did to Headwind Storm-runner. I believe it will take a generation to tame the wild herd—that's years of hay and medicine, and for what? We don't need them; we can breed our own animals. But those wild Kihlari are worth a fortune."

She shifted her weight and leaned against her throne. "I'm not suggesting we sell them to private buyers, but to the empire's zoological society. It will be good riddance, and the clans will come around when they hear how much the steeds are worth. We'll split the profits with them, less our rescue expenses. War with the giants is inevitable now, and this way we won't have to pay for it." She tightened her lips. "There is no downside here."

General Tsun addressed the treasurer. "How much will war with the giants cost our clan? Surely we can fund it without selling those precious steeds."

Lilliam slammed down her fist. "Our treasury won't support a war with three hordes. Not now."

The Fifth Clan treasurer nodded in agreement.

The general snapped his eyes to Lilliam, brows furrowed. "But we're not in famine or drought. Isn't our treasury strong?"

"Finances are a matter for treasurers and queens," Lilliam growled. "Not for generals."

Tsun's chest ballooned and his scarred face reddened. He stood to pace the room.

Rahkki risked a glance at Lilliam's fine clothing. Fortress workers reported that the queen was as loose with the treasury as a child. They gossiped about shipments from Daakur that arrived often at their port in Cinder Bay, carrying silks and spices, jewels, presents, foreign sweets, and books—all for Lilliam and her daughters. She hired overqualified tutors and imported expensive

Daakuran servants for her private quarters. She'd once spent ten thousand dramals on a new saddle for her stallion, Mahrsan.

Tuni's face reddened. "I don't understand. You've increased our tithes for five of the last eight years, your Land Guard eats almost for free, and your Borla charges for medicine that used to be free to the clan. Why do we need *more* money?"

The general tapped Tuni's arm, a warning to stop talking, and Rahkki wondered if Tuni was also part of the uprising.

Queen Lilliam ignored the Headwind while an attendant brought her a crystal glass full of water and fresh mint leaves. Rahkki stiffened. All glass came from the empire; her cup was an expensive import and more evidence of Lilliam's waste.

"What you need to know," the queen continued, her blue eyes sweeping the room, "is that I've chosen a solution that will fund the war, rid us of the giants for good, and replenish our treasury." Lilliam stood. "Enough discussion. I proclaim it. We're selling those wild steeds to Daakur." She took a breath and added with less confidence, "After we rescue them."

I'Lenna tilted her head toward Rahkki and whispered,

"What does she mean, *rid us of the giants for good*?"

"I think it means exactly that," he whispered back. "No more giants."

"None? That's brutal."

He agreed. No one liked the giants, but invading their camps and murdering all of them—even their children—it felt wrong.

Lilliam shifted beneath the weight of her unborn child. "First steps," she said. "We need more reliable information about the giants and the wild herd than what we have gleaned from two overexcited children."

I'Lenna huffed and crossed her arms.

The queen called for Harak, and he darted forward with a familiar smile dancing across his lips.

Her fondness for the handsome Headwind softened her expression. "After morning bells tomorrow, you will lead a patrol to Mount Crim to scout the hordes."

Harak bent at the waist. "Yes, my queen."

"And take Stormrunner with you," she said. "Initiate our newest Rider."

All eyes turned to Rahkki, and he instantly felt younger and shorter.

The queen continued. "The boy knows where he last saw the giants, and his Flier is connected to the wild herd.

She dragged Stormrunner straight to them yesterday; she can do it again. Yes?"

"Yes, my queen," Harak agreed.

"Keep the boy . . . *safe*," she added.

Rahkki's belly clenched. The word *safe* had never sounded more threatening.

Harak grinned. "Yes, my queen." He flipped back his golden hair, ringing the bells tied within, and strode out of the command chamber.

Lilliam rose and left with her guards, her hand resting lightly on her belly. She caught Rahkki's eye and snarled at him. "Don't be useless, Rider. Go."

Rahkki bowed and reluctantly left I'Lenna's side. He'd have to find her later to tell her about the uprising. He jogged into the courtyard and caught up to Harak as they returned to Sula, who was still tied to the hitching post. "What do I do?" Rahkki asked the Headwind. "Sula and I don't have armor yet."

Harak bopped Rahkki on the forehead. "Get some, little Rider, before morning."

"But—"

Harak ignored him as he called to another Rider and strode away.

Rahkki halted beside his silver mare. She'd never

worn a saddle before, and he didn't have one to put on her. He needed to fly to Uncle's right now and ask for coin.

Sula whinnied at him, irritated and scolding.

"I'm sorry I left you here so long," he said to her, "but I have good news. We're scouting tomorrow." Rahkki untied her rope, amazed that she hadn't broken free on her own. With a small prayer to the wind spirits, he climbed onto her back. "You're so patient," he said, complimenting her.

But Rahkki should have known better.

As soon as she was free, Sula tossed her head and bolted across the courtyard, almost throwing Rahkki off her back. Years of riding young horses saved him as he counterbalanced and grabbed her mane.

"Whoa!" he cried. But his wild mare lifted off, and her wings swirled dirt into his eyes as they swooped up and out of Fort Prowl.

10

THE BET

ECHOFROST CLEARED THE WALLS OF THE FOR-
tress and sailed toward the Kihlari barn, passing Harak,
who stalked swiftly across the yard. It had only been a day
since she'd returned, and her resolve to act obedient had
already dissolved.

She spied Rizah, coasting across the blue sky with
Tuni. They were off-duty, flying for pleasure. "Rizah!" she
whinnied.

The palomino startled and braked, hovering at cloud
level. The wind tossed her white and gold forelock to the
side. "Where's your tack?" she asked. "How is Rahkki
guiding you?"

Tack was the Kihlari word for all the accruements

Landwalkers used on their mounts: saddles, bridles, halters, and the like. "I don't need tack to fly," Echofrost snorted.

"But *he* does," Rizah nickered, her green eyes shining. "He can't join the Sky Guard without armor and tack."

"But we're Paired," Echofrost neighed. Had she been branded for *nothing*?

"You can't fight against giants unprotected, Sula, and neither can Rahkki. But don't worry; he'll buy what you need. He has to."

Mollified, Echofrost asked, "When will we fly east to rescue my herd?"

The palomino narrowed her eyes. "I don't know. War is complicated, Sula."

"Not really," the silver mare replied.

Tuni spoke to Rahkki. "What did I tell you about controlling that mare? Harak won't let you fly bareback, or without armor, and he won't let you fly at all if you can't keep Sula in formation."

"I know," Rahkki answered. "I'm taking Sula to Uncle's now and then to the trading post for armor. We'll have everything we need by tomorrow."

She frowned. "You shouldn't be scouting. It's too soon since you Paired and neither of you are trained yet, and the queen knows that. Please be careful."

"I will." Rahkki finished his conversation with Tuni, tugged on Echofrost's mane, and pointed north. She felt his rapid heartbeat and noted his trembling legs. She'd frightened him when she'd bolted skyward; she'd have to be more sensitive about his fears in the future. But now he was pointing, and she understood what that meant.

With a parting whinny to Rizah, Echofrost flattened her neck and followed Rahkki's finger north. The boy clutched her mane hard, his pulse thrumming. When the rice farm swept into view, she understood that this was where Rahkki had wanted to go. Perhaps he kept armor here.

She angled her purple wings and descended, landing lightly near Darthan's hut. The boy slipped off of her back, pale and shaking, but he did not tie her up. The Pair stood side by side and faced Uncle Darthan, who rocked on a chair, resting in the shade. Smoke poured out from between his lips, startling Echofrost. Did Landwalkers breathe fire? But the scent of his smoke was sweet, almost pleasant.

"You and Sula have been to Brim," Darthan said, eyeing their bandages. "Did you visit your brother?"

"Yes." Rahkki sat cross-legged at his uncle's feet and

caught his breath. "Is Brauk going to be okay, you think?"

He shrugged. "That is up to Brauk."

To quell her impatience, Echofrost dropped her head and grazed on the sweet wild grass that grew around Darthan's hut.

After a long pause between the two Landwalkers, Darthan exhaled another stream of smoke and smiled at Rahkki.

"Uncle Darthan, I need to talk with you." Rahkki glanced at Echofrost. "I—"

Before he could continue, Uncle Darthan said, "I bet two rounds on you yesterday at odds of twenty to one. Do you know what that means?"

Rahkki let go of his tension and grinned. "It means you're rich."

Darthan knocked a clump of ashes to the ground. "It's true that I won forty rounds, a small fortune, and that's exactly why I won't be getting it. If Lilliam pays me, it will bankrupt the clan. She's refused to settle her bet on grounds of hardship."

"No!" Rahkki blinked at him. "She can't do that!"

"She can and she did, but she had to settle with me another way, to show good faith. I ended up with something far more valuable than four thousand dramals."

Darthan's lips curled into a slow smile. "Last night she met with the queens from the other clans to unseal our pact. They agreed. The farm is mine again."

Rahkki grinned. "So you'll still end up stinking rich!"

Darthan met Rahkki's gaze. "I'll earn a living, Rahkki, which is all I ever wanted." He leaned against the wide carved back of his chair. "But I won't have any new rice to sell until after the harvest, and that is moons away. Until then, I'm broke."

"Oh," he whispered. Rahkki slumped, looking drained.

"I know you need armor and hay for Sula, and armor for yourself," Darthan said. "But I can't help you. Not yet."

"It's not fair."

Darthan chuckled. "Remember what I told you about wanting life to be fair?"

Rahkki kicked the ground. "You told me not to do it."

Darthan nodded, his dark eyes thoughtful. "That's right, so you'll need to find a different sponsor, or you'll need to wait."

"I can't wait." Rahkki picked at his nails and glanced at Echofrost again.

She nickered to him as if he could understand her. "Where is my armor? Where's yours?"

Rahkki shifted. "I fly out tomorrow with Harak to

scout the hordes. We're preparing for war."

Darthan grimaced, exhaling his sweet smoke between tight lips. "The timing is bad," he grumbled. "And you can't trust Harak, Rahkki."

"I never have," answered the boy.

"I know, but there's more to it now," Darthan added, his voice low. "The clan is plotting against Lilliam and the queen knows about it, but not who's behind it. She doesn't trust anyone—not her crown princess and not the Stormrunners. Me, you, Brauk, and I'Lenna—we top her list of possible assassins."

Rahkki snorted. "Like I'Lenna would overthrow her own mother."

Darthan's dark eyes glimmered. "She might."

Rahkki tensed. "Uncle!"

Echofrost flared her wings, feeling the anger emanating off Rahkki and then wondered at her growing attunement toward him. It was as if they were members of the same herd.

Darthan exhaled. "Look, I don't like to speak ill of your friend, Rahkki, but there are rumors that she's behind it. You ought to stay away from her."

"It's not her. It's General Tsun," Rahkki answered. "*He's* leading the uprising, and he wants us to join him."

Darthan leaned forward. "He said this to you?"

The boy nodded.

Darthan stood and began pacing. "No, I won't lend the Stormrunner name to this rebellion. We aren't traitors, but we have to prepare, store weapons. And now that the pact is unsealed, you boys aren't safe. Lilliam has every right to rid the clan of her bloodborn predecessors, without repercussion."

"Why hasn't she then?"

"Until the rebels move against her, she won't dare harm any of us—not outright. It would trigger the uprising she wants to avoid. And since you're friends with her daughter—who she believes wants her throne—you're the one she'll go after first. Lilliam could easily arrange an 'accident' and be done with you."

Rahkki sobered. "I'll be careful, but I don't believe I'Lenna is behind it. She doesn't want the throne, she told me." He wiped his face. "I hope the clan saves the wild herd before this uprising, but Sula and I can't help without armor. Brauk's set won't fit me, and Kol's won't fit Sula." He touched his satchel. "I have a game of stones, an old beetle cage, and a few of Sula's feathers. What else can I sell?"

"Talk to Koko, she may have spare equipment you can borrow."

Rahkki turned to Echofrost, his golden eyes probing hers. He slipped hesitantly onto her back and nudged her south. "I'll try," he said to Darthan.

Echofrost lifted off and flew back the way they'd come. Taking action calmed her, and at least she was out flying and not locked in a stall.

As they soared south toward the Kihlari stable, Rahkki sat up in excitement. "Look! There's I'Lenna."

Because of Rahkki's excited pointing, Echofrost scanned the terrain below and spotted the crown princess. I'Lenna stood beside the River Tsallan, deep in a private conversation with a soldier.

"It's General Tsun," Rahkki growled, urging Echofrost toward the princess.

But odd movements in the eastern jungle drew Echofrost's attention away. The trees were shaking and swaying in a defined pathway, leading toward the fortress. It reminded her of when she and Storm Herd had first spotted Granak. He was so large; he'd snapped trees in half and knocked them over as he'd moved. Curious, she arched her neck and whinnied a warning to Rahkki.

But her cub had also noticed the disturbance, and it took his attention off I'Lenna and the general. He leaned toward this new danger. Echofrost banked and changed course, flying toward the creature in the jungle.

If it was Granak, they were safe because the dragon couldn't fly, but whatever it was—it was heading directly toward the Fifth Clan settlement.

Using his legs and hands to cue her, Rahkki urged Echofrost to fly lower. She cruised over the treetops toward the swaying forest canopy.

Suddenly the source of the jostling trees came into view. It wasn't Granak.

It was giants!

11

PARLAY

ECHOFROST'S WINGS STUTTERED AS SHE BRAKED
and hovered above the trees. Below her dangling hooves,
she counted a pack of fifteen Gorlanders, a small flight
of burner dragons, two elephants, and a gigantic fanged
cat—all tromping toward Fort Prowl. She swooped closer,
noticing their weapons weren't drawn. A pegasus whinny
rang out from behind the last elephant.

She recognized it and whinnied back. "Redfire!" Echofrost dived toward the giants. Redfire had been a captain
in Desert Herd's army in Anok, and he'd taught Echofrost
how to sharpen her hooves and add power to her kicks.
He'd been captured with the rest of Storm Herd—but now
he was here! She descended toward him.

Rahkki shouted at her. "No, don't fly closer, it's too dangerous!" He kicked Echofrost and pulled her mane. "You don't listen!"

Echofrost ignored the boy and glided toward the rear of the frightening group. There was Redfire, tied to the saddle of a cow elephant. The lead giants, three adult males, grunted at her but did not threaten the lone mare and boy. They continued their steadfast march toward Fort Prowl.

Redfire reared toward her. "Echofrost," he neighed, "there's a Landwalker on your back."

"I know," she sputtered, relief flooding her at the sound of his voice. "What are you doing here? How's Dewberry?"

The tall copper chestnut strained against his tether, and the annoyed elephant trumpeted at him. Redfire ceased tugging. "Dewberry is—" His voice choked off for a moment, and dread filled Echofrost. "She's stressed. The foals are sucking the life from her."

"Foals?" Echofrost cried.

He nodded. "We think so. Since our capture, Dewberry's belly has doubled in size. She's finally eating and resting, and yes, we believe there are two."

Twins! Echofrost's heart bulged at the news and she blinked back tears. Her brother, Bumblewind, would never meet his foals and the unfairness of that crushed her. "I've joined the Sky Guard army with this cub," she whinnied to Redfire. "We're going to rescue Storm Herd."

Four of the smallest giants trotted toward Redfire and then walked beside him. They stared up at Echofrost, flashing their small tusks. They had smooth faces and bright-red hair, and she realized they were children. "What is this?" Echofrost asked, sweeping her eyes across the group. "Why have they brought you here?"

"I don't know." Redfire narrowed his eyes at Rahkki, who was clinging tightly to Echofrost with his arms and legs. "Do you trust the Landwalkers?" he asked.

"Of course not," she answered. "But I need them to save you. Where are you being held? Is anyone injured? How is Hazelwind?"

"Hazelwind is angry. He blames himself for our capture, but otherwise he's fine. Some are injured, but most of us are battle ready." Redfire lashed his tail at the Gorlan children, warning them to stay back, and continued. "The giants are hiding us in a valley at the top of the mountains. Tall cliffs surround it, so you have to fly real high to spot us, or you have to travel through a pass overland. The mouth of the valley is narrow, and the cliff walls are full of dark caves. It's the perfect place to trap an army of Landwalkers."

The three giants leading the group roared at Echofrost when she flew too close to Redfire.

"Back off, Sula," Rahkki urged, tugging helplessly at her mane.

Echofrost glided higher to appease Rahkki and the giants. She continued speaking with Redfire. "If the valley is open to the sky, then the flying army can't get trapped, right?"

"True," he said.

"How are you kept?"

But Redfire didn't have time to answer. Day Patrol had flown back from scouting the western border of the Sandwen settlement and spotted the giants.

"RAID!" Harak bellowed.

Rahkki urged Echofrost toward the Headwind. "Let's go," he pleaded.

"I'll be back, Redfire!" Echofrost neighed as she surged toward Harak and his stallion, Ilan.

"It's not a raid; they brought their pups!" Rahkki shouted over the hot breeze. "Stand down!"

Harak jerked his stallion around and rocketed toward Rahkki and Echofrost. "Don't tell me what to do, yeah." The Pair flew past and swooped over the Gorlan party, all eighty of Harak's Riders and Fliers trailing behind him.

The giants halted and lifted their weapons.

Harak yanked Ilan into a hover, dropped his reins, and gestured, speaking Gorlish with his hands. The three largest Gorlan males gestured back. After much hand signaling, the giants lowered their weapons, and Harak motioned them to continue their journey toward Fort Prowl. "They've come to talk," he announced to his patrol.

Echofrost and Rahkki followed the group as they emerged out of the jungle and marched past the supply barn that the giants had burned down the last time they'd raided.

The Gorlander's miniature dragons flocked onto the back of the bigger bull elephant and chortled at the Sandwens. The Fifth Clan ceased what they were doing to watch the small procession of Gorlanders and their beasts pass by. Parents collected children and raced into their huts. Their small faces gaped from the windows.

The saber cat snarled, her eyes darting hungrily toward the penned animals near the Sandwen homes. A teenage giant rode on the cat's back, guiding her with a hackamore bridle. The cat, as large as Echofrost, had bearlike shoulders and powerful haunches. She snapped her thick tail back and forth.

Since joining the Fifth Clan militia, Echofrost had

expected to fight giants, but had forgotten about their cats and elephants, which were just as fierce and dangerous. She glanced at Harak's Riders, noting how lithe and fragile they suddenly appeared. But their fast arrows and sharp blades bolstered her, and the fact that giants couldn't fly.

"Open the gates and call the queen," Headwind Harak commanded as they approached the fort. "The Gorlanders have come to parlay."

12

THE SOUP

SINCE THE GORLANDERS AND THEIR BEASTS wouldn't fit inside the queen's command chamber, General Tsun and the Headwinds cleared the courtyard for the parlay. All nonmilitary Sandwens were escorted out except for the Borla and the clan treasurer.

With some pride, Rahkki realized he was permitted to stay. And Sula didn't need any prompting to attend; she dropped toward the courtyard so fast he lost his breath. At the last moment, she flared her light purple end-feathers and landed smoothly beside Tuni and Rizah. The mares nickered greetings to each other, and Rahkki wondered if Sula had made friends with the golden pinto.

The vast flagstone courtyard, flanked by thirty-length-high walls, quickly shrank as the Gorlan party filled its center. While they awaited Queen Lilliam, Rahkki studied the Gorlanders.

Their great size made the Sandwens appear as dolls and their weapons as toys in comparison. As the giants sat or squatted, their bodies slammed heavily upon the flagstone and their loud, grunting breaths filled the air. Their soil-stained fingers took up considerable space in their laps.

The three largest males crouched together, facing the throne that had been carried out for Queen Lilliam. Rahkki's eyes trailed up their huge bodies, noting the stitching in their goatskin wraps, their waterskins, and the bludgeons strapped to their backs. Thick claws grew from their toes and fingers, and a double set of tusks grew out over their lips. Short red fur covered only their chests, shoulders, and upper backs. Long hair in varying shades of red grew from their heads and down their short necks. They seemed half beast, half man, a confusing combination.

The three alpha males each wore a decorative collar, and Brauk had once explained what this meant. *The giants are governed by the largest males*, he'd said. *And you'll know their kings and princes not just by their size,*

but also by the wreaths they wear around their necks. The
kings wear full wreaths, and the princes wear half wreaths.
They're made of gems, ivory, or saber tusks, depending on
the horde.

By their half wreaths, Rahkki understood he was
standing only several lengths from the Gorlan princes of
Highland, Great Cave, and Fire Hordes. He leaned toward
Tuni. "Have the Gorlanders ever come to bargain with us
before?"

She whispered back. "No, but your mother tried to
arrange this for years. She believed the giants could be
reasonable."

The four Gorlan children, who had walked next to the
wild stallion, now gathered close to the Highland Horde
prince, tugging on his goatskin and signing rapid questions to him in Gorlish. The bulky prince pushed them
gently aside, but they swarmed him anew, their faces crinkled with curiosity. Rahkki guessed by his patience with
them that the Highland prince was their sire.

The smallest youngster, a female with tangled red
hair, could not sit still. Her bright-blue eyes darted
around the circle of giants and Sandwens, and a happy
rumbling sound emitted from her throat. She spied
Rahkki watching her and flashed him her milk-white

teeth. Was that a Gorlish smile?

"Why did they bring their pups?" he asked Tuni.

"To prove they mean no harm," she answered. "But look, they're armed. And those animals, the elephants, the saber cat, and the little dragons, can be counted as weapons too, especially the saber cat. Stay on your guard, Rahkki. If this goes sideways, get aboard Sula and fly." She kept her brown eyes trained on the giants as she spoke.

General Tsun jogged through the gates, out of breath, and Rahkki remembered that he'd seen the man speaking with I'Lenna by the river. Rahkki glanced around, but the princess was nowhere to be found.

The general approached the Gorlan princes and signed to them in Gorlish. Giants didn't bother to learn the Sandwen language, probably because they didn't possess the agile tongues necessary to speak it; but all soldiers, Riders, generals, and reigning queens learned simple Gorlish. Better to understand the enemy than not, the Sandwens believed.

Rahkki's mother had begun teaching him Gorlish sign language when he was one year old. "Let's put those busy fingers to use," she'd liked to say. And Rahkki was signing with his mother before other kids his age could communicate at all. He watched General Tsun's hands now, but the gestures blurred into one another. "What's he saying?" he asked Tuni.

She leaned closer, translating. "The general announced that our queen is preparing to emerge."

The Gorlan princes grunted toward the larger of the two elephants that stood outside their circle. The bull's attendants reached into his packs and withdrew four bowls and a covered pot. Carefully, as though it were very fragile, the smaller giants carried the pot toward the princes and gently set it before them. Next, they set the four empty bowls beside it and waited.

A moment passed and then Queen Lilliam emerged, draped in red robes. She'd tied back her long black hair, and her dark-blue eyes scanned the Gorlanders. With one hand on her protruding belly, she stalked toward her throne, chin high, back straight. Her iron crown circled her head. The youngest princesses, Rayni and Jor, followed her out, a reciprocal gesture since the Highland prince had brought his royal children. I'Lenna was not present, and her absence hollowed Rahkki's heart.

General Tsun, speaking in both Sandwen and Gorlish, welcomed the hordes on behalf of the queen.

"Land to skies, can't Lilliam do anything for herself," Tuni muttered.

The three princes approached the throne together, and one called for the captured chestnut stallion to be brought forth. A giant led the prancing wild Kihlara toward the throne. The winged horse was tall, lean, and naturally, brilliantly shiny, with sharp-angled golden wings, a deep chest, and a tiny waist. Built more like a wasp than a Kihlara, Rahkki guessed that the stallion's massive rib cage housed an equally gigantic set of lungs and a muscular heart. With his light body, this copper stallion could probably fly higher and faster than most steeds.

The surrounding Sandwens came to the same conclusion. "We have to keep that one for our clan," one Rider said to another.

Above Rahkki, the flicker of black-edged blue wings caught his attention. He watched as I'Lenna and Firo descended from the sky and landed neatly near the queen. Lilliam scowled, and I'Lenna dropped her eyes and scurried to her place beside her sisters.

Rahkki let out his breath. I'Lenna appeared unharmed after her conversation with General Tsun, but what had they spoken about?

Then the Highland prince began signing in Gorlish, and Tuni explained to Rahkki what was happening. "They're offering to trade the captured herd for their stolen land." She huffed at the word *stolen*, but Rahkki knew it was true; his clan had taken the land by force.

The general whispered the offer into Lilliam's ear, and her nostrils flared.

"This is good," Rahkki said, his hope blossoming. "The queen will agree, right?" A deal like this would stop the war with the giants, save the wild herd, *and* bring peace between the hordes and the Sandwens.

"Wait." Tuni slowly raised her hand as she studied the conversation between the giants and the general. "The Gorlanders won't discuss this further until Lilliam has shared soup with them." Tuni exhaled, shaking her head. "Giants," she muttered.

The wild red stallion was led away, and the Gorlan attendants returned to the pot they'd brought from Mount Crim. With a grace belying their size, they untied the lid and removed it. Steam rose from the large container, and everyone present leaned closer. Gorlan horde soup was legendary, and Rahkki stood on his tiptoes, wanting to see it for himself.

Odd lumps bobbed in the yellow broth as the attendants

stirred it, and Rahkki's gut lurched. Gorlan camps and their entire culture centered round their massive cauldrons of soup. Broths often simmered for years, even decades. The older the soup, the better it tasted to the giants; and each member of the horde contributed, tossing in whatever animal or plant they'd harvested during the day. Each meal for a Gorlander's entire life was scooped directly from the communal pot.

And when the giants warred, they attacked one another's cauldrons, tipping them over or tossing coal into the broth to spoil it. Once spoiled, a horde would have to start over with a fresh broth. And since they believed that a young soup would weaken an entire generation of giants, losing an old soup was a terrible blow to a horde.

But when the giants were at peace, they shared soup—and right now the giants were offering to share with the Sandwens. "Finally the hordes have something worthwhile to trade," Tuni whispered, glancing at the red stallion. "This could be the end of our thousand-year war."

Rahkki's scalp tingled with pleasure. This also meant the giants hadn't harmed Sula's wild herd, not yet.

The attendants ladled a creamy broth into each of the carved wooden bowls and then handed the steaming soup to each Gorlan prince. The older of the two attendants approached Lilliam with the final bowl, which was much smaller: a human-size bowl.

The crowd of Riders and Land Guard soldiers quieted. Only the sound of shuffling hooves and feet, soft nickers, and the unexpectedly savory aroma of the Gorlan broth filled the air. The older attendant, a male Gorlander about twelve lengths tall, halted at Lilliam's throne with her bowl in his gigantic hands. He bowed toward her while the other attendant signed in Gorlish.

Tuni summarized. "They say they are proud to honor our queen with a portion of soup before negotiating. It's a mixture of broth from each horde, and the combined age of the serving comes to seventy-five years. It has nourished two generations of giants." Tuni lifted a brow. "They're extremely proud of it."

The attendant handed the bowl to Lilliam as if presenting her with a newborn baby.

Tuni relaxed her shoulders, her warm eyes finding Rahkki's. "This is incredible," she said. "In the Gorlan culture, sharing soup creates kinship. They will be honor bound to come to peaceful terms with us after sharing soup with Lilliam. When your mother tried to arrange this, the giants weren't as receptive."

"So there will be no war?"

Tuni smiled. "Nope. All Lilliam has to do is eat the soup."

"How do you know all this?" Rahkki asked.

Tuni adjusted the baldric that held her sword, and the oiled leather creaked in response. "Your mother studied Gorlan culture in Daakur, where there are many books about the giants. When she returned, she taught us."

Rahkki glanced at Queen Lilliam, who stared suspiciously at the soup. He understood her hesitation. It was said that giants put everything in their broth—from insects, snakes, and rodents, to spiny plants and vines, and even Sandwen children. In fact, whenever a child went missing in the clan, his people didn't blame the dangerous jungle—they blamed the giants.

Because of this, making peace with them was all the more important. So why was Lilliam hesitating? Rahkki glanced at Princess I'Lenna, noting her horrified expression. His friend tried to speak to her mother, but Lilliam shushed her. An uncomfortable pause fell upon the hordes as the Sandwen queen whispered heatedly with her general.

"Queen Lilliam knows she has to eat the soup, right?" Rahkki whispered to Tuni. "And why is General Tsun translating for her; doesn't she speak Gorlish?"

Tuni paled, and her eyes flicked across the circle to Meela Swift, the woman who'd replaced Brauk as Headwind. Meela's green eyes were as round as Daakuran marbles. Even Harak had blanched. Tuni's hand shifted back to her sword. "Rahkki, I think you'd better get out of here."

"I don't—"

But he never finished the sentence.

13

FIGHT

ECHOFROST STARTLED WHEN LILLIAM HEAVED
out of her chair and swiped the bowl of Gorlan soup toward
her general. "Why don't *you* eat it?" she snarled. But when
her hand struck the bowl, it tipped out of the giant's paw
and clattered onto the flagstone. The yellow broth spilled,
as thick as blood, and spread toward Lilliam's sandals.
The bowl wobbled, landing upside down.

Silence descended.

The Gorlan princes stared at the spilled soup, their
faces turning as red as their hair. They rose and pounded
the flagstone with their fists, threw back their heads, and
roared. The noise struck Echofrost's chest, rolling through
her like thunder.

"Go!" Tuni shoved Rahkki as she swung her body onto Rizah's back. "Now!"

Rahkki plunged toward Echofrost and they collided; he fell. Huge bare feet slapped the stone around him as the giants closed ranks against the Sandwens. Rahkki rolled out of the way as a Gorlan foot dropped toward him. Then he leaped to his feet, snatched Echofrost's mane, and hauled himself aboard. She pushed off the hard stone and sprang toward the clouds.

The tiny fire-breathing dragons filled the sky, chortling and hissing. Echofrost dodged them as they swarmed the Sandwens and shot jets of blue, then red flames out of their mouths. The soldiers ducked behind their shields.

Echofrost galloped toward the heights, pumping her wings and swirling straight up like a bat. Rahkki gripped her mane tight and squeezed his legs. She felt a tremor shudder through him.

Princess I'Lenna had thrown her sisters onto Shysong's back and leaped up behind them. The blue roan paddled through the sky, panting at the effort to carry all three. Echofrost soared toward her friend, and they hovered side by side. "Where's Redfire?" Echofrost had lost sight of their friend in the melee.

"They retied him to that elephant."

Echofrost squinted, her eyes telescoping fifty wing-lengths to the scene below. She glimpsed Redfire's copper hide as the cow elephant trotted across the courtyard, dragging the stallion behind her. A giant had mounted the beast and they shambled toward the gates, which the Sandwens were shutting.

The Sky Guard ascended. Guiding their pegasi with their legs, the Riders fired arrows at the Gorlanders. The queen's private guards had whisked Lilliam into the command chamber, and fortress guards defended the entrance.

The small Gorlan party, outnumbered and outraged, gathered close to retreat.

"Surround them!" General Tsun shouted. The Land Guard soldiers circled the giants, their *sawa* swords flashing in the sunlight.

Rahkki shouted over the wind to I'Lenna. "Why didn't your mother eat the soup?"

I'Lenna's sisters sat in front of her, crying; but Echofrost saw fury, not sadness, smoldering in the older girl's dark eyes. "She doesn't speak Gorlish," I'Lenna answered, and spat toward the ground. "I told her to learn. I tried to teach her." She tugged on Shysong's reins, flying the mare in a wide circle.

Below, the giants slammed Sandwens across the

courtyard. "I should be fighting." Rahkki bent to urge Echofrost toward the battle.

"You're not ready," I'Lenna cried. "You don't even have armor!"

But Echofrost needed no urging. She dived toward the battle, whinnying to Shysong. "The Sandwens are going to trap the giants inside the courtyard. We have to free Redfire."

But then the bull elephant rammed the unlocked gates, flinging them wide open.

Led by the two elephants, the Gorlanders rushed out and their huge strides carried them swiftly toward the jungle. The burners took up the rear, blasting the Sandwens with their coldest flames. The purple fire froze the Sandwen swords, covering the metal in frost, and the soldiers dropped them, crying out when the icy blasts reached their fingers. Chirping in delight, the dragons protected the giants' retreat into the forest.

Echofrost swooped after the Gorlanders, and the Fire Horde prince spotted her. He signed to his trained dragons. A cluster of the burners massed together and flew at her, combining their flames into a huge blue ball of fire. She tucked her wings and dived to avoid being struck.

Rahkki floated off her back but kept hold of her mane. *He's learning to stay with me,* she thought.

The dragons dived down, shooting hot jets at the new Pair. Rahkki cringed when the flames licked the back of his neck. Echofrost smelled burned hair. She flew sideways, then angled toward the clouds. The dragons chased her. *Blast it!* She couldn't lose the swift the little beasts. She retreated, and when the tiny dragons realized it, they turned and followed their masters into the jungle.

Echofrost glided back to Shysong. "I couldn't get to Redfire," she neighed. Gazing down, they watched the Sandwens scurry around the courtyard and the damaged gates like ants.

Shysong blinked her large ice-blue eyes. "Whatever just happened down there, I don't think it's good for Storm Herd."

Echofrost stamped the sky as anger scorched her heart. "I agree, and as much as I can't stand it, we still need the Landwalkers' help to free Storm Herd. Nothing has changed." She glanced at the roan and the three young cubs riding on her back, then down at the furious and shocked Sandwens. "Redfire told me that Dewberry is having twins."

"Twins," Shysong gasped. "We have to rescue her before they're born."

Echofrost flattened her ears, and with fresh resolve, she said, "We will."

∽ 14 ∽

THE BLANKET

THE LAND GUARD AND SKY GUARD ARMIES COL-
lected in the courtyard. Rahkki wanted to ask I'Lenna
about her meeting with General Tsun, but there was
no time. The wild mares glided into the courtyard. Firo
touched down first and the princesses rode her toward
their private chambers inside the fortress. Rahkki and
Sula landed near the hitching post. Rahkki slid off his
silver mare, feeling miserable. He'd had no control over
Sula during the Gorlan skirmish. His mare did whatever
she wanted. He'd never be able to pilot her well.

"We should go after the giants right now," Harak
snapped at Tuni.

Rahkki was close enough to the Headwinds to

eavesdrop. He grew still and melted into his surroundings. All stable grooms knew how to vanish while in plain sight. Spying on Riders was, in fact, one of their favorite pastimes, and Rahkki had once been Brauk's stable groom.

"The Gorlanders came in peace," Tuni snarled back. "We're the ones who blew the parlay." Her eyes cut toward the command chamber where the queen had disappeared.

Harak pushed his stallion against Tuni's mare. "The giants want farmland that is on *our* soil, yeah. Lilliam would never have agreed to their demands, soup or no soup."

Tuni's soft-brown eyes darkened with rage. "She could have told them that without offending all three hordes. War is inevitable now."

Harak jerked on Ilan's reins, driving the nervous stallion even harder into Tuni's mare. "Are you questioning our queen?"

Tuni pressed her lips together. Rizah flattened her ears, threatening to kick Ilan.

Meela pranced toward them aboard Jax. "The giants will be back with warriors from all three hordes and their battle beasts. We can't let that happen to our village. We need to strike first—in *their* territory."

Harak nodded. "I agree."

"We have no choice now," Tuni grumbled.

"Wipe that sour look off your face, Hightower," Harak snarled, "or I might start questioning your devotion to our ruler, yeah?"

"Riders!" General Tsun marched toward them, his flint-blue eyes trained on the Headwinds. "The queen won't hold Council tonight, she's not feeling well, but she's spoken her commands. Forget the scouting mission tomorrow, no time for that now. She's sending us to Mount Crim, a full battalion of Riders and soldiers. Our orders are to destroy the hordes and retrieve the wild Kihlari. There is much to do to get ready. We leave in two days' time."

A heavy silence fell on the group, and Rahkki held his breath. This is what Sula wanted, to save her friends. It was finally happening.

"We'll leave a ghost detail behind to protect the clan from predators," the general added, looking around at the stunned faces. "Have you heard me? We're going to war."

"We hear you," the three Headwinds answered in unison.

"Then prepare! Ready your fighters, sharpen your weapons, and mend your tack and armor. You have two days." General Tsun stalked away, his fists clenched.

The Headwinds dispersed. Tuni mounted Rizah and was about to leave when she spotted Rahkki, eavesdropping in the shadows. She trotted Rizah toward him. "You're a Rider, but you don't have to go with us," she said. "You can stay back and protect the clan."

Rahkki shook his head. "Sula won't stay back. She knows the giants have her friends."

"Friends?" Tuni frowned. "Rahkki, I'm not sure Sula is as aware of things as you believe."

He snorted. "She is; I know it. Sula will follow the Sky Guard to Mount Crim, with or without me."

Tuni flipped her dark-red locks off her shoulders and let out a pent-up breath. "All right, but you both need armor. If you don't have it by tomorrow, I'll clip Sula's flight feathers and ground her myself. That will keep you two home."

"You wouldn't!" he cried.

Tuni's eyes glistened. "The feathers will grow back, but I have to look after *you*, Rahkki. Who else will?"

He straightened. "I'm a Rider, and I'm almost thirteen. *I'll* look after me."

She softened. "Just get the armor by tomorrow night. Promise?"

He nodded, feeling sullen. "My mother would have eaten the soup."

"The Pantheress? Yes," Tuni agreed. "She'd have eaten it and asked for seconds." The Headwind peered skyward and grabbed Rizah's mane. "Yah, Rizah!" The golden pinto whinnied and soared up and out of the courtyard, her gold-edged pink feathers twinkling in the sunlight.

Rahkki turned to Sula, filled with sadness. When he was a prince, buying a set of armor for himself and his Flier would have been as easy as ordering a chunk of honeycomb at the Clan Gathering. Now the dramals he needed were so out of reach they might as well have been stars. "I can't afford new armor," he said to his mare. "But maybe Uncle is right. Maybe Koko has some old stuff for us." Deep down, he didn't believe she did—armor was too precious to go unused—but he led his mare to the Kihlari stable anyway, hoping for a miracle.

When he arrived, he led Sula into her stall and then hunted about for Koko. He found her, finishing her instructions to the grooms. News of the war had traveled like a firestorm through the clan, and the grooms had gathered around Koko like squirrels, their eyes bright, their heads cocked.

"Check the tack, fix ev'ry tear an' broken stitch," she said. "Pack 'xtra straps, spare bridles, an' tools. Yur marchin' wit the soldiers so yuh can care for the steeds. Don' forgit nothin'. Now git." The grooms scattered.

Koko swung around, spotted Rahkki, and squared up. "Yuh pack the same gear fur yur wildin', since yuh don' got a groom ta do it."

"I would, but I don't have any gear yet," he said helplessly.

Koko swept her gaze across Rahkki, considering him a moment, then sighed. "I got tack yuh can borrow, but no armor. Come on."

He followed her into the tack room. Koko pushed her thick blond hair off her face as she dug through trunks of old equipment, and Rahkki watched the muscles ripple in her shoulders. The girl was powerful strong and as unflappable as a spit dragon. She would make an excellent warrior. "Do you want to be a Rider?" he asked.

Koko froze, her head deep inside a trunk. Her answer echoed up to him. "Course I do." She heaved out an old saddle, chose a bridle, and faced him. "Can't afford a Flier though." Her brown eyes settled hard on Rahkki. Like Mut, she'd tried to win the wild mare at the contest, but

Sula had easily thrown her. "Maybe I'll git one a those wildlin's after we save 'em."

"The queen is selling them to Daakur." That fact soured his stomach. How would Sula react when her friends were freed and then sold? He didn't want to find out. Somehow, he would stop that sale.

Koko rocked back on her heels. "Sellin' 'em ain' righ'." She tossed him a long look and then closed the tack room door so they were alone.

Rahkki stood up, wondering what she wanted. Outside, he heard grooms rushing about the stable, calling to each other and arguing as their excitement mounted.

Koko lowered her voice. "Join the uprisin', Rahkki. Git tha' crazy queen off yur mutha's throne."

Rahkki stilled. "You know—"

"I know the general talked to yuh."

"Bloody rain," he muttered, sweat prickling his scalp. "I told him I won't join. No future queen will be able to trust the Fifth Clan if we're traitors."

"It's more dangerous ta keep 'er, Rahkki," Koko retorted. "Granak didn' eat the sow offerin', did yuh 'ear tha'? An' now this mess wit the soup—the queen's lost 'er 'ead."

Rahkki braced. "I won't join." He met her hot gaze.

After a moment, Koko sighed and handed him the tack she'd found. "Here, yuh can 'ave this. An' git yur mutha's Kihlara blanket outta here b'fore it gits ruined." She pointed at a closed trunk. "After your wildlin' kicked Brauk, I stowed it there."

Koko left the room, and Rahkki approached the trunk she'd indicated. He opened the lid, catching a glint of blue fabric. At the winged-horse auction, Sula had worn this ceremonial blanket that had once belonged to Reyella's winged stallion, Drael. Brauk had said it would encourage higher bidding, but after Sula kicked Brauk, she'd been led back to her stall and Koko must have taken it off her.

He lifted the trunk lid higher and removed the soft blanket. Decorated with tassels and jewels and trimmed in white fur, it filled his hands with memories. He pressed it to his nose and inhaled. This blanket was one of the few treasures Rahkki and Brauk still possessed that had belonged to their mother. Brauk had gambled or sold everything else during the dark years following her death.

But this custom-made blanket, as soft as a flower petal, was worth two hundred dramals, maybe more. Staring at it, Rahkki clenched the material into his fists. Suddenly he knew how to get the money for the armor, but his throat squeezed tight at the thought. If there were any other way, he'd take it. But this was the best option—and also the worst.

Tomorrow morning, he'd fly Sula to the trading post at Cinder Bay. The Sandwen clans bartered with one another for most of their goods and supplies, but some things— like metalwork, books, foreign spices, fine fabrics, and armor—had to be purchased from the empire. And since the empire also purchased items from the Sandwens, a trading post had been set up on the Sandwen side of Cinder Bay. Daily ferry service transported the Daakuran merchants to and from the post.

Rahkki fingered the precious fabric. Tomorrow, he would sell Drael's blanket.

⟊ 15 ⟊

THE DESCENDANTS

ALONE IN HER STALL, ECHOFROST MUNCHED HER hay and downed her grain because she knew it kept her strong. It seemed obvious to her that the giants had come in peace—the group was small and they'd brought their cubs—it was also obvious that the meeting with the Sandwens had not gone well. Redfire was heading back to Storm Herd, still a captive, but she was relieved to know her friends were alive and that Dewberry's foals were safe, still unborn.

Around her, the Kihlari stable blazed with activity as grooms rushed up and down the aisles, gathering tack, Kihlara armor, saddlebags, and grooming kits. Echofrost spied Jax, Meela's stallion, standing nearby while a groom massaged lineament oil into his tired muscles. "When is the Sky Guard flying to Mount Crim? Do you know?" Echofrost asked him.

The gold dun nodded absently. "Soon. A day, maybe two. We'll end our war with the giants forever."

Echofrost's heart stammered. "Good—that's good!"

In the neighboring stall, Kol reared. "I should be going!" He rammed the divider between them with his chest. "This is your fault."

Angling her head to see him better, Echofrost studied the stallion. Kol's tail twitched madly, and his eyes rolled back, showing the whites. This powerful Flier hadn't been exercised in days. Pegasi in Anok adopted a similar state of distress when they were injured and couldn't fly. There was only one cure for what ailed Kol—the wind in his feathers and his lungs full of clouds.

"You need to get out and fly," she prescribed.

Kol's brown eyes bored into hers. "If my Rider wasn't injured, I *would* be out." He spun another circle, his hooves scraping the floor.

"This is ridiculous," she huffed. "You should be free to fly when you want."

Kol's anger crumpled. "I miss Brauk," he whinnied. "I want him back."

"You depend on him too much; it isn't right."

"I love Brauk," Kol said. "You'll see; you'll love Rahkki too."

"Never," she whinnied. "I don't make friends with wolves or horses or birds, so why would I make friends with a *boy*?"

But a memory flew up in her mind. The immortal stallion named Star had befriended Crabwing, a bird that lived on the coast of Anok. His adoration for Crabwing had shone in his eyes each time he told a story about the silly, lazy bird. *I guess pegasi do sometimes make friends with other creatures*, she thought. *But then, Star was not like most pegasi.*

Echofrost snorted away her thoughts. "Brauk is your *captor*, not your friend. You love him because he lets you out of your stall and takes you flying. But if he set you free, you could fly when you wanted. You could find a mate and sire foals. You could *truly* live. This is not living." She kicked the wall between them.

"You're wrong," Kol whinnied, but with less conviction.

A spotted Kihlara mare across the aisle spoke. "Isn't it frightening to live in the wild?" she asked Echofrost.

"Not when you live with a herd," she replied. "We watch out for one another. We have patrols scanning for predators and scouts searching for the best grasslands. Our foals fly moments after they're born. By the time they're weaned, they can fly to the clouds. We migrate twice a year to avoid bad weather. It's very safe as long as we're together."

More Kihlari lifted their heads and listened to Echofrost. When she'd first arrived at this barn, they'd rejected the idea of living wild. Now she sensed their curiosity budding. "You all lived wild, once," she reminded them.

"You still think we're the lost descendants of those ancient Lake Herd steeds?" the spotted mare asked.

Echofrost nodded. "Yes. Lake Herd lived in the interior of Anok, in the Flatlands. The steeds all vanished four hundred years ago, right around the time your ancestors arrived here." She fluffed her feathers, remembering tales she'd heard about the ancient pegasi. "They were excellent wind surfers. I wish I could have attended their flight school."

"Flight school?" Kol eyed her suspiciously. "So you aren't born knowing how to fly. You have to learn?"

She shook her white mane. "Yes and no. Pegasus foals fly moments after their birth, but we do learn about wind currents, elevations, and advanced maneuvers from our instructors."

Triumph flared in the stallion's eyes. "Just like I learn from Brauk."

"Okay, okay, I guess it's a little bit the same," Echofrost admitted. "But an experienced pegasus can teach you a lot more about flying than a Landwalker. You don't need Brauk. What you need is more practice and a better teacher."

"Like you?"

"No, like Hazelwind or Dewberry. Redfire—that chestnut stallion who was with the giants—he can ride the jet streams and fly to where the blue sky turns black."

"That's impossible," a white stallion scoffed.

Echofrost glanced at him. "It's not. My friend Morningleaf rode a jet stream once. And the ancient mare Raincloud once flew to where the blue sky turns black sky to escape a cruel over-stallion."

"Your homeland does not sound safe." Kol tossed his yellow-streaked red mane. "Not at all."

Echofrost shrugged. "It's no more dangerous than living with dragons and giants and Landwalkers, except our herd protects us."

"Is it true you keep your foals forever?" the spotted mare interrupted.

"We do," Echofrost answered. "A herd is a huge family

made up of smaller families. We guard our foals and keep them close. When they're grown, they raise their families in the same herd they were born to. Sometimes a pegasus leaves, but it's rare." Echofrost decided not to mention the wars with foreign herds, the occasional stolen foals, or the raids. That was life in Anok. The Kihlari here could choose to live in peace.

Kol's tension eased. "Do you sleep outside?"

Echofrost whinnied, amused. "Most of us, but Desert Herd pegasi sleep in caves, and Jungle Herd steeds build nests high in the trees." She noticed that all the Kihlari were listening now. Their eager faces and innocent questions made her eyes sting with tears. These pegasi had been *robbed* of their birthright and turned into slaves. Overcome by the injustice of it, she nickered to them softly. "Once we free Storm Herd from the giants, you should join us. Try living free."

The Kihlari flinched backward. "And leave our Riders as Halves?" Tension shot through the barn. Some Kihlari trembled; others pawed the floor.

"Blast it," Echofrost muttered, suddenly understanding. The Kihlari had bonded to their Riders as deeply as she'd bonded to her mother and friends in Anok. The thought of leaving was as distressful to the Kihlari as losing a herd would be to a pegasus. Their instinct to stick together was working *against* them. But they would get over their attachment to Landwalkers in time; Echofrost believed that.

"Just think about it," she nickered to them. "You don't have to do anything you don't want to do. But if you want to raise a family of your own, you'll never have that here. Never."

The Kihlari grew silent and retreated to the backs of their stalls, clearly overwhelmed. Kol tilted his head, considering Echofrost. "If Brauk doesn't heal, I'll be a Half," he stated flatly. "They'll send me to the Ruk."

Echofrost leaned toward him. "You have a place with Storm Herd, if you want it."

Kol sighed and dropped his head. "I just want Brauk." He sagged against his wall.

Echofrost didn't know how to soothe the big stallion. She returned to her dry hay and chewed it mindlessly. *I need to get these steeds out of the barn and into the sky*, she thought. *They've never tasted freedom, or flown without a Rider, but once they do, they will love it.* She closed her eyes and drifted into a fitful sleep.

16

UNTETHERED

LATER THAT AFTERNOON, RAHKKI AND THE other Riders met with the three Headwinds in the training yard for a briefing.

"It'll take the soldiers five days to march to Mount Crim once we embark," Tuni said. "Our first orders are to protect the Land Guard," Tuni said. "Their pack animals and cooking fires will attract droolers and panthers—we are to slay them on sight. The army will stick to the clan travelways for as long as they can."

Harak interjected. "When we get to the mountain, we'll set up base camp and send scouts to find the wild Kihlari, yeah. Our queen wants them alive, unharmed." He met each Rider's eyes. "We'll halter the steeds and slice their flight feathers so we can drag them home. Got that, Riders?"

They each nodded, except Rahkki. He met Harak's stare, his anger bubbling. When the meeting was over, Harak yanked Rahkki aside, his green eyes as cold as emeralds. "You better have that armor by the time we leave," he snipped. "I'm counting on that viper you ride to lead us straight to her herd, yeah." He released Rahkki, boarded Ilan, and coasted toward Fort Prowl.

Rahkki left the yard and went straight to visit Brauk, but Brim shook her head. "He's not here. I moved him to your uncle's farm. Ossi Finn is with him, she's his new caretaker."

"Mut Finn's sister!" Rahkki blurted.

"That's the one." Brim chuckled. "She's a good sort, Rahkki."

"If you say so," he mumbled. Rahkki thought about the fine ceremonial blanket he was going to sell. "Soon I'll have the coin to pay you back, Brim."

She gave him a stern look. "I'm an animal doctor, Rahkki. You can pay me when you bring me an animal." She sent him off with a hug and a new pouch of tea.

Rahkki decided to head to Uncle's farm right away, to ask Brauk's permission before he sold their mother's blanket. He stopped by the Kihlari stable to pick up Sula, but when he arrived to retrieve her, his eyes landed on Kol. The dejected stallion drooped in his stall, head low, tail down, probably bored out of his mind. "Kol," Rahkki gasped.

The chestnut whirled around and whinnied a sharp reprimand at his former caretaker.

Guilt gutted Rahkki. "I'm sorry, boy, so sorry. Land to skies, I've left you locked in here." Rahkki wiped the tears that pricked his eyes. He snatched Kol's halter and strapped it onto the stallion's head. "You're coming with us."

He quickly haltered Sula and led both winged horses out of the stable, scanning the Fifth Clan settlement as he did so. On the hillside, the villagers were fortifying their supplies and their homes against attack. Metal sang as soldiers and Riders sharpened blades. Cooking fires glowed as clansfolk smoked meat. And clay ovens steamed as grooms baked grain patties for the five-day march to Mount Crim.

People tromped everywhere, preparing for war, and Rahkki wasn't in the mood to be teased or laughed at for walking his Flier instead of flying her, so he skirted the border of his settlement along the jungle's edge. He crept softly, listening for Granak. The dragon had not eaten the sow, and that meant the beast was hungry.

While they traveled, Sula and Kol nosed him impatiently. They wanted to fly but he preferred to walk, so he ignored them. Overhead, the clouds darkened, threatening rain. A band of orangutans hooted within the nearby trees, but the usual noise of the jungle had subdued, perhaps because of the recent appearance of the giants.

When they arrived at Darthan's hut, Rahkki led the steeds toward the barn. Kol balked at the doorway, his hide twitching. *He needs to fly*, Rahkki thought, but he didn't want to take the stallion up himself, and Brauk couldn't ride yet.

He glanced from Kol to Sula. His wild mare knew how to fly by herself. Why couldn't he let both steeds loose to have some fun? Smiling at the idea, Rahkki slid off their halters.

Sula's eyes widened. Kol tensed.

"Go on," Rahkki urged. "Shoo! Get!" He waved his arms at them.

A happy whinny burst from Sula's lips as she leaped into the sky. Kol flared his wings, glanced around, and then galloped away, bucking and lifting off. He trailed the silver mare toward the clouds. She hovered, waiting for him. When he caught her, the two soared toward the River Tsallan. All Kihlari enjoyed water, and Rahkki wondered if they'd go for a swim.

Still smiling, Rahkki entered Darthan's hut to find a crackling fire and his brother lying on a cot, his eyes closed. "Ay, Uncle, ay, Brauk," he greeted, shrugging off his satchel and rushing to his brother's side.

A red-haired female sat near, about Brauk's age. She extended her wrists. "Ay Rahkki, I'm Ossi Finn."

He clasped her wrists, noting her pale-blue eyes, freckles, and mischievous smile. He'd seen her around, of course, but had never spoken to her. He liked her instantly.

"I'll fix you a plate," Darthan offered, and he began fussing over the platters cooling on his table.

Rahkki knelt beside his brother's cot. Brauk had taken all the bells and beads out of his hair. The black locks hung long and loose, reaching well past his shoulders. He lay flat, his head propped on a firm pillow. His tan skin was pale, and when he opened his gold eyes, they were as dark as amber. "Hey," Rahkki said.

"Hey," his brother answered.

Darthan interrupted, handing Rahkki a plate. "Either of you want some more?" he asked Brauk and Ossi.

They shook their heads, and Ossi moved to a low-backed

chair to watch the fire dance in Darthan's hearth.

Rahkki hadn't eaten since breakfast. As Darthan and Ossi chattered quietly, he sat next to Brauk and filled his starving belly. The meal was delicious, a feast of bamboo-skewered pork, slow-grilled wild mushrooms, fried rice, boiled duck eggs, fresh-sliced melons, and coconut milk. Brauk watched him eat as the conversation in the hut turned toward the giants. Ossi had informed the Stormrunners about the failed parlay, but since Rahkki had witnessed it, he filled them in on the finer details.

"I should be going to war, not lazing here like a Half," Brauk muttered, glaring at his unmoving legs.

Uncle Darthan stiffened, then relaxed. He was a Half. His Flier, Tor, had died of heart failure years ago. Tor was Drael's twin, and this brought Rahkki's mind back to the reason for his visit. He stood and retrieved Drael's ceremonial blanket from his satchel, causing Ossi to leap out of her chair. "That's beautiful!" she exclaimed.

"Ah, you found Drael's blanket," Darthan said. "I wondered where it had gone."

"Koko had it," Rahkki answered, fixing his eyes on Brauk. "But . . . I'm going to sell it."

Brauk's head reared upward. "You're what!" He gritted

his teeth. "That blanket belonged to our mother's stallion."

Rahkki flinched, struck by Brauk's hollow, anguished tone. "I know. But Brauk, we need the dramals. How else am I supposed to care for my Flier?"

"You shouldn't have bought that wild mare in the first place." Brauk grunted, clenching his fists.

"I didn't buy her; I won her."

"Bloody rain, you know what I mean." Brauk spat at Rahkki's feet. "That viper almost killed me, and now you want to sell Drael's blanket to feed her. Just let her go. Get rid of her."

"But she won't go," Rahkki explained. "She wants the Fifth Clan to free her herd."

Brauk groaned. "There you go again, putting thoughts into that mare's head that aren't there. She's an animal, Rahkki. A stupid animal."

Rahkki leaned away. "Why do you hate Sula so much?"

Brauk slammed his unfeeling legs with his fists. "Did you really just ask me that?"

Rahkki blanched. "I'm sorry."

Brauk spat on the floor again. Desperate, Rahkki continued. "Look, I can't replace the hay and grain we lost in the last giant raid. If I can't feed Kol or Sula, they'll both be sent to the Ruk. The rations you stored are gone, Brauk. We have nothing left . . . except this blanket."

Brauk froze at the mention of the Ruk, his eyes glistening. "Sun and stars," he hissed. "I see you have to do it, Rahkki—but Sula? She deserves nothing."

Rahkki exhaled. At least he had permission, however painful. "There's someone here to see you," Rahkki said, changing the subject. With a sly smile at Darthan, Rahkki opened the front door and whistled for Kol. The bright stallion soared up from the river and coasted toward Rahkki. Upon landing, the large-boned Flier trotted into the hut and headed straight toward Brauk. Ossi dived out of the way.

"Land to skies, he's big," she said, laughing.

The stallion lowered his head, sniffing Brauk's hair. "Kol . . . my boy." Brauk's eyes moistened as he scratched behind his stallion's ears and stroked his round jaw. Kol nickered, filled with pleasure. "We'll be flying again soon," Brauk whispered into Kol's pricked ear. "Just you, me, and the sky."

Rahkki left the hut to check on Sula, and Darthan followed. The mare was in the barn, nickering to Lutegar, Uncle's swamp buffalo. The two creatures had briefly shared a stall after giants had attacked the rice farm during the last raid. Sula arched her neck, her eyes luminous as she watched Rahkki and Darthan approach.

"She's a fine braya," Uncle said.

"You don't hate her, do you?"

Darthan hunched to inspect Sula's sharpened hooves. "She's not mean, she's wild," he said. Then Darthan pointed. "How do the wild steeds know to sharpen their hooves? I think our steeds can learn from them."

"I'm sure they can," Rahkki said, happy his uncle felt the way he did—that the Kihlari were more intelligent than most Sandwens believed. He paused for a moment. "I'm flying to Mount Crim with the Sky Guard. I didn't know if you'd heard."

"I did." Darthan nodded slowly. "The tension in our clan is about to snap, Rahkki. Perhaps this war with the giants will unite us—you know, common enemy?"

"Maybe." Rahkki changed the subject. "When are you leaving for Daakur?"

"I'm packed and ready," Darthan replied. "Catching the last ferry out tonight."

Rahkki's heart fluttered. "Thank you. I hope you find out something about Reyella."

Clattering hooves caught their attention. Kol exited the hut and winged across the grass, whinnying to Sula.

The silver mare left the barn and joined him. The two Fliers galloped into the sky just as the clouds shuddered and drizzled warm rain. Undaunted, the pair soared overhead, gliding and circling and nickering.

"She's already teaching him," Darthan said, his expression awed.

"Teaching him what?"

"Her ways." Rahkki and his uncle retired to the porch and watched the two steeds fly, untethered and free.

17

TACK

THE NEXT MORNING, ECHOFROST AND KOL FOL-
lowed Rahkki overland back to the Kihlari stable. "He
better get over his fear of flying before the war," Kol nickered.

Echofrost nodded, enjoying the truce between them.
The joy of unencumbered flight had opened Kol's mind last
night, and he'd spent the evening drilling her with questions about living wild. He learned that a lead mare and
an over-stallion governed a herd, but that Star had begun
a new practice. The supernatural stallion had appointed
a Council to make decisions. Kol learned that Anokian
armies were sectioned into battalions led by captains; that
herds utilized *sky herders*, agile mares who used speed and

a secret language to confuse and drive their enemies into traps; that medicine mares treated the sick and injured; and that wild steeds mated for life. Under-stallions and mares raised their foals as a family. Kol also learned that wild Kihlari called themselves *pegasi*.

"You don't live like wild horses at all," Kol had commented.

"Why would we? We're not horses," Echofrost had whinnied, annoyed.

Now the shiny chestnut fluttered his feathers, looking happy for the first time since Echofrost had injured Brauk. "I want to learn more," he said. "I want to fly higher, faster, farther. It's so much easier without . . . without Brauk." Kol's voice faded, and Echofrost saw guilt tumbling in his eyes, and perhaps possibilities.

She eyed his muscle tone, his plumage, his hooves; and she guessed he was fourteen years old, maybe older, but still quite young for a pegasus. He had plenty of time to learn, to start a herd of his own, or to join hers. But she wouldn't press him, not today.

Now, they arrived at the Kihlari stable amid much neighing and questioning from Kol's friends.

Where have you been?

What did Sula do to you?

"I'm fine," Kol resounded. He stared across the rows and rows of stalls. "Why *are* we kept locked up?" he asked aloud, and this began a heated debate that swept through the barn like a wildfire.

Rahkki had disappeared into the tack room, returning with an old bridle dangling from his fingertips. Echofrost spied it and backed away. She and Rahkki had been managing just fine without any Landwalker entrapments.

"I'm sorry," the boy said, "but it's time you got used to this. I oiled the leather; it's soft now." He brought the bridle closer, and the shiny metal bit glinted in the sunrays that streamed through the barn window. He tried to slide it in Echofrost's mouth.

She reared, and Rahkki covered his head as her sharp hooves ripped the bridle out of his hands. It fell onto the straw, where she thrashed it like a snake. When she finished, she was shaking.

Kol nudged Echofrost. "If you want to fly with the Sky Guard, you have to wear that, and a saddle, and armor. You're teaching me to be wild; let me teach you how to be tame."

Rahkki bent over, breathing through his nose and

clenching his fists. "I'm trying to *help* you," he said, lifting the bridle out of the straw.

Tears filled Echofrost's eyes. She glanced at Kol, "I think it's easier to go from tame to free than the other way around."

"I know Rahkki well," Kol nickered. "He's cared for me since I Paired with Brauk. The boy is gentle. He won't hurt you. Just trust him."

Echofrost glared at the bit, then peered out the barn window toward Mount Crim and Storm Herd, exhaling a mighty breath. She would wear this contraption if it helped save her brother's unborn foals and her best friend, Hazelwind. She lowered her head.

Rahkki slid the cold metal into her mouth. The bit clanged against her teeth and then settled into the wide space between them. Rahkki left and returned with a saddle and saddle pad that he placed on her back.

"You look pretty," Kol whinnied.

She rolled her eyes. "You're hopeless, you know that?" But when Rahkki tightened the girth around her barrel, Echofrost bucked in shock and accidentally knocked her Rider into the wall.

"Careful!" Kol scolded.

Rahkki rolled to his feet, finished buckling her tack with trembling fingers, and led her into the Sky Guard training yard. Kol remained behind to devour his hay and grain. The other Riders quieted at the sight of Echofrost wearing tack.

Tuni, who sat in the shade playing stones with a friend, stood up. "Ay, ay, Stormrunner!" she called, smiling. "Look at Sula!" Tuni walked across the trampled yard and inspected Echofrost.

"The bridle is scratched already," Rahkki said, looking embarrassed.

Tuni grinned. "So what? She's wearing it! Well done." Tuni removed one of Rizah's pink-and-gold feathers from her wrist and tied it to Rahkki's belt. "We haven't formally welcomed you," she said, dipping her head. "Congratulations to the new Pair."

Harak approached next. His green eyes were as sinister as ever as he tied one of Ilan's feathers next to Rizah's on Rahkki's belt. Then he smacked Rahkki, making him stumble. "Welcome to the rest of your life." He tossed Echofrost a ferocious glare and glided away.

Then the Riders who weren't on patrol or practicing drills fell in line. They tied the feathers of their mounts

137

onto her cub's belt and murmured words to them both.

Afterward, Rahkki led Echofrost out of the yard and placed one hand on the saddle, one on her mane, and one booted foot into her saddle stirrup. "Don't move," he pleaded as he hauled himself onto her back.

Echofrost flinched, but soon noticed that her cub felt more stable in a saddle than he did bareback. *I don't like it, but this tack helps him*, she decided.

Rahkki clutched her shining white mane and took up the reins, holding them loosely. "Let's fly," he said, nudging her skyward. Echofrost whinnied and flared her wings. Her purple-hued feathers glistened in the sunlight as she kicked off the grass.

Using his legs and leaving the reins alone, Rahkki guided Echofrost southeast toward the beach at Cinder Bay, home of the trading post. The Fifth Clan settlement shrank as they soared away.

Echofrost inhaled, long and deep, drinking in the swirling scents of jungle mulch, salted air, and mist-laden clouds. The rain forest spread below, an undulating, screeching blanket of green leaves. To the north, she spied the glimmering Dark Water ocean, and to the east rose Mount Crim. She glided effortlessly, growing quickly accustomed to Rahkki's slight weight as he stroked her neck. She allowed his touch without flinching, surprised that it didn't annoy her.

After a short while, a figure appeared below, flying between the trees. "Who's that?" Rahkki wondered.

Rahkki and Echofrost were not alone.

C·❦·18·❦·ᄀ

THE CROWN PRINCESS

A MOMENT AFTER SPOTTING THE INTERLOPERS, Rahkki recognized them, and his heart quickened. "Ay, I'Lenna!" he called to the princess and her winged mount. Sula nickered a joyful greeting to I'Lenna's mare, Firo.

"Fly down here," the princess shouted, her voice jingling like the charms on her anklets.

Rahkki leaned eagerly over Sula's neck, and his mare sank toward the jungle, leaving his belly floating behind him. Sula angled her purple feathers and glided slowly next to her wild friend. They whinnied to each other in excited conversation.

"I need to fly low so the Sky Guard doesn't spot me," I'Lenna explained. "I'm supposed to be in my room 'resting.'" The princess grimaced. "Whenever my mom is tired, she makes *me* rest. It's annoying."

Rahkki laughed.

"But when Firo and I saw you from my bedroom window, we had to join you." She eyed his silver mare. "Saddle and bridle, I'm impressed. You two are having a good day."

"I am," Rahkki agreed. "But Sula's not happy."

"She'll get used to it. Firo did." I'Lenna patted her roan's shiny neck, her adoration beaming from her eyes, and Rahkki wondered how it would feel to have I'Lenna look at him like that.

"So where are you two going?" she asked.

"To the trading post. I need armor before we leave tomorrow." He nodded toward Sula. "We both do."

"You're going shopping?" I'Lenna asked, eyes widening. "That's perfect. I need a few things myself." The princess stretched tall and watched the trees blur past them. Her skinny sun-tanned arms guided Firo with sure gentleness, and Rahkki noticed that she'd changed from her usual dress into smooth leather riding breeches and a blue silk blouse—expensive clothes from Daakur. As usual, her jasmine perfume floated behind her, and an exotic blackstone necklace dangled around her neck.

He studied her. When had I'Lenna started wearing

perfume and jewelry? He remembered the days when they were younger, when they were dirt smudged, scab kneed, and poorly shod. He glanced at the threads unwinding from his cotton shirt and his rough boots. He smoothed his hair, wondering when he'd last combed it. But instead of feeling abandoned by I'Lenna's sleek composure, he felt a sudden, urgent desire to keep up with her.

As they flew in companionable silence, Rahkki realized this was a good time to ask I'Lenna about her conversation with General Tsun. "I saw you with the general yesterday," he started.

"What? You couldn't have." I'Lenna's grin faltered. "I stay far away from all that business, Rahkki."

"But—but I saw you," he said. "The general—"

"Sun and stars, Rahkki! The general wants to oust my mother. He's my enemy." She shook her head. "You must be confused."

"Oh, okay," Rahkki said, but he *knew* it was her. His thoughts screeched: *I'Lenna just* lied *to me! Why? Doesn't she trust me?* As his mind swirled, he studied her with fresh eyes. How much did he really know about the crown princess? She had access to secret tunnels, she stole candy and medicine for the villagers, she disobeyed her mother, and she snuck into his bedroom.

And when he thought back, I'Lenna and General Tsun had been relaxed during their conversation by the river, their expressions pleasant. But General Tsun wanted to overthrow Queen Lilliam, and I'Lenna knew it, so why had she been so calm with him? Was she spying on him? Or was she *helping* him? Goose bumps erupted down Rahkki's arms. Land to skies, could *he* trust I'Lenna?

The two fell silent as they glided between the trees. Occasionally a large branch forced Sula to duck or twirl, making Rahkki's head spin; but the jungle here was not dense, and the small mares fit well enough between the palms. Tiny golden monkeys shrieked at them as they passed by.

Rahkki broke the silence first. "So you know all about the rebellion?" he asked.

"Of course." I'Lenna reached between their flying mares and took Rahkki's hand, her fingers hot on his palm. "My mother believes we're plotting to kill her." She said this as casually as one asks for extra nutmeg on their rice.

"She thinks *we're* plotting—you and I?" Rahkki cried. "You're serious?"

"As a dragon."

"But you don't want your mother's throne, do you?"

"Want it?" I'Lenna snorted. "Absolutely not, but I am the crown princess. Authority falls to me if anything happens to her."

Rahkki felt sullen. "General Tsun is the one *actually* plotting against her. He's the real threat."

I'Lenna ignored Rahkki's comment. "The people of the clan loved your mother, but they hate mine. You and Brauk threaten her. You always have. Be careful on the march to Mount Crim. I don't believe my mother intends for you to come home alive."

Rahkki stared at her. "I hear you, I'Lenna, but if your mother thinks you and I are plotting, then I'm not sure that *this* is being careful." He glanced at her hand, which was still holding his.

I'Lenna let go of him, and her brown eyes slid from his head to his boots and then settled back on his face. "Trust me, Rahkki—if I'm caught with you again, *I'll* be the one who pays."

"I'Lenna!"

"Don't worry, I can handle my mother." I'Lenna's voice was firm.

Rahkki believed I'Lenna would have better luck handling a poisonous jellyfish than her mother. His eyes searched her face. "I don't understand. If our friendship is so dangerous, then why are you here with me?"

Her expression softened. "Because you're the only kid my age who owns a flying horse. Who else can I do this with?" She grinned and kicked Firo forward. "Race you to the trading post!"

Rahkki leaned into Sula's mane and clucked at her like she was a horse. But Sula didn't need any encouragement. She pinned her wings and blasted after her wild friend.

19

THE TRADING POST

MOMENTS LATER, RAHKKI AND SULA BURST OUT
of the rain forest. His mare flapped her wings, coasting
toward the southeastern shoreline of Cinder Bay. The
emerald inlet glittered in the sunlight, and a light breeze
prickled the surface. Stingrays glided in the shallows, ele-
gant and wing shaped. Farther out, curling waves broke
against protective reefs. Seabirds soared on updrafts,
then dived down, beaks open.

The sand here was fine and light, unlike the black
sand in the north. The cooling breeze that wafted across
the bay provided Rahkki a welcome relief from the inland
heat. Several boats from Daakur floated dreamily, moored

in the shallows. Sula and Firo flared their nostrils, drinking in the scents from far away.

The trading post, a small expanse of shacks and colorful tents, flickered like a mirage on the hot sand. Rahkki hadn't been here in over a year. Everything was too expensive, and most of what he needed he was able to make himself. For the rest, he darted silvery fish in the river, caught fighting beetles in the jungle, or whittled toys and tools and then traded them for the things he could not make or sew.

The Daakuran merchants, who dressed in soft cloths like I'Lenna's silk, paused their activities to stare in admiration at the winged steeds as they coasted closer. Since the empire protected the sacred Kihlari, no amount of coin could purchase one from the Sandwen clans, but that didn't stop the Daakuran people from wishing.

Sula and Firo dropped toward the beach, speeding in so fast that a concerned outlander shrieked and ran for cover. I'Lenna smirked as the dazzling mares angled their wings, caught the wind, and braked with a loud, feathery snap. Then they alighted onto the sand, as silent and as gentle as butterflies.

Several merchants clapped, and Rahkki wiped his

mouth as saliva flooded it. *Don't throw up*, he told himself.

He and I'Lenna dismounted and led their winged mares toward the trading tents, taking stock of the wares on display. Items hung on racks, tinkling softly in the breeze, or rested on shelves inside the tents—the goods were spotless and undented, seams were tight, and edges were sharp. There was pottery, Daakuran forged iron, wooden carvings, hearth goods, bright fabrics, spices, shining armor, books, weapons, and artwork. The scent of new leather, fragrant oils, and exotic meats filled Rahkki's nostrils, and Sula's too. His mare skittered sideways, bobbing her head and snorting at the strange place. "Shh," he said, resting his hand on her mane.

Rather than shrugging him off, Sula quieted, and Rahkki felt a rush of pleasure at the progress they'd made together. "Come on," he said to I'Lenna, and they walked toward the tents.

Overwhelmed by the foreign finery, doubts began filling Rahkki's mind. Drael's beautiful Kihlara blanket morphed in his imagination—changing from a precious artifact into a sodden, frayed, and smelly Sandwen relic. How many dramals would it fetch? Too few, he guessed.

On the beach, three Daakuran outlanders were loading a dinghy full of spices and furs. Two young burners, just purchased from the First Clan traders, fluttered within an intricate blackwood cage set on the bow of the boat. The tiny fire-breathing dragons hissed in outrage and shot out every color of fire in their arsenal—from incinerating blue to the coldest purple—but they could not affect the impervious and fireproof blackwood cage.

"Poor dragons," I'Lenna murmured. "Heading to the zoo, I imagine."

Other Daakurans haggled, some dined. A few Sandwens lingered, doing business or chatting with the traders, but most of the clans didn't travel here until after the napping hour. Rahkki didn't recognize anyone from his clan except Tuni's mother, Kashik.

Kashik Hightower cooked here each day and sold her food to the hungry shoppers, turning a high profit that kept Tuni and Rizah well supplied with armor and hay. From Kashik's tent, Rahkki smelled simmering pork soup, fried snake, rice wine, and honeyed fruit.

"Ay, Rahkki," Kashik called to him over the pot of soup.

"Ay, Kashi," he greeted, using her nickname.

"Cup of broth? No charge for the new Rider." She winked at him.

"Thank you, maybe later," he answered.

I'Lenna touched Rahkki's arm. "I need some things for Firo; I'll be in there." She pointed to the leather smith's tent. She tied Firo to a hitching post and entered, greeting the trader in polished Talu, the language of the empire.

Just then a figure strode out of the metal smith's tent next door, surprising Rahkki. It was Ossi's brother, Mut.

Mut spotted Rahkki standing beside his Kihlara mare and froze, his face twisting. Rahkki halted, waiting as Mut's eyes raked across Sula's wings and wiry muscles. Envy radiated off Mut like heat rays off sand. "You trained her to wear tack already?"

"Not really," Rahkki said, shrugging. "She's cooperating, that's all."

Mut reached absently to pet Sula's neck, but she whinnied a sharp warning to stay back. He quickly withdrew his hand. "I still don't get why she chose *you*," he remarked bitterly.

Rahkki's cheeks burned hotter because he knew Sula was only using him to save her friends. Maybe she was starting to like him, to trust him, but Rahkki was not fooled. Sula was too wild for him to keep forever. When she no longer needed him, she'd fly away, leaving him a Half. His throat tightened. *Don't think about it.*

Mut's eyes drifted to Firo tied to the hitching post. "I

wish they'd let us try to win the roan mare too. I'Lenna could have any Kihlara in the clans, couldn't she? Why'd her mother have to buy her that one?"

Rahkki didn't know what to say. Three years ago, Mut had bragged to everyone that his father was going to buy him a Flier for his sixteenth birthday. The following summer, his dad used the money to abandon his Sandwen family and marry a Daakuran woman. Now he worked in a cobbler's shop in the empire, making boots. Mut's father had sold his son's dreams to buy himself a new life.

The older boy seemed to sense Rahkki's mounting pity, and he stood taller, brightening. "At least I get to kill giants." He spat on the sand and tucked his thumbs into his breeches. "The queen drafted all the teens into the Land Guard. I just ordered my armor and weapons." Mut showed Rahkki his rations paper, marked by General Tsun. Land soldiers received free food and gear, since joining the Land Guard army was mandatory for most Sandwens.

Rahkki felt suddenly cold as he imagined Mut Finn battling the elephant-riding giants, racing toward death, when he should be swimming with his friends and playing in the jungle. This was the queen's fault! Rahkki considered Koko's warning that keeping the uneducated queen was more dangerous than ousting her. He had to admit she made a fine point.

"What are you doing here anyway?" Mut asked, narrowing his eyes. "You buying?" He loomed over Rahkki, eyeing his satchel. Mut had robbed Rahkki on several occasions in the past, but Rahkki held his ground.

"I'm selling," he said coolly, and he hoped that was true. Everything depended on how much coin he received in exchange for Drael's ceremonial blanket.

Mut lost interest. "Doubt they'll want anything you got." He bent over laughing as he walked toward his family's land pony tied in the shade. He released the pinto from the thin palm tree, leaped onto his back, and galloped into the jungle.

Rahkki turned and walked past the metal smith's tent. It was time to find out what the bejeweled blanket was worth.

20

NEGOTIATION

"AY," RAHKKI SAID AS HE ENTERED THE EXPORT tent. A Daakuran female sat behind a wide teak desk. Her assistant worked near the shelves, organizing their stock, and an armed soldier guarded their treasury and wares.

"Ay," the woman greeted, but after a cursory glance at Rahkki's tattered clothing, she frowned. "There's a free table outside, broken stuff and whatnot. Take what you like." She spoke to him in his language and then returned to her papers, dismissing him.

Rahkki cleared his throat and switched to Talu. "Actually, I have something to sell."

Startled, she pushed her curly black hair out of her face and peered more closely at him. Her skin was smooth, unwrinkled by the sun. Her clothes were soft and fine, the colors pale. Like all Daakurans, she appeared freshly bathed. Even her nails were clean. She slid her papers aside and gave him her full attention. "Well, what do you have?"

He approached her desk, opened his satchel, and lifted out Drael's ceremonial blanket, spreading it across her desk. Awed silence followed, and Rahkki viewed the blanket with fresh eyes. The fabric was *stunning* in comparison to the finery around it. His imagination had tricked him! Rahkki's heart swelled with pride and sorrow. "I'm selling this," he said, his voice shaky.

The woman stood up fast and came around to finger the fabric. Her assistant dropped what was in her hands and joined them, whispering over the merchant woman's shoulder. They examined the intricate beadwork, the seams, the texture, and the tassels. Next, the trader produced a jeweler's eyeglass and examined the precious stones one by one. Then she returned to her seat behind the desk and stared intently at Rahkki. Outside, Sula stretched and folded her wings. "Is this that mare's blanket?" the woman asked, nodding toward his silver Flier.

Rahkki shook his head.

She let out her breath, her eyes drifting down to his scuffed boots. "Did you steal it?"

"No!" His outrage burned as pure as a smokeless fire. "I'm Rahkki Stormrunner, bloodborn prince of the Fifth Clan. This blanket belonged to my mother, Queen Reyella Stormrunner. Her Kihlara stallion wore it."

"You're a prince?"

"Yes," he snapped. "And no." He would always be bloodborn, a Sandwen prince, but he'd been cast adrift from any particular throne.

The Daakuran woman leaned back, appearing amused and impressed at the same time. "I'm Willa Green," she said. "Just Willa Green, no fancy titles like you."

Rahkki nodded, waiting, and Willa continued. "So you're one of those bloodborn kids, a descendant of the Seven Sisters?"

"That's right."

Her eyes sparkled. "Are you magical?"

Rahkki frowned. "No, I'm not magical."

She appraised him like she'd appraised the blanket, studying his face, the feathers tied to his belt, the stitching on his satchel.

He felt like a trinket—a Sandwen doll—the kind they

sold in droves at the port in Daakur. "How much for the blanket?" he pressed. His Talu was rusty, and his head had begun to ache from using it.

"I'll tell you in just a moment." She returned her attention to the fabric, counting the different types of jewels and crystals. Then she produced a fresh parchment and began scratching symbols on it. She mumbled as she worked, counting numbers and thinking. Her assistant helped, scanning the seams for damage and signs of wear, and then relaying the information to the trader.

Rahkki was at Willa's mercy. If she didn't purchase the blanket, he and Sula would have to fly to Daakur and sell it in the empire. That would take time, and it was dangerous for a kid. He could speak Talu, but he couldn't read it, so he'd be dependent on the help of strangers to navigate. He had no coin to lease a room, so he'd have to sleep in the borderlands. And besides all that, the Daakurans didn't hold Sandwens in high regard. Only their queens and merchants were treated well in Daakur, and that was in part because they traveled with armed warriors and in part because everyone who had money to spend was treated well.

He closed his eyes, and his mother's long dark hair and kind eyes flickered across his mind. How could he sell this last piece of her? Just then Sula nickered, as if encouraging him, and Rahkki let out his breath. He was doing the right thing. He had no choice.

He turned his attention back to Willa, hoping for a large offer, because on top of Sula's expenses, he also had to feed Brauk's stallion, Kol; and he wanted to reimburse Brim for Brauk's medicine. Rahkki was hoping for two full rounds. That would be enough to meet his immediate needs. He tried not to fidget.

"Okay," Willa finally said. "I'll give you three rounds."

"Three rounds!" Rahkki gaped at her. Three rounds were more than he'd hoped for!

She frowned. "It's the best I can do, Rahkki Storm-rider . . . Stormraider. . . ." She struggled to remember his name, then gave up. "If you don't like it, go to Daakur."

He couldn't speak. Three rounds was a fortune. Did Willa have that much coin in her treasury? No wonder she had a guard.

She tapped her fingers as she waited for him to agree, then she exhaled. "All right, look, I'll throw in a spyglass. I bought it off a sailor just today. Here." She handed Rahkki a seaman's spyglass.

He was about to object, since he had no use for a spy-glass, but then he realized it was something he could sell or trade later. He took it, pretending to study it for flaws.

"So, do we have a deal?" Willa pressed.

He squinted at her and noticed her right eye twitching. It lasted just a second and then vanished; otherwise her expression seemed carved of stone. Traders were known for giving low figures. What if the blanket was worth *more* than three rounds? But Rahkki didn't want to risk losing the deal by questioning Willa, and three rounds more than suited his needs. He fingered the blanket, imagining how his mother's stallion must have looked wearing it, and tears moistened his eyes. "Well—"

"There you are!" I'Lenna glided into the export tent and caught sight of the glimmering Kihlara blanket, and her breath hitched. "Are you *selling* that, Rahkki?"

The Daakuran trader grimaced. "Ay, Princess I'Lenna."

"Ay, Willa." I'Lenna narrowed her eyes at the trader. "What did you offer him?"

Rahkki answered. "Three rounds and a spyglass."

"Huh." I'Lenna swooped the fabric off the desk and lifted her chin. "I don't think so. Five rounds."

Rahkki blanched. I'Lenna was going to unwind his negotiation!

But Willa glared at the princess, her expression resigned. "Three and a half."

I'Lenna leaned over the desk, eye to eye with Willa, and raised one eyebrow. "Four rounds or I'll buy it off the boy myself and sell it in Daakur for eight."

It was Willa's turn to blanch. "All right, all right, four rounds." She plucked the spyglass out of Rahkki's fingers. "But I'm keeping this."

"Deal," I'Lenna said. She spat on her hand and offered it to the trader—a Sandwen gesture. Willa pursed her lips, spat, and slapped hands with the princess. Then she motioned to a guard, and he counted out four full coins of the Realm and placed them in Rahkki's palm.

"Sign here," Willa said, sliding over a piece of parchment and a quill.

Rahkki stared at it. He didn't know how to write or read.

I'Lenna whisked the quill off the desk and spoke as she wrote on the paper. "Rahkki Stormrunner, son of Reyella Stormrunner, bloodborn prince of the Fifth Clan." She finished the signature with a mighty flourish of the quill.

Willa took the signed receipt, blew on the ink to dry it,

and then dismissed them with a wave.

Rahkki followed I'Lenna out of the tent, stunned. His mother's blanket was gone, but in its place were *four* full coins of the Realm, worth four *hundred* dramals. A Sandwen villager could live for years on such funds. They paused when they were out of earshot. Rahkki stared at the coins and whispered in wonder, "I can't believe it."

I'Lenna snorted like a horse. "Willa Green knows what that blanket is worth in Daakur. Anything related to our Kihlari steeds is a collector's item there. Willa got a good deal, but so did you. Four rounds will go far in the clans, and we don't have time to fly to Daakur."

"How do you know all this?" Rahkki asked. I'Lenna had been raised in the same village he had. She'd played in the same mud, listened to the same stories, and eaten the same foods; but at this moment, she seemed from another world.

"My mom doesn't just take me to Daakur to visit museums, Rahkki," I'Lenna said, laughing. "We shop. We haggle. I learned from the best." She paused, tugging self-consciously on her blue silk blouse. "Did that blanket belong to your mother?"

He nodded.

"I'm sorry," she said gently, and they each felt the bitter sting of the past.

Rahkki shrugged. "It's not your fault, I'Lenna."

The princess straightened. "Still, I'm sorry." The sun sloped overhead, traveling quickly west. "I have to be back before end of light. Let's get your armor and go home." She smiled, wide and carefree, dazzling him, and then she turned to Firo.

As Rahkki watched the crown princess cuddle and coo to her wild mare, he fought hard against his rising doubts about her. I'Lenna had just helped him, but she'd also lied to him about meeting with the general—and hidden things were dangerous. The jungle had taught him that. Predators hid and then ambushed. You never saw them until their fangs were upon you.

But in spite of her lie, I'Lenna was his friend, his true friend. Rahkki didn't know much, but he believed that.

21

ARMOR

ECHOFROST HAD WATCHED RAHKKI TRADE THE Kihlara blanket she'd worn at the Sandwen auction for four large stamped coins. "Now he can help me," she nickered to Shysong.

"He looks sad," the roan mare nickered back.

Echofrost shrugged her wings. "Rahkki always looks sad."

"I'm serious," Shysong said. "I don't think he wanted to give that blanket away. It's special to him." She turned to Echofrost. "That cub really cares about you. He's made your fight his fight."

Echofrost peered more intently at Rahkki. He had done many hard things since they'd met, and all for her.

162

"He reminds me of Star," she said.

Shysong snorted, pointing her black-edged feathers at the undersized Sandwen boy. "How does that cub remind you of the most powerful pegasus in Anok?"

"They both do hard things," Echofrost answered. "In spite of the fact that no one believes in them."

"I believe in Star," Shysong said, lashing her black tail.

"That's because you met him *after* he'd proved himself. I knew Star when he was a colt, when the over-stallions wanted him dead and when members of his own herd betrayed him. It's the same with Rahkki—the leader of his clan fears him, but Rahkki is . . . he's innocent." Echofrost inhaled sharply. "I'm going to get him killed, I know it. Look at him!"

They both gazed at Rahkki. He and I'Lenna had returned from the tents, and now the little cub was struggling to lift her heavy packages off the ground. The roan mare huffed. "Don't worry so much, Echofrost. The Sky Guard will protect him."

"I'm not sure they will," the silver mare answered, remembering how Harak abused the boy.

Rahkki and I'Lenna finished loading her packages, and then they led the mares to another tent, this one full of chest plates, helmets, shields, and other protective wear. "Finally," Echofrost nickered. "He's going to get our armor."

The metal smith stood from where he'd been pounding out a helmet and approached them, bowing low to I'Lenna. "Ay, Princess Whitehall." He turned to Rahkki. "You must be Rahkki Stormrunner."

"I am," said the cub. "How did you know?"

"I keep track of the new Pairings in the clans. I'm Dolfo." He extended his crossed wrists and Rahkki did the same; they quickly clasped and released. "Let's get you two outfitted."

Echofrost relaxed her wings, a sign that she was not hostile, and then the measuring began. She stood very still as the stranger used a thin rope to mark the width and depth of her chest, the size of her head and her flanks, and the length of her neck. Then he began fitting pieces onto her.

"I don't like this," Echofrost whinnied, beginning to tremble as each piece was affixed to her body with leather straps. She felt trapped even though the armor was notched and layered to move as she moved.

"No, it's good," Shysong nickered. "Look, it protects your vital areas. You're not fighting creatures your own size."

"Right." She pawed at the tent floor to release her agitation.

Next Dolfo measured Rahkki and then adjusted their armor. Echofrost studied the dark metal. It was crafted perfectly to fit the body of a Kihlara Flier. She was growing accustomed to Landwalker creations, but the intricacy of this metalwork reminded her of their incomprehensible power. But without their weapons, armor, homes, tools, and animals—Landwalkers would not survive well. How had the weakest become the strongest?

As they all waited for the armor to be adjusted, a Sandwen woman brought each cub a bowl of fish soup and two stalks of sugarcane for the pegasi. As the cubs slurped their meals, Shysong and Echofrost sucked the sweetness out of the sugarcane and then grazed on tangy sea grasses.

Far offshore, a pod of dolphins swam by, their backs wet and rolling. This beach was warm and the water flat, very unlike the western coast of Anok, which was windy and cold, rough surfed and whitecapped. After a while, I'Lenna curled in the shade and closed her eyes. Rahkki left them to browse the tents alone, and Echofrost watched him purchase items and stash them in his carrying bag.

When Dolfo was finished, he called for them. "I charge

one full round per set of armor," he said. "But I'll take off twenty dramals from each of your sets because they're small, requiring much less metal and leather than what I usually use."

Rahkki glanced at I'Lenna, and she nodded approval. Rahkki handed two gold coins to Dolfo, and then the man counted back forty bronze dramals. The Landwalkers slapped hands. "We'll wear the armor home," Rahkki said.

Dolfo nodded. "Good idea. Best to get used to it right away." He pointed to Echofrost. "She's going to have some trouble lifting off at first."

Echofrost pranced on the sand as Rahkki dressed her. The adjustments Dolfo had made pleased her. The small annoyances where the metal had poked or scratched her hide were gone. He'd smoothed the chinks and bulges, narrowed and widened the metal in the right places, making it fit like a second hide.

"You look tough," Shysong whinnied, admiring her friend. Echofrost noticed that even Rahkki appeared larger and stronger in his armor.

Rahkki thanked Dolfo, who returned to his tent. Then he handed I'Lenna a wrapped package.

She took it, startled. "What's this?"

A flush crossed Rahkki's cheeks. "It's a late birthday present."

"Should I open it now?"

Rahkki shrugged. "Open it whenever you want."

She clutched the present to her chest and then placed it gently in her satchel. "I'm going to wait. What else did you get?"

Rahkki tapped his bag. "Hot pepper for Darthan, new boots for me, and a champion fighting beetle for Brauk. He needs something to do while he's healing."

"That's a nice present," she admitted. "But the hot pepper—you know that's the strongest spice in Daakur, right? It burns."

"The hotter the better for Darthan."

I'Lenna glanced west, toward home. "We should get back."

Rahkki nodded and climbed onto Echofrost's back. She stumbled sideways under the weight of the boy and their two sets of armor. "I'll never get off the ground," she complained to Shysong.

"Try a running start," her friend suggested.

Echofrost hadn't anticipated this problem. With Rahkki leaning slightly forward, she galloped down the beach where the sand was moist and hard. She spread her wings and flapped. They lifted a winglength off the shore. Echofrost flapped harder, straining her wings. "Blast it!" she whinnied. "Until I get used to this, I don't want to fly too high."

I'Lenna urged Shysong forward, and they caught up to Echofrost. The four of them cruised into the jungle, with Echofrost concentrating on staying aloft. Soon, warm sweat ran between her ears, and her wing muscles ached. They flew low and straight. They were almost back to the village when Echofrost spotted a bubbling stream. "I need water!" She landed near its banks with a hard stumble.

I'Lenna and Shysong fluttered down next to her. Rahkki guessed Echofrost's needs and slid off her back to give her a rest. I'Lenna dismounted too, and they let the mares drink in peace. Echofrost thrust her muzzle into the cool liquid and sucked long, deep mouthfuls.

I'Lenna reached into her satchel and pulled out two white candies. "Peppermints," she said to Rahkki, her voice teasing.

"You got more?"

"I have an endless supply." I'Lenna whirled, running away.

The princess zipped passed Echofrost, startling her. Then Rahkki rushed by, chasing I'Lenna. His armor clanged as he smacked into tree branches, and the princess squealed when he caught her.

Rahkki laughed with her, and I'Lenna handed him the treat she held in her hand. The cubs rested in the leaves, staring up at the branches swaying overhead while sucking on their peppermints. Echofrost kept her ears pricked for danger, but the oppressive heat seemed to have squelched the jungle's inhabitants. She scanned the trees. Monkeys were alarmists, and right now they were quiet. The area must be safe.

I'Lenna sat up, selected a fallen tree branch, and began stripping off the leaves one by one. A soft, flowing croon emitted from her mouth.

"Two in the jungle
One in the sea
Three in the fortress
None with me.
Strong as dragons, my children grow.
Fast as arrows, my children go.
Two in the jungle

One in the sea
Three in the fortress
None with me."

Echofrost also rested and inspected her armor. Now she and Rahkki were ready to battle the giants, and her heart fluttered with excitement. They would free Hazelwind, Dewberry, and Storm Herd; and it would be happening soon!

"*Hsssss!*"

"What was that?" Rahkki whispered as he yanked I'Lenna upright.

"I—I don't know." They all turned. Close behind them, waking from his slumber in the shadows, yawned a dragon.

Granak!

22

GRANAK

"DON'T MOVE," I'LENNA WHISPERED AS SHE AND Rahkki stared up at the black-scaled dragon. The boy hadn't heard Granak coming because the dragon was already there. He'd been so still in sleep that even the monkeys hadn't realized his presence.

Drool dripped from Granak's jaws in a gleaming stream as he blinked into the sunlight. He hadn't seen the kids—yet. The dragon's tail disappeared into the jungle behind him, and bright colors flickered across his irides-cent black scales. Rahkki remembered right then that Granak had refused to eat the Fifth Clan sow. "He's hun-gry," he whispered.

The dragon's forked yellow tongue whisked in and out.

He swayed his head, tasting the air. His ribs expanded and then shrank with a loud hissing noise.

"We're downwind; he can't smell us," I'Lenna whispered back.

The wild mares stood at least a hundred lengths away, also frozen in place, staring up at the giant lizard. If they moved, he'd hear them.

Granak stepped forward, and his thick leg bent a tall sapling in half. The mares quietly spread their wings. Sula glanced at Rahkki as though calculating her odds of reaching him before the dragon did.

Lowering his mighty head, Granak tasted the wind, revealing short serrated teeth. His long tail, naturally armored with bumpy scales, crashed between the trees.

Suddenly a cross breeze swept through the jungle. It lifted I'Lenna's long hair and fluttered Rahkki's tunic.

Granak cocked his head and twisted it, clearly smelling their scent. His dark round eyes flitted, then focused . . . on them. "*Hsssssss.*"

"Run!" I'Lenna shouted.

She and Rahkki bolted. The mares leaped off the ground. But one gigantic step put the dragon right behind Rahkki and I'Lenna as they skittered between the trees, holding hands, pulling each other faster. Rahkki's heart hammered; his eyes blurred. He and I'Lenna yanked each other over roots and stumps, racing toward their village. Their Kihlara mares flew low, darting between the palms.

Granak dropped his head and charged. The rain forest screamed to life as birds, deer, monkeys, insects, and rodents scattered. A band of orangutans swung from vine to vine, screeching at Rahkki and I'Lenna as if scolding them for waking the dragon.

Rahkki skidded around a huge kapok tree and yanked I'Lenna down so hard she cried out. "Hide!" They quickly pushed vines and leaves over their bodies, but Granak reared back and uprooted their tree with his massive clawed foot. Thick roots popped out of the soil, throwing Rahkki and I'Lenna into the air. The broken kapok groaned, a dying monster. Granak's toxic drool dripped down, sliming the jungle floor.

The kids bounced onto the dirt. "This way!" I'Lenna shouted. She dragged Rahkki toward a cleared animal path where they could run faster, still holding hands.

Leaves and dirt had fallen into I'Lenna's hair; her shoulder was cut and bleeding. Granak thundered after them, and the tight trees mercifully slowed him.

An image of I'Lenna caught between the reptile's jaws flashed through Rahkki's mind so sharply that he heard her bones crunching in his ears. His friend was going to get eaten if he didn't do something right now! Rahkki flicked his wrist, breaking her grasp on it.

"Rahkki, no!" I'Lenna screamed.

But then he was gone, running opposite her and waving his arms at Granak. "Over here!" he shouted.

"Rahkki!" I'Lenna yelled. "Stop it! What are you doing?"

Granak's round eyes rolled toward the boy. His shimmering scales quivered. Rahkki ran as fast as he could, luring the dragon away from I'Lenna. *This bleeding armor is going to get me killed*, he thought, hating how the extra weight slowed him down. Then ahead, he spied his village.

Echofrost caught up to the black dragon. "We have to help the cubs," she whinnied to Shysong.

The roan pinned her ears, and the pair swooped down, attacking like angry birds. Echofrost landed a barrage of kicks to Granak's head. Shysong cracked him hard across his ear hole.

The dragon peered up.

Echofrost rose higher, fighting against the heaviness of her armor. Granak flicked out his tongue, almost reaching her, and saliva pooled at his feet. He hissed with a sharp contraction of his ribs.

Echofrost coiled back her legs and glided a circle around the monster's head, hoping that her bright feathers would keep his attention off the cubs. Below, Rahkki waved his arms, also trying to tease the dragon away. The princess had turned and was running toward Rahkki. Echofrost saw that these two were going to kill themselves trying to save each other. "Get the kids," she neighed to Shysong.

The roan mare peeled off and dived toward I'Lenna.

Her quick movement attracted the lizard, and he stomped after her, picking up speed.

"Behind you!" Echofrost whinnied.

The lizard's huge foot swung at the roan, just grazing Shysong's wing. She spun out of control.

"Get to the village! Get help!" Rahkki shouted.

I'Lenna glanced at him, her cheeks blazing.

"Please," he mouthed.

She turned and bolted toward the clan, toward help. Shysong spun into a tree and collapsed.

"Firo!" I'Lenna ran back for her fallen mare.

Echofrost gritted her teeth and flew into the dragon's line of vision, angling her body so that her shiny armor reflected the sun into his eyes. The lizard paused, blinded.

I'Lenna caught up to Shysong. The mare's wing drooped, and she couldn't fly, but she could run fast. The princess leaped onto her back, and the pair galloped toward the village.

"Sula, watch out!" Rahkki shouted.

Echofrost pinned her ears. The cub was trying to save her, but she had wings; she didn't need saving!

The black dragon heard the boy and charged Rahkki, cracking a tall palm tree in half. The trunk fell toward the cub, and Echofrost swooped down. She knocked the boy clear just as the tree landed where he'd been standing.

Granak sprang, jaws wide.

Echofrost thrust her tail toward Rahkki, and he snatched the end of it. "Go, go, go!" he cried. She galloped toward the village, dragging Rahkki through the brush behind her.

The lizard followed, shoving his way through the dense forest, hissing in frustration. His long tongue flicked over their heads. Echofrost flapped her wings, and Rahkki dangled beneath her as she lifted a few lengths off the jungle floor. Rahkki's weight, plus all the heavy armor, kept her from flying higher.

Echofrost spied the fortress and the Kihlari training

yard ahead. She flattened her neck, beating her wings harder and faster.

I'Lenna and Shysong had already arrived, and the princess must have told the guards about Granak. Warning bells clanged from Fort Prowl, but something was wrong. The Landwalkers were fleeing *into* the fortress, *into* the barns, and *into* their huts. Two gate guards seized I'Lenna and dragged her, kicking and shouting, into the fortress. Doors slammed. Gates closed.

Help was not coming!

Echofrost surged forward, but the dragon was right behind her. Her muscles burned, her wings ached. She flew as fast as she could. Then suddenly Rahkki lost his grip on her tail and his weight was gone. She rocketed forward.

Echofrost landed, her lungs burning. Rahkki hit the dirt in the Kihlari training yard and rolled onto his side.

Granak burst out of the tree line and halted over the small boy, his shadow covering the yard. He roared, whipping his head toward Rahkki.

"Help him!" I'Lenna screamed from the southernmost tower. Queen Lilliam snatched her daughter's ear, yanked her into the tower, slammed the door, and returned to watching the dragon.

Granak swiped his huge paw and slammed Rahkki's chest. The boy tumbled across the yard.

Echofrost brayed for help, but no Kihlari answered.

Rahkki's clanmates stared in openmouthed horror as the dragon clubbed the boy again. The queen, watching from the fortress wall, chewed her lip, breathless.

And then Granak leaned in for the kill.

23

COMMANDER OF DRAGONS

RAHKKI TUMBLED ACROSS THE SOIL, HIS BODY
vibrating from the power of the dragon's paw. His armor
clanged, protecting his skin, and his satchel tore open,
spilling the contents. Rahkki landed on his back, head
spinning. Granak's black-scaled face filled his vision,
blocking out the sun and dwarfing the trees. Purple, blue,
and orange colors slithered across his scales. His toxic
drool dripped down, and rivulets of venom flowed toward
Rahkki.

The boy wheezed, trying to push himself upright.
Where were the Riders, the soldiers? He'd glimpsed the
queen, staring at him from the fortress wall. But the Sky
Guard Riders had raced into the barn, and their faces now

stared back at him through the windows.

Understanding dawned. *No one* would battle the Fifth Clan's guardian mascot. Rahkki should have guessed that.

Granak crept closer, mouth open, his short teeth curved like small Daakuran swords.

An explosive mixture of fear and anger unfroze Rahkki's muscles. He was not going to die this way!

The dragon slid his tongue toward Rahkki, and the whoosh of his breath blew the boy's hair back. Sure of his target now, Granak poised to bite.

Rahkki grasped for his dagger but it had been flung out of reach. Desperate, he glanced around and spotted something else he could use to fight. Turning and flopping himself onto his spilled belongings, Rahkki opened the sack of hot pepper and grabbed a handful.

Granak lunged, and Rahkki tossed the powdered red spice straight into the dragon's open mouth.

Granak reared back with a roar and shook his great head. Drool flew in every direction. Rahkki rolled over and hid his mouth and eyes from the toxic saliva. Granak smacked his lips and then roared again in pain, a sharp keening wail, a sound Rahkki had never heard in the jungle.

The boy crawled slowly away, holding up his hand and letting the breeze carry the hot pepper's scent toward the dragon.

Granak tracked him; his eyelids flickering as if his mind was trying to decide—was Rahkki predator or prey? Instinct drove him to hunt the boy even as the dragon's eyes began to water.

I'm backing away from him. Rahkki thought. *But I should be moving forward. Show him I'm not afraid.*

Rahkki wobbled to his feet, thrust his hand higher, and strode forward. "Go back, Granak," he shouted. "Back to the jungle!"

The lizard lashed his ridged tail.

"Back!" Rahkki repeated. His heart slammed his rib cage, and his breath caught in his throat. The beast loomed over him, hesitant, angry, injured.

Rahkki lifted his voice. "By the Seven Sisters of the Realm, leave me be. I am your *prince!*" He blew on his hand, sending the final grains of hot pepper flying into the dragon's nose and eyes.

Granak stamped his front paws, his body shivering with pain and fury, but he obeyed! He turned and thudded away, disappearing into the thick foliage.

The orphan prince stood alone and alive as absolute

silence filled the Fifth Clan settlement. His clanfolk stared, their mouths hanging open.

Sula was the first to react. She lifted off and glided to her Rider's side. The boy wrapped his arms around her neck, suddenly trembling. She steadied him, holding his weight with her wings. He leaned into her. "Let's get this armor off our backs." He retrieved his satchel and dagger, and then he and his mare walked toward the Kihlari stable together.

The villagers on the hillside emerged from their huts and knelt, facing Rahkki. Atop the fortress walls, land soldiers and guards squatted, lowering their heads to him. Rahkki's heart tumbled. *What is happening?*

Only Queen Lilliam and her Borla stood upright, their lips pursed. Lilliam's face twisted into an expression that Rahkki had never seen her wear before. It wasn't anger or hatred—what was that look?

He walked on, feeling embarrassed by the awed stares of his clan. The Riders had emerged from the stable and formed a line leading to the barn doors. Rahkki had to pass all of them to get to the armory inside. He crossed Tuni's path first. "How did you do that?" she asked, her brown eyes aglow. "Was that . . . magic?"

"I—" Rahkki was about to tell the truth, but then he pinned that unusual expression on Lilliam's face—it was *fear*. The queen was afraid of him.

Exhaling, Rahkki realized how things must have looked to his clan. Likely they hadn't noticed the spiced powder he threw at Granak because they were too far away. What *they* saw was a dragon obeying a boy. Not just *any* dragon, but the guardian mascot of their clan, and not just *any* boy, but a bloodborn descendant of the Seven Sisters. Rahkki Stormrunner had ordered the Father of Dragons to return to the jungle, and the beast had complied. It was a powerful display. Clearly it had impacted the clan and frightened the queen.

Rahkki clucked to himself, thinking fast. He should press his advantage. That's what his brother, Brauk, would do. And hadn't Brauk once instructed him never to dispute his own legend? Rahkki hadn't *actually* commanded Granak, but would it hurt to let his clan believe he had? Weren't all legends just stories? His thoughts jumbled and twisted, and then he made up his mind. Perhaps the clan's belief that he commanded dragons would protect him from Queen Lilliam.

So Rahkki nodded at Tuni, committing himself to the

lie, and kept walking. As he disappeared into the barn, his clan erupted into speculative whispering. Rahkki's neck flushed, and he felt silly as his sapling legend sprouted a new branch behind him.

$\mathcal{C}\!\!\curvearrowleft\!\!24\!\!\curvearrowright\!\!\mathcal{D}$

HERO

RAHKKI LED SULA INTO THE ARMORY AND removed their shields and breastplates, her flank plates, their helmets, and his arm and calf guards. His body was still shaking, and his breaths came fast and shallow. Once the armor was off, Rahkki felt a hundred times lighter. It wouldn't be too heavy once he was used to it, but that would take time. Sula nickered at him, seeming happy to be free of the metal also.

Once they'd both caught their breath, Rahkki led Sula outside to rinse her sweat-streaked hide. Then he returned her to her stall and added an extra scoop of grain to her feeder. "You rest and eat," he said. "We leave with the armies in the morning."

The mare tossed her sparkling white mane and his heart swelled. Sula was a good Flier; she hadn't abandoned him to the dragon. He patted his torn satchel. The weight of the coins inside meant he could afford to keep her for as long as it took to save her friends. Rahkki took his first deep breath since he'd won her.

As he returned to the armory, Rahkki's thoughts switched to I'Lenna. Lilliam had witnessed her daughter blasting out of the jungle, screaming for help. Then Rahkki had emerged right behind her, chased by a dragon. *Trust me*, I'Lenna had said on their way to the trading post. *If I'm caught with you again, I'll be the one who pays.* He wondered how the queen would punish her eldest daughter for their latest forbidden adventure.

Sighing with pain, Rahkki cleaned and buffed his and Sula's new armor with quick strokes of a cloth. Both sets were dented and scuffed. The dragon's claw had etched four long stripes down Rahkki's breastplate, disrupting the intricate engravings. Already the armor had saved his life.

Once everything was clean, Rahkki packed it neatly into the trunk that Harak had assigned to him. Then, using a needle and sinew kept on hand for the Riders to repair their belts and scabbards, Rahkki sewed the strap back onto his torn satchel.

Next Rahkki visited the small supply shed located inside the Ruk. The giants had burned down the larger one once used by the Sky Guard. He found Koko inside, rubbing her temple as she tallied the bales. "Ay, Stormrunner," she greeted. "Wha's all the fuss ou' there?"

"Granak was in the woods," he explained, deciding not to elaborate on the details. "But he's gone now."

Koko nodded. "So, wha' yuh want?"

"I need some things for Sula and Kol."

Rahkki placed an order for sixty bales of hay—thirty for Sula and thirty for Kol. He also ordered twenty sacks of grain and six packets of Flush, a medicine that killed parasites and worms in Kihlari steeds and horses. His brother's chestnut stallion had been raised on Flush, but Sula had not, so he didn't buy any for her. Rahkki guessed that her body naturally killed parasites.

The boy opened his satchel. "How much?"

Koko blew her hair out of her face and leaned against the wall. "Hol' up, Stormrunner, I gotta figure it."

He sat on a hay bale and waited.

The girl's tongue poked between her teeth as she

leaned over her parchment. Koko could clean armor, trim hooves, sharpen weapons, stitch leather, handle the most ferocious Kihlari—and their equally ferocious Riders—with misleading ease; but when it came to figuring sums, she struggled to write the calculations. *Much simpler ta do it in my 'ead*, she'd told him once. But the queen required paper receipts.

Finally, Koko finished, tore off a parchment, and slapped it onto Rahkki's palm. "The total's righ'," she said as if he'd question it.

Rahkki glanced at the price and hid his shock—ninety-one dramals! But he didn't doubt its accuracy. Kihlari were expensive; it was the sole reason why so few Sandwens could afford them. Rahkki handed over a single gold round and received nine dramals in change. Between the armor, the feed, and the gifts and boots he'd purchased, the bloodborn prince had spent a small fortune in one day, but he still had a small fortune left—one round and thirty-nine dramals, which he'd save until he needed to order hay again.

He exhaled, comforted by the weight of the remaining coins. For now, his future was secure. He could reimburse Brim and Ossi for Brauk's care, and feed Sula and Kol during the coming monsoon rains. Rahkki placed his change at the bottom of his satchel and mumbled a thank-you to Koko.

Exiting the supply barn, he smacked into the hard body of a white winged mare. A royal guard sat astride her and, behind them, rode Queen Lilliam aboard her blood-bay stallion, Mahrsan. Rahkki quickly scanned the area. They were alone, out of sight of others. His gut tightened.

"My queen," he said to Lilliam, dipping his head.

She was dressed in soft brown leggings and a white tunic that flowed around her pregnant belly. Her dark hair hung loose but heavy with adornments: Mahrsan's feathers, sparkling gems, and shells from the east. A choker made of sea pearls circled her neck, tiny painted bones pierced her ears, and jewel-encrusted anklets jingled each time she kicked her flying steed. Rahkki guessed that Lilliam had traded heavily with the other clans during the recent Clan Gathering.

Now she urged Mahrsan closer to Rahkki. Her eyes bored into his, as piercing as the bones that lanced her earlobes. "I want to know *exactly* how you tamed that dragon?"

"I didn't tame him, my queen."

"Don't quibble with me, Stormrunner. Granak obeyed *your* command. How? Why?" She grimaced suddenly, her hand flying to her extended belly.

Rahkki kept his expression blank, but his brow dampened as he began to worry. Which was more hazardous to him: the truth or the lie?

Lilliam curved her lips, showing her teeth. "I saw what I saw. You commanded the Fifth Clan mascot. If you hold his favor, then you're invincible, Stormrunner."

Invincible! Rahkki had claimed no such thing.

"And you saved my daughter's life in the jungle." She raked her eyes across his small body. "I owe you for that."

"You don't owe me, my queen," Rahkki said. His voice cracked on the word *queen*.

Lilliam laughed, deep and throaty. "You're as humble and unambitious as my crown princess—two bloodborns who want nothing more from life than to eat candy and fly pretty horses." She circled him, and Mahrsan's sapphire wings grazed Rahkki's cheek. Lilliam continued. "Allow me to glorify you, my humble prince. "

Rahkki braced himself—no reward from Lilliam could be good for him.

"Tomorrow we ride out to slay those nasty giants once and for all, and I want *you* on the front line. You and your mare will lead the charge *from the ground*." The queen winced as another pain seized her stomach.

"The ground?" he sputtered. "But I'm a Rider?"

Lilliam continued, "You're a *hero*, Stormrunner, and so I'm offering you the more honored position of Battle Mage, leader of the front lines. You will be the first to fight. You and your wild braya will inspire my soldiers."

Rahkki blanched. The Fifth Clan hadn't utilized a Battle Mage in centuries. Mages were specially trained soldiers, educated in magic, warfare, and strategy. Daakur employed them in their armies, but the Sandwen clans held a sour view of magic and had done away with the practice. "But I'm not a Battle Mage. I'm not trained for that," Rahkki said. He wasn't trained as a Rider either, but he knew better than to mention it.

Lilliam ran her tongue across her lower lip and smirked at him. "You're not trained for anything, are you? But you're a natural mage—Rahkki the Commander of Dragons. My army will follow you to their deaths. You're *that* incredible."

Rahkki felt the blood drain from his face. Battle Mage was the most dangerous position in *any* army. He and Sula would face the Gorlan hordes, their elephants, and their saber cats first and up close, with all military support *behind* them and the Sky Guard army high *above* them. Rahkki knew exactly what Lilliam was doing. She was trying to get him killed, and fast.

"Do you have something to say, Stormrunner?" the queen asked.

He was about to tell the truth, that he'd commanded no dragons, but then he saw it again, the flash of real fear in her eyes. Lilliam had treated him worse than a dog since he was four years old, but now that had changed. He had her on her back foot, and she was desperate. She'd kill him eventually anyway, he thought, remembering the time her Borla had refused to treat his injuries, just days before the auction.

But her fear had put her on the defensive and now was not the time to show weakness. Now was the time to press harder. The thought made him grin, and he probably looked crazy when he answered. "I'd be honored to lead the armies as your Battle Mage, my queen."

She narrowed her eyes.

He smiled wider and dipped his head as though she'd just granted him a wish.

Lilliam grunted and tugged on her left rein, turning Mahrsan away. "The Fifth Clan marches tomorrow.

Report to General Tsun at dawn, before the last morning bell rings. If you fail to appear, you will be arrested for desertion."

She thinks I'll run away, he realized, but continued smiling. "Yes, my queen."

Lilliam and Mahrsan sped toward the clouds, and her mounted guard lifted off and joined her. She rode Mahrsan in a hunched position, and Rahkki guessed her child would soon be born.

In the past, a run-in with Lilliam would have scared him. But today it wasn't fear that welled within Rahkki but anger, hot and unexpected. It gushed through him like a rain-full river. He clenched his fists, battling back the urge to find General Tsun and commit the Stormrunner name to the rebellion.

Instead he closed his eyes. The hatred blasting through him felt like power, but false power. The rage would control him if he let it, like it controlled his brother, and that wasn't good for Rahkki or anyone else. He drew deep breaths until the hot feelings passed. Then he headed to the room he'd once shared with Brauk to prepare for tomorrow's march. As he climbed the circling stone stairs, Rahkki knew that his short time with Sula was coming to an end. Win or lose, after this battle with the giants, she would leave him. He pushed open his bedroom door, feeling suddenly exhausted and sad.

As he walked in, a voice from the corner startled him. "I didn't know you could talk to dragons."

C 25 O

THE IDEA

RAHKKI WHIPPED AROUND TO SEE PRINCESS I'Lenna rocking back and forth on his dressing chair, holding the birthday gift he'd purchased at the trading post in her lap. She'd lighted his oil lamps, and laid a small feast on his wooden table. He slammed his door and locked it. "Are you okay?" he whispered. "I saw your mom drag you off the wall."

I'Lenna wiped the dust off her breeches, laughing. "My mother *fined* me. I have to pay her fifty dramals, which is silly because she pays me fifty dramals each high moon as an allowance. Basically, I don't get paid this month." I'Lenna shook her head and shrugged.

"You're not afraid of your mother at all, are you?"

Rahkki said. I'Lenna's left ear was still bright red where the queen had grabbed it earlier.

"Ah, Rahkki, that's not true," she answered, flashing him a thin smile.

Rahkki sat at his table and stared at the food I'Lenna had brought, not feeling hungry at all.

The princess leaned closer, her eyes shining. "I can't believe you stood up to Granak! You should be dead."

He noticed she'd changed into solid black riding pants and a smooth dark vest, the leather custom fitted to her thin frame. Her dagger hung from a sheath belted around her waist, her long hair was tied back in a high ponytail, and she wore iron-toed black boots. "Are you going somewhere?" he asked.

"Yes, but don't change the subject. How did you talk to that dragon, and why didn't you do it sooner? Firo got hurt, you know. Why did you let it chase us if you knew you could stop it?"

"How is Firo?" he asked, remembering that the roan mare had fallen and hurt her wing.

"She's bruised but recovering," I'Lenna said. "Now stop avoiding my question." She peered into his eyes. "Did you use magic?"

"No." He laughed. "I don't believe in magic."

"I do," she said.

"That's because you can afford it—I can't." He was referring to the questionable business of trading coin for enchantments that was common in Daakur. "Anyway, I didn't use magic. It was the hot pepper I bought at the trading post, the gift for my uncle. I threw it into Granak's mouth."

I'Lenna squealed and covered her lips. "He didn't like that!"

Rahkki grinned. "No, he didn't."

When her chuckles subsided, I'Lenna held up the wrapped present. "May I open my gift?"

Rahkki flushed. "Yeah, whenever you want."

She drew her chair closer to him, her hands trembling as she tore the thin paper. She opened the package and stared at the object within, her mouth wide.

"Do you like it?" he asked.

"You got me a book," she whispered. She turned the gift over in her hands and then flipped the pages.

He nodded. "You read Talu, don't you? You speak it so well, I just thought—"

I'Lenna smiled. "I do, and this copy is illustrated. It's beautiful, Rahkki."

"It's about the first Kihlari who landed here four

hundred years ago. But it's a Daakuran version of our story, so probably all wrong."

She laughed. "The Daakurans always flub our tales. Did you read it?"

He shook his head. "I can't read Talu."

They stared at each other for a long moment. I'Lenna knew so much more than he did, and it struck Rahkki that when he'd lost his mother, he'd also lost his education. He sighed. "Happy late birthday."

"Thank you." I'Lenna hugged the book to her chest and then slid it into her bag.

They started eating, and as they piled their plates, Rahkki pointed out I'Lenna's thick leather vest, dark breeches, and dagger. "So . . . ," he said, "you're dressed to kill."

I'Lenna laughed so hard that the rice milk she'd been drinking spurted out of her nose. "I'm dressed to *blend*," she corrected. "I'm going to the village for a while, you know, to hang out with the regular kids. The dagger is . . . just in case."

"That sounds nice," Rahkki said with a hearty exhale.

"What's wrong?" I'Lenna asked.

Rahkki repeated his earlier conversation with the queen.

"The front lines!" I'Lenna cried. "But you're a Rider, not a Battle Mage. Fly away. Just go. You have Sula; you can make good time if you leave right now." She stood and paced.

"No, I want to help Sula free her friends. I'm not much of a fighter, I'Lenna. I probably wouldn't be any safer in the sky."

The coming battle still didn't feel real to Rahkki, more like a game. If only he could throw hot pepper at the giants and the elephants—if only he could help Sula without killing anything. Then an idea struck Rahkki—an idea so simple that it just might work! He tugged on I'Lenna's belt. "Will you sneak me out of my room?"

She grinned. "Can a bat see in the dark?"

"Actually, they—"

I'Lenna smacked his arm. "Of course I will, I am at your service, Commander of Dragons and Battle Mage—have I forgotten something?"

"Thrower of Hot Pepper?"

"Right," she said. "And Saver of Princesses too." I'Lenna bowed to him, and they burst into giggles. She strode to the fireplace, blocked his view, and then there was a soft click as she pushed open the hidden door.

Rahkki ran forward. "Land to skies, I'Lenna. I've

studied every inch of that fireplace. There's no latch, no hook, no weakness. There's no way to open it. Are *you* using magic?"

I'Lenna laughed, delighted. "Just because you don't understand something doesn't make it magical."

"Right," he said, appearing doubtful. "Give me just a minute." Rahkki emptied a waterskin bag he would need for his plan, retrieved a candle and lit it, then followed the princess into the darkness.

Must and mold spores filled Rahkki's nostrils as they silently traveled through the maze of tunnels. The walls leaked water. Moss, cool and spongy, slicked the hard floor.

As the tunnel angled downward, Rahkki shifted his weight so he wouldn't slide into I'Lenna. Soon came the sound of rushing water as they rounded a bend. They were in the deep belly of Fort Prowl now. Here the lower tunnels collected rainwater and expelled it through a series of grates.

Rahkki recognized the table and chairs he'd spotted his first time in the tunnels. Fresh fruit rinds littered the floor, but the writing parchments were gone. It appeared that people met here, perhaps dangerous people. He glanced at the back of I'Lenna's head, remembering how she'd shoved him away from the table last time. A second look at her dark outfit and dagger made him wonder, was she really heading to the village to *play*? He shook his head; it wasn't his business.

"Come on, keep walking," I'Lenna urged. They stepped into the flowing water and waded knee-deep the rest of the way.

When they reached the grate, I'Lenna unlocked it. They emerged from the fortress near the jungle's edge. Warm winds struck Rahkki, flipping up his dark hair. Overhead, the sky was indigo black, star spotted, and layered in drifting clouds. Fractured warbles, chirps, and screams emitted from the forest canopy beyond. "Thanks for getting me outside," Rahkki said.

"Any time." I'Lenna glanced at the culvert. "I'm leaving the drainage grate open, but be back before midnight. It's *very* important you aren't late. Do you promise me?"

"Yes," he answered.

I'Lenna swept her gaze across Rahkki's small frame. "Tomorrow you go to war. I can't believe it." She leaned forward and hugged him. "This isn't good-bye. This is for luck." He hugged her back, and then I'Lenna slunk into the shadows and disappeared, heading toward the Fifth Clan village.

Rahkki sped to the clearing where the dragon had

attacked him. The puddle of poison drool was still there. Rahkki glanced at the guards that strolled the walls of Fort Prowl, high on the hill. So far they hadn't spotted him in the dark shadows. Rahkki dipped his empty waterskin into the toxic saliva, careful not to let it touch his skin, and filled it. "This will stop the giants," he whispered, and then headed to the Kihlari stable to fetch Sula. He wanted to spend every last moment with her while he still could.

26

DRAGON DROOL

ECHOFROST STARTLED WHEN THE BARN DOOR
opened and Rahkki slipped into the stable. The tame
steeds greeted her cub with soft nickers. He was popular
with the Kihlari, she'd noticed. Rahkki approached her
stall, and she whinnied at him, wondering why he'd come
to visit her at night.

"Shh," he whispered, touching his finger to his lips.
He patted Kol next door and then invited Echofrost out of
her stall.

As they emerged from the stable, the moon had shifted
to the sky's zenith. Rahkki guided Echofrost across the
clearing and through a ditch and then back into Fort Prowl
through a dark cave-like tunnel. She snorted, mistrustful

of the watery walls and low ceiling, but Rahkki proceeded with enough confidence to calm her.

Soon, they paused at an opening that led to a larger chamber. She ducked her head and entered while he closed the passageway behind them. The room they stood in smelled like Rahkki, and Echofrost realized he'd brought her to his sleeping den.

Attached to the walls, flickering torches produced small radials of light. Rahkki took one and used it to start a larger fire in the stone hollow from which they'd arrived.

Standing so close to the flames frightened Echofrost more than any dragon or giant. She had no defenses for fire, so she crowded to the back of Rahkki's small den. For now, the fire was staying put and obeying her cub.

As usual, Rahkki spoke to her as if she could understand him. "We're going to win this war, Sula, and I won't have to kill anyone." He held up a waterskin. "This is Granak's drool. Watch!" The cub was excited, and Echofrost grew curious.

He poured the liquid from the waterskin into a large pot that hung over the fire. Soon, it bubbled merrily, and a sharp acrid stench filled the room. Rahkki opened his shutters, letting fresh air sweep out the bad smell.

"Brim told me how she makes Brauk's sleep medicine," he chattered. "She boils all the toxins out of the dragon drool, and it turns into medicine that makes people and animals go to sleep." He flashed his short white teeth and gestured toward the boiling pot. "I'm going to treat my darts with this and knock the giants out, Sula. No one will know they're sleeping. They'll think I killed them. That's how we'll win this war and save your friends."

His chest puffed, and Echofrost watched her cub stir the pot, sensing his pride.

He glanced at her, his face glowing orange in the firelight. "And then I'm going to let you go." He changed out of his wet clothing, and Echofrost glimpsed the brand on his shoulder, the one that matched hers. "I'll be a Half when you leave," he murmured. "I'll be bad luck." He smirked and donned a clean white shirt that reached his calves. "So nothing will change for me."

Rahkki extinguished the fire by dumping a bucket of cooled ash over it. He left the pot where it was and approached her with his head bent. His familiar essence wafted from his mouth, and she inhaled it through her nostrils, then blew out softly, exchanging breath with him.

He leaned against her chest, and his fingers darted up

her neck, scratching and massaging the muscular crest. She sighed. This felt very good to her. But after several moments, she grew nervous, overcome by their differences. She stepped back, and he let her go.

Rahkki climbed into his soft sleeping nest and quickly fell asleep.

Her eyelids drooped, tired from the long day, but excitement trilled her heart. All around the yard and the fortress today, soldiers had been preparing to leave. Soon, they'd face the giants and slay the beasts. Storm Herd would be free.

She closed her eyes and imagined Hazelwind. His large eyes, his long forelock, and his strong arched neck. They'd been partners in war since she was a yearling. But now when she looked at him, she pictured regal buckskin fillies and stubborn gray colts. She imagined a family flying together, coasting on the breeze. She envisioned a vast plain of grass and crystal-blue lakes—their new home.

She'd thought that freedom meant answering to no one, but she'd been wrong. Freedom meant *choosing* her bonds, because a pegasus could not live alone or act only for oneself. A herd, a friend, a mate—they were tethers too, but not the kind that tied her to the ground. They would help her fly faster, farther, higher, and she would help them do the same. She exhaled, shifting from hoof to hoof. Tomorrow she would begin rectifying her mistakes. Her true enemy wasn't the giants or the Landwalkers—it was her own selfish pride.

27

LEGENDS AND LIES

A HARD KNOCK AT RAHKKI'S DOOR WOKE ECHO-
frost. Her cub leaped out of bed, and they both rushed to
his window and glanced outside. The sky was pale silver,
warming to gold at the rim of the jungle. "I'm going to
be late!" Rahkki grabbed the door handle and pulled. It
creaked open, revealing a Land Guard solider standing in
the hall holding a cloth sack. "Soldiers get free rations,"
he said.

"But I'm a Rider," Rahkki said, then remembered he
was also a Battle Mage.

The Land Guard soldier shrugged. "Queen's orders."
He tossed the sack at Rahkki. "And you better hurry."

"Right, thanks." The soldier left, and Rahkki faced

Echofrost. "It's time." He'd ordered hay and grain brought to his room late last night, and now he fed her the leftovers, adding baked rice and roasted millet from the feast I'Lenna had left him.

Echofrost watched Rahkki don smooth leather breeches and a vest while she chewed her breakfast. He leaped and squatted, dancing around his little den, swinging his arms. The leather flexed as it warmed to him.

When finished, Rahkki poured the now-cooled dragon drool out of the pot and into his waterskin, filling it. He led Echofrost into the hall and down the stairs. Outside, he climbed onto her back and pointed. "Armory!"

Echofrost dimly recognized the word and took off, flying toward the Kihlari stable. The warm pre-dawn breeze filled her lungs and swept away the anxiety she'd felt while trapped in Rahkki's small den. When they arrived at the stable, it was bustling. The Sky Guard Riders were awake and saddling their Fliers. Rizah nickered to Echofrost. "Full armor today, Sula!"

The Kihlari steeds who were ready to fly had lined up in the yard, their Riders standing at their sides, checking their weapons.

Rahkki tossed his food ration to a stable girl. "Here, you can have this. I'm not hungry."

She grinned. "Thanks, Stormrunner!"

Rahkki retrieved their tack and armor and soon had Echofrost expertly dressed for battle. He secured his engraved black metal tight around his chest and back, lending him the strong lean shape of a Sandwen male. Next he strapped hard black shields onto his forearms, followed by a pair of tall, heeled riding boots. He led her out of the stable, where a deep familiar voice called to him. "Hey, brother."

"Brauk?" Rahkki and Echofrost whipped around to see the elder Stormrunner laid out in a wheeled cart that was attached to Kol. Brauk's wane head was propped up so that he could see. Ossi Fin stood at Kol's side, holding his lead rope, and Echofrost spied his uncle walking beside the cart.

Ossi tugged Kol's rope, and the stallion pranced forward, pulling his injured Rider's cart with great pride through the yard, but the Riders present avoided eye contact with Brauk.

Rahkki rushed to his brother, grabbed his hand, and kissed it. Echofrost followed, feeling hesitant when Brauk glared at her.

"Word is you're a Battle Mage?" Brauk grumbled. "Is General Tsun behind this?"

"Queen Lilliam assigned me," Rahkki answered.

"Bloody rain! She is trying to get you killed."

Rahkki shrugged. "She says she's glorifying me."

"That's rich." Brauk's laughter rolled from his chest, deep and bitter. "Will you take us to those palms, Ossi," he asked the woman. She clucked to Kol, leading the stallion away to a cluster of palm trees. Rahkki, Echofrost, and Uncle Darthan followed.

When they were out of earshot of the other Riders, Brauk lowered his voice and held Rahkki's wrist. "Watch your back out there, Rahkki. War is brewing in our clan between the rebels and the queen's loyalists."

"I know, I know," Rahkki said, blowing strands of hair off his forehead. "I'm staying out of it, just like everyone keeps telling me."

"Good," Darthan interjected. "It's got nothing to do with you."

"Are you back from Daakur already?" Rahkki asked Darthan, "Did you find anything out about Reyella?"

"Aye. I ferried over yesterday morning and spent all day on the docks, came back last night." Darthan grimaced. "And Rahkki, you were right; your mother escaped."

"Really?!" His body tensed. "You found her!" Echofrost flinched at the sharp tone in Rahkki's voice.

Uncle placed a steadying hand on the boy. "No, not yet, but I talked to a horse trader, an old man who's worked on the docks since I was a kid. He remembers a pregnant Sandwen woman arriving one rainy night with two guards, about eight years ago. They were in bad shape, exhausted and injured."

"That's her—that's our mom, right?"

Ossi shifted uncomfortably, and Brauk wiped the hair out of his eyes. "Don't get too excited," Brauk grumbled. "Uncle lost her trail on the docks. If it was our mom, no one knows where she went next."

"Is that true?" Rahkki turned to his uncle, eyes glistening.

Darthan nodded. "The trader tried to sell her a horse because she was injured and not walking well—"

"If she was hurt, then how'd she get across Cinder Bay? Who were the guards? Did the trader tell you what the woman looked like?"

"Rahkki, calm down," Darthan whispered. "I don't know much. He said she had dark hair, and she was soaking wet; but listen to this." Darthan's eyes flickered. "She traded a jeweled ring for two horses for her guards to ride but said she didn't need one for herself, said she *already had a mount.*"

"What mount?" Rahkki asked.

Echofrost sensed her cub's excitement and stress. She nickered to him. When were they going to fight giants! But no one paid her any attention.

Darthan's lips twisted into a half smile. "Drael could have flown Reyella across the water."

"That's enough," Brauk snapped. "Rahkki and I watched that stallion die."

"I didn't," Rahkki said.

"You just don't remember," Brauk interjected.

Uncle Darthan stiffened, speaking to Rahkki's brother. "You saw black magna spiders wrap Drael in silk, but you don't know if they made it back to their web with him. Drael wouldn't be the first meal that ever escaped. If he did break free, Drael would have found your mother. . . ."

"Black magnas got Drael?" Rahkki cried, his breath speeding.

Brauk tossed back his hair. "You see," he said to Darthan. "This search is just stirring up bad memories. Besides, if Reyella's alive, tell me this; why hasn't she come home?"

Darthan pulled Rahkki close and touched Brauk's knee. "I don't know the answer to that, boys. But after this war, I'm going back to Daakur. I won't stop until I find out what happened to my sister and her baby."

Brauk suddenly turned his attention to Echofrost, startling her, and said, "Why don't you tell Rahkki *my* news, Uncle?"

"What news?" Rahkki's eyes bounced between Brauk and Darthan.

It was Ossi who answered. "Brim is concerned because your brother still can't move his legs. The damage might be . . . it could be permanent," she said softly.

Tears erupted and streaked Rahkki's face. "No," he whispered.

"What did I tell you about crying?" Brauk said, ruffling his brother's hair.

Rahkki sank toward Brauk and laid his head on his chest. Brauk put his arm around his shoulder, and they were all silent for a moment.

Echofrost watched the Landwalkers, sensing currents of friction, fear, and grief.

Brauk gently pushed Rahkki off him. "Don't worry about me," he grunted, setting his jaw. "We have to keep *you* alive, Rahkki."

Her cub nodded.

"Listen," Brauk continued. "The rumors about you are growing—that you command dragons and that the princess has enchanted you." Brauk rubbed his face, now avoiding eye contact with Echofrost. "You should end these tales, Brother. None are true, right?"

"No, but you're the one who told me to let my legend bloom," Rahkki sputtered.

"Well, yours has sprouted into a big fat stinkweed," Brauk mumbled, frowning. "You need to kill these rumors that you're magical. The queen and her loyalists are afraid of you—that makes you a target."

Rahkki ground his boot into the dirt. "When it comes to rumors, does it matter if they're true or not? Isn't that the point of them?"

"Right," Brauk said, exhaling slowly. "If you deny them, you'll just add weight to them. But the worst rumor is that you slink off with that ambitious little princess in the dead of night to do Granak knows what."

"Ambitious!"

"Rahkki, hush," Uncle warned. Then he also turned on Brauk. "What are you getting at?"

Brauk lifted his head higher, gesturing toward the fortress. "Who do you two think is plotting to usurp the queen?" Brauk's golden eyes bored into Rahkki's as he continued. "Think about it. Who gains the most from Lilliam's assassination?"

"The crown princess," Ossi breathed. "She's the first heir."

Rahkki pulled away, the vein in his neck throbbing. "No." He shook his head. "I'Lenna doesn't want the throne. General Tsun is leading the rebellion; he asked me to join him."

"The general can't rule the clan, Rahkki," Brauk said, wiping his face with a cloth. "He needs a bloodborn heir to take over; otherwise every princess in the Realm will line up to claim our throne. And do you really think he's working with a princess from another clan? No one in the Fifth would support that. It has to be I'Lenna."

Rahkki swallowed.

Brauk gave a satisfied nod. "This is an inside job, Rahkki. I'Lenna is lying to you."

"She wouldn't!" Rahkki shouted.

Echofrost flared her wings as the tension between the brothers increased.

Brauk dropped Rahkki's wrist. "Believe what you will, Rahkki, the damage is already done. The queen knows there's a plot, and she doesn't trust anyone but Harak." Brauk gestured toward the Land Guard soldiers assembling at the base of Fort Prowl. "There are assassins in that army who are loyal to Lilliam, and you're a target."

Then he glared at Echofrost. "This is your fault."

Rahkki stared at his brother. "Why are you so angry?"

"Angry! I'm bloody scared is what I am. I haven't taught you how to fight, how to fly—anything. And now you're a Battle Mage and I'm grounded. How did this happen?"

"I'm sorry," Rahkki said.

Brauk groaned. "Don't be sorry, be smart. Here, take this." Brauk handed Rahkki an amulet. "Ossi made it for you."

The red-haired woman flushed. "It will protect you. I added flecks of iron for protection, rice seeds for provision, and Kol's feathers for luck and swiftness in battle."

Darthan handed Rahkki an open bag filled with food and other items that Echofrost didn't recognize. "Take this too."

"But I get free rations," Rahkki said.

"Don't eat their food!" Uncle and Brauk shouted at the same time. "It's not safe. Never forget you're a target," Brauk added. "All Stormrunners are enemies to the crown, according to Lilliam."

Rahkki nodded and took the package, tucking it into his satchel. Then he removed most of the coins he'd earned selling the Kihlari blanket. "Hold these for me," he said, handing the coins to Brauk. "I'll keep the rest for the march, in case I need to buy medicine."

"No." Brauk crossed his arms. "Give those to Darthan. I'll—I'll lose them."

"That reminds me," Rahkki said. "I got you a present." He reached back into his satchel and produced a small box and a gilded cage. When he opened it, a wiggling insect scurried onto his palm. "A new fighting beetle and battle cage, something to do while you're . . . healing."

Rahkki let the insect crawl onto Brauk's hand, and his brother softened. "Thanks, Rahkki, he's a bruiser." Brauk placed the beetle inside the golden cage and winced as he readjusted himself.

Echofrost whinnied at the Landwalkers and lashed her tail.

Brauk's eyes flicked toward her. "Listen, Rahkki, as much as I dislike your Flier, *she* knows how to fight, so let her. And Rahkki, there's no shame in flying away. By Granak, you're ten years old."

"Twelve."

Brauk laughed, and his face tightened with pain. "Just come back to me, okay?"

Rahkki's eyes filled with tears, and Brauk reached up and thwacked him. "Don't make me hurt you, Brother."

Rahkki leaned over the cart and hugged Brauk.

Echofrost's heart twisted with sadness. She knew what it was like to love a brother, but she and Rahkki needed to focus. She lifted her head and whinnied more forcefully.

Uncle Darthan hugged Rahkki in a quick embrace and then squatted down to look at him. He drew a line down Rahkki's chest, right over his heart. "Remember, you have your mother's blood in your veins. Reyella Stormrunner, the Pantheress of the Fifth Clan, is with you. You're made of her."

Rahkki nodded. "I understand."

Harak flew down from the sky on Ilan. "You, Battle Mage," he said, smirking at the title. "Report to General Tsun before the last morning bell, yeah. If you're late, I'll arrest you for desertion."

Rahkki nodded to his family as he mounted Echofrost. The waterskin bag full of dragon drool hung off his belt. He checked his sharpened quills—he'd chosen his blowgun over his bow—felt for his sword and his dagger. When satisfied, he urged Echofrost into a gallop and she kicked off the ground, soaring toward the fallows.

She trumpeted the pegasus cry to battle just as the sun cracked the horizon.

That's when the screaming began.

⟨∘28∘⟩

BATTLE MAGE

AS SULA ASCENDED, RAHKKI SPOTTED A COMMO-
tion below—the stable girl who'd taken his breakfast
rations was on the ground, convulsing in the dirt. Another
groom screamed for help as white froth poured from the
girl's mouth.

"Get Brim Carver," Rahkki shouted down to the other
grooms. "Tell her the girl's been poisoned. Hurry!" He
scowled at the fortress. *Queen's orders*, the soldier had
said when he tossed Rahkki the bag of food. Was Lilliam
already trying to kill him?

"The Borla is a better healer," a boy yelled up to Rahkki, shading his eyes from the sunrays creeping over the
trees.

The Borla is probably the one who made the poison, but Rahkki didn't say this. "Brim's closer!" he shouted, and the two grooms bolted toward Brim's shed.

The morning bells began to ring, and Rahkki wiped his brow. He had to report to General Tsun before the final bell clanged. Brim was already out and sprinting toward the two grooms, her wrinkled legs a blur.

Darthan and Brauk had predicted this, and Rahkki now realized there'd be more attempts on his life. If he'd eaten his rations in his room and died, the queen could have removed his body and claimed he'd run away because of the war. Luckily, he'd been too nervous to eat but he felt terrible for the poor groom. Rahkki rubbed his temple. He should have told the truth about Granak. Now his misunderstood power over the clan mascot and his friendship with the crown princess had pushed Lilliam over the edge.

As the tolling morning bells reached their crescendo, Rahkki flexed his heels, about to dig them into Sula's ribs. He stopped himself midthrust. Now was not the time to risk a fight with his wildling mare. Instead he clucked and used the reins to direct her toward the Land Guard army, which had assembled in the lowland fallows. "We can't be late. Hurry!"

But Sula was eager—he felt it in her muscles—and

this sped her flight. They soared toward the fallows, the grass rolling beneath them, and they landed beside General Tsun just as the final bell tolled.

"Rahkki Stormrunner reporting," he announced. Sula pranced, her nostrils wide and her eyes round.

"I was beginning to think you weren't coming," said the general. He was dressed in the thick armor of the Land Guard soldiers. It was constructed to absorb blows at close range while a Riders' lighter-weight armor was designed to deflect sharp hurled objects, not absorb punches from giants. While Rahkki's new set was beautiful and unique, black metal with intricate silver carvings, it was not right for ground battle.

General Tsun motioned Rahkki closer. The man's nostrils flared; the wind ruffled his short platinum hair. "You're no Battle Mage," he said. "You're leading the Land Guard as a figurehead, understand. But I'm in charge."

Rahkki nodded. "I understand."

"This is all just a ruse to get you killed, you know that right? You can't trust *anyone*."

Rahkki met the general's fierce blue eyes, shocked to hear someone of this man's rank say it out loud. "Yes, General."

He clasped Rahkki's arm and leaned closer, his body

touching Sula's wing. The mare pranced sideways, but the general kept close to her. "It's not too late to join us," he said quietly, adding the unusual hand gesture Rahkki had seen before: a closed fist and then four fingers pointed down. "It's the sign of the rebellion. It's our signal," the general explained.

"Is I'Lenna behind the uprising?" Rahkki asked.

The general backed away. "Who told you that?"

When Rahkki didn't answer, the general narrowed his small blue eyes, and then he exhaled slowly. "You have until the end of this march to choose sides, Stormrunner. Here, I've assigned a special detail to protect you." He waved over a group of four teenagers, led by Mut Finn.

"*They're* my protectors?" Rahkki sputtered.

The general lowered his voice. "It's no secret the queen wants you dead, Rahkki, and most of my soldiers are loyal to her. I can't risk assigning any of them to guard you. But these kids"—he waved at Mut's group—"were recruited by me two days ago. I *know* they're not assassins."

A buffalo horn blew, two short bursts, and the armies solidified their formations, preparing for departure. The general tightened his belt, glancing from Rahkki to Mut. "Are you two ready to fight some giants?"

"Yes, General," they answered as he strode away.

Mut fidgeted with his sheathed dagger. "You really screwed up, Stormrunner," he said. "You should be up there, not marching with us." He glanced at the Sky Guard flying overhead.

"I'm lucky to be here at all," Rahkki rasped. "Someone poisoned my rations this morning."

Mut harrumphed. "By the end of this battle, I suspect we'll all be dead." The red-haired teen peered at Rahkki with new respect. It was an expression Rahkki had observed several times since he'd commanded Granak. "Not you though," Mut added. "Some say you can't be killed."

Rahkki ignored that and studied Mut's team, noticing they wore used, ill-fitting armor meant for larger people. He recognized the head groom in spite of the helmet that left her face in shadows. "Koko? You're fighting too?"

She tipped her head. "Ay, Rahkki. I'm good with a sword, an' I can 'elp wit the wild steeds, when we catch 'em."

Another kid stepped forward, and Mut introduced him. "You know Jul Ranger. He's Meela Swift's apprentice." Mut nudged the final member of their shoddy team, a huge lumbering boy. "And I think you know my friend, Tambor Woodson."

"Call me Tam," the boy drawled.

Rahkki peered at Tam. He was one of the teens who'd dunked him in pig slop when Rahkki was ten years old. He slapped palms with the teen anyway, quickly forgiving Tam's childhood pranks in light of what lie ahead. "We're all in danger," Rahkki whispered. "And it's my fault. I shouldn't have lied."

Mut squared his wide shoulders. "Lied about what?"

Rahkki lowered his voice again. "I didn't command that dragon."

Mut's body jerked like he'd been struck. He squeezed Rahkki's arm, yanking him close. "We all saw you do it, and denying it can't save you now. Land to skies, your power is the *only* thing we believe in!" Mut searched Rahkki's face. "This war is about two things: killing giants and selling those wild steeds to make the queen richer. But we don't believe in Lilliam, we believe in *you*—the bloodborn son of the Seven Sisters. We'll fight for *you*, Rahkki. Not for Lilliam." Mut spat on the ground. "I *saw* you speak to Granak, and I watched him obey you; that's no lie."

Mut lifted his chin, his eyes fever-bright. The teen was scared but also inspired. It occurred to Rahkki again how dramatic it must have appeared when he commanded their guardian mascot to retreat—and then the massive dragon had done it, had left!

No one had noticed the fine, spiced powder Rahkki had thrown into Granak's mouth. They didn't understand the trick. I'Lenna's words echoed in his mind: *Just because you don't understand something doesn't make it magical.* But that wasn't true—if you didn't understand something, then magic was the *only* explanation, right? Perhaps that was the very definition of magic: *things yet to be understood.*

Rahkki loosed a breath. "You're right, I shouldn't deny it." The fire in Mut's eyes was faith—and Rahkki decided to let it burn since it gave Mut hope. But the fifteen-year-old seemed younger now, with his eyes aglow, especially in comparison to the callused warriors standing behind him.

"You'll use your powers to protect us, right?" Mut added.

Rahkki nodded, but his legs felt suddenly weak. His special team was supposed to protect *him*!

He urged Sula into a slow trot, and he and his team made their way to the head of the front line.

On his way there, Rahkki scanned the troops. There were about two hundred land soldiers, one hundred riders on warhorses, a hundred and fifty archers, and three hundred and eighty flying Pairs. Forty buffalo stood intermixed with the soldiers. The beasts were packed high with supplies, including the ropes and halters that would be used to steal the wild herd from the giants.

Steam rose from the ground as the heat of the new day touched the cooler soil. Horses snorted. Men and women shifted in their boots, their fresh-polished armor squeaking. Overhead, the Sky Guard army swooped and circled, waiting for the signal from Rahkki to move out. General Tsun sat astride a warhorse in the midcenter of the ground forces.

The Borla, with his team of apprentices, stood at the head of the army speaking over the warriors and blessing the battle. Next, Lilliam would speak to the troops.

"Where's the queen?" Rahkki asked, suddenly noticing her absence. "Where are the princesses?"

"Busy," Jul Ranger answered. "The baby is coming, and the princesses stayed with their mother."

Sula nickered, growing impatient. Rahkki wrapped his hands in her long, sparkling white mane, which flowed out from beneath the shield that crested her neck. When he'd dressed her, he'd braided purple feathers into her hair and threaded spiked beads throughout her tail. He'd also tied two of her purple feathers onto each of his wrists. Her ears poked through the Kihlara helmet that protected her forehead. Her large black eyes glittered as she pawed the field.

The army stilled and waited. It was time.

Rahkki stood at the helm of the ground forces and drew a deep breath. He felt like an imposter. His clan was impressed with him for all the wrong reasons. He'd never imagined that his dream to save Sula's wild herd would lead to this—heading the Land Guard army as a Battle Mage, something he wanted even less than Pairing with a Sky Guard Flier.

He raised his arm, and all eyes turned to him. Rahkki pressed Sula's side, and she pranced forward. He turned his head toward his troops, dropped his arm, and bellowed in his biggest voice. "To war!"

"To war!" the Sandwen warriors hollered, raising their voices in unified aggression. The lines of men and women marched forward, cradling their spears. They had a five-day walk to Mount Crim if they maintained an even and efficient pace.

With Rahkki and Sula in the lead, the armies marched into the jungle, heading toward the giants.

29

THE LAKE

ECHOFROST FLEXED FOR TAKEOFF, BUT RAHKKI tugged gently on her reins and said, "No." Annoyed, she folded her wings and trudged overland, feeling ridiculous. The Sky Guard glided overhead, and she whinnied to Rizah, "Why am I walking on the ground?"

The golden pinto squinted at her. "I don't know," she whinnied. "You should be up here with us."

Echofrost stamped the soil. "We could fly to the mountains so much faster."

"The land soldiers can't," Rizah neighed, "and we need all of our forces for this battle."

"So how long will this walk take?"

"About five days." Rizah drifted higher, flying in the

awkward formation of the Sky Guard. The tame steeds didn't seem to understand drafting. They flew in straight lines, battling the air currents instead of riding them. Echofrost snorted. If the Kihlari joined Storm Herd, she'd teach them the proper way to fly long distances.

A thorny branch scraped Echofrost's hide as she trotted through the brush. Her new armor squeaked and weighed her down, but she had to admit, traveling over land was probably easier than flying, at least until her muscles grew used to the battle gear.

Her cub sat tall on her back, and the soldiers shuffled along behind them. Yellow rays of sunlight pierced the canopy in dusty stripes, warming her hide. A sloth dozed, sitting in a crisscross of tree branches, and insects bit her in flurries, disturbed by her hooves. She swished her long white tail and bobbed her head in a steady rhythm. Growing up with Star, who'd been born unable to fly, she'd learned how to travel like a horse.

Allowing herself to relax, Echofrost enjoyed the warm air that hung heavy between the trees and the morning drizzle that beaded on the wide sharp leaves around her. Steam rolled along the jungle floor, hiding her hooves. Small deer and large rodents scurried away from the Land Guard as they shifted through the trees. Rahkki's hips rolled with her stride, and his warm body on hers multiplied the heat of the day, but she was content. They were on their way to free Hazelwind, Dewberry, and Storm Herd, finally.

Four exhausting days passed and now it was early evening. "Camp ho!" blared General Tsun, and the Landwalker army emerged from the jungle and set down their packs. Ahead was a flat blue lake, reflective in the slanting light of evening. Echofrost scented the breeze. Predators lurked, she detected their foul odors, but they soon retreated, frightened by all the noisy Landwalkers, buffalo, warhorses, and circling Kihlari steeds.

Quickly, the horses and buffalo were staked, patrols were assigned, and then half the warriors shed their armor and clothing and sprinted for the lake, hollering like children.

Rahkki slid off Echofrost's back and settled beneath a shady lime tree. Koko, Mut, Jul, and Tam staked their things nearby. "We're almost there," Rahkki whispered to Echofrost, nodding toward Mount Crim. The mountain loomed ahead, its peaks shrouded in mist.

Rahkki removed the engraved metal shields that

protected Echofrost's chest and flanks. He massaged a soothing balm into her tired muscles. Afterward, he traced pungent oil down her spine, and Echofrost recognized its scent. Medicine mares in Anok used the same oil for the same purpose: repelling insects.

Around the temporary encampment, soldiers and Riders patrolled for danger. So far, they'd lost two soldiers and three horses. A long-fanged tiger had carried off one man, and a viper bit the other. The three horses had died in leopard attacks.

Echofrost absorbed all she witnessed without emotion, keeping her thoughts centered on Hazelwind, Dewberry, Redfire, Graystone, and the rest of Storm Herd.

Rahkki tugged on Echofrost's mane. "Come on, girl, let's go swimming. Who's coming?" he asked his team.

Koko ambled closer, flipping back her hair. "There's gators in there," she drawled, rolling her thick-muscled shoulders.

"So?"

"So, I ain't fond of 'em."

"That's because your parents raised you on a beach," Jul said. "We've been messing with gators since we were tots."

"And dragons," Mut added. With a pretend snarl, he

leaped onto Koko's back, knocked her over, and tickled her.

"Get off me, yuh Gorlan-blooded freak." Koko broke his grasp on her, reared up, and tumbled Mut to the ground, her blond hair swinging.

Jul burst into laughter.

Rahkki slipped off his vest and boots, leaving on only his trousers. "Race you all to the lake!" He tore off, getting a head start, and Echofrost coasted beside him.

"Not fair," Mut shouted, sprinting toward the lake on foot, followed by the others. Koko crossed her arms, refusing to follow.

Unburdened, Echofrost felt light and free. She left Rahkki briefly, soaring toward the clouds and inhaling the mist. Mount Crim towered east of the lake, its peaks ragged and spiked. Tomorrow they would ascend to the home of the Gorlan giants and free Storm Herd. The knowledge brought pleasure that whipped through her like a hot spring wind.

She coasted, gliding without effort. The land sprawled below, lush and green. Cinder Bay glimmered in the distance, the turquoise water so clear that she spotted dark coral reefs below the surface. The lake where the soldiers swam appeared small from the clouds, but by contrast, the jungle was enormous, stretching as far south and west as her eyes could see, an endless ocean of waving branches and ambitious trees, taller than any in Anok. Slick blue stripes marked the various rivers that channeled water through the rain forest. The open spaces teemed with herd animals that grazed as the sun dropped, lured by the cooler temperatures of evening.

"Sula!" Rahkki called from the lake.

She dived down and landed on the water, folding her purple wings and paddling on the surface like a duck. Rahkki climbed onto her back and did a flip into the water.

Echofrost dived into the clear depths with her cub. She'd spied alligators resting on the shore, so she kept a wary eye. Rahkki swam somersaults, as graceful as a seal pup, and then kicked up for a breath. He returned and clutched her tail, and she pulled him through the water. They frolicked until the sun vanished, twirling and twisting and diving.

Once Storm Herd was free, Echofrost would move on, find a new and safer home. She would never see her cub again, and it occurred to her she would miss Rahkki.

They kicked to the surface and Rahkki sprawled across her back, splashing the water with his fingertips, chattering nonstop—about what, she could only guess. His small earnest face, round golden eyes, and thin frame had become so familiar to her that she sometimes forgot he was a Landwalker.

When he was finished swimming and the last rays of the sun had retracted from the sky, they returned to the camp. Rahkki absently stroked the crest of her neck. This had become a habit between them at end of day. Nothing about the cub disgusted Echofrost like it used to. She'd grown to accept and even enjoy his warm touch, his woody breath, and his lilting voice.

It was inexplicable, but her heart had expanded just enough to fit this small boy neatly inside.

30

DRAEL

AFTER THE SWIM, RAHKKI'S TEAM LEFT TO explore the camp before the sun set. Each evening, soldiers and Riders entertained at a central campfire, telling stories, frying honeycomb, singing, and drumming. Tonight there would be no fire or singing—they were too close to Mount Crim—but there would be quiet storytelling. Rahkki had noticed the tales growing darker and more frightening as each day passed. Sula didn't like the gatherings; there were too many people, so tonight he stayed with her by the lime tree. He dined on Darthan's rice cakes and fish jerky while Sula grazed on wild grasses.

Rahkki startled when a leopard spider leaped down from the lime tree and snatched his dried fish right out of his hand. "Bloody rain!" he yelped, and Sula flared her wings.

The black-and-tan spider, about the size of Rahkki's head, hung from its silk thread and turned its eight shimmering eyes on the boy. Four of its long legs gripped the piece of fish, the other four clutched the silk, but it continued to glare at Rahkki, working its jaws.

"Get," he said, shooing it away.

The heavy creature lost interest in the boy and retreated, rising effortlessly back into the tree. There it rolled the fish in silk, spinning the sticky thread from its hairy abdomen and wrapping the meal tight.

Rahkki stared, transfixed. The spider's motions and its glistening silk reminded him of what Brauk had said about Drael being killed by black magnas. Waves of nausea rolled through Rahkki. He wasn't afraid of spiders, but he knew he'd seen this before: a spider wrapping its prey. Could it be that more of his memories from the night Lilliam attacked his mother were returning? And what if Drael had survived the black magnas attack? Rahkki's heart stuttered—that bay stallion had been his first, and his best, friend.

Rahkki finished the rest of meal and then curled into his bedroll. He slept fitful, his mind churning. He dreamed about the evening his mother disappeared. After he and Brauk were safe on Drael's back, Reyella had leaped over Rahkki's low-burning fire and vanished through the flames. Lilliam, whose hands were curled as if still around Rahkki's throat, had screamed, "I will find you!"

After Reyella vanished, Brauk, Rahkki, and Drael had galloped down the long hallway. Lilliam had shouted for her personal guards—hired soldiers she'd brought with her from the Second Clan to help her overthrow Reyella Stormrunner. The guards burst from the shadows and blocked Drael.

The stallion had whirled and kicked, hurtling guards into walls. Rahkki rode in front of Brauk, his fists clenched around Drael's black mane. The boys rode bareback with no bridle to guide Drael and no saddle to keep them secure, but Drael knew what was needed: to get the young princes out of the fortress.

Rahkki had dared a glance at Brauk. His brother was thirteen years old and already strong and fast from wrestling and hunting. And he was fearless too—he baited small dragons, rode untrained horses, flew Drael to breathless heights—but his face that night was round and young and twisted with terror. "Yah!" he'd shouted to Drael.

The stallion charged past the final guard, lowered his head, and leaped straight into the shuttered window, smashing it to pieces. Slivers of wood sliced Rahkki's arms, and he'd yelped with pain. The last soldier hollered and drew his bow. Seconds later, an arrow whistled toward them. Brauk leaned over Rahkki, shielding him, grunting when the arrow grazed his ribs, drawing blood. Then another flew, and it plunged into Brauk's shoulder. Drael, who was also injured, had wheezed for air and sunk toward land. "No, Drael, fly!" Brauk had cried.

And there Rahkki's memory had dropped a veil these past eight years. He'd remembered nothing except showing up at Darthan's farm ten days later, starving and weak. But now, in his sleep, that veil shattered just like the shuttered window, and he suddenly remembered everything. . . .

"Something's wrong with Dee Dee!" Rahkki screamed after they burst through the window. He was four years old, and he couldn't pronounce Drael, which meant "diamond" in Talu. Upon hearing Rahkki's words, the small bay stallion rallied, pumping his wings and regaining his altitude. He flew deep into the jungle, his breath coming in rapid bursts.

Rahkki glanced back and saw tears streaming down his brother's cheeks. Then he studied Drael—his best friend in the world. What was wrong with the stallion? Why did he sound like he was full of holes?

That's when Rahkki noticed the blood. It dripped down the stallion's chest and fell toward land. "Dee Dee's hurt!" he screamed at Brauk.

"We have to land him," Brauk hollered.

They'd flown so fast they'd reached the Western Wilds, the lands that were uninhabited by Sandwens. Rain burst from the clouds, soaking them instantly. Brauk guided Drael to the animal paths. The bay stallion stumbled upon landing and then crashed onto his side. Rahkki and Brauk tumbled off his back and into a clump of dark vines and ferns. Lightning cracked and thunder roared across the sky.

Rahkki rolled to his feet and rushed to Drael's head. A long sharp sliver of wood was embedded in the stallion's chest like a spear. Rahkki ignored it and lay beside Drael's chiseled and perfect muzzle. His tears dripped onto the stallion's face. They mixed with the rain as he stroked the bay's cheek and listened to his soft breaths.

Brauk sat a distance away, his gold eyes as blank as the moon.

Drael heaved a breath and groaned in a deep rumble. Blood pooled between his teeth.

"Don't die," Rahkki pleaded. "Please don't die."

The stallion rolled his dark-brown eyes toward the young boy.

"I love you," Rahkki whispered to him. "You're my best friend."

Drael shut his eyelids.

"Dee Dee, no!"

The small stallion's amber feathers gave a defiant rattle as his wings settled around him. His breaths slowed.

A blast of lightning struck, revealing danger. "Run!" Brauk had shouted, and he grabbed Rahkki's nightdress in his fist, yanking him upright. "Black magnas!"

Scurrying toward them from the west came an army of gigantic black spiders. Snapping mandibles, thousands of glittering eyes, and razor-spiked black legs filled Rahkki's vision. Brauk picked up a sharp stick.

The closest spider had reared back and shot a band of silk at them. Brauk ducked, tugging Rahkki with him. Then he charged the waist-high spider and smashed it across its fangs. The magna reared again, shooting silk that struck Brauk's face. The spider gripped the thread with its hairy claws and reeled Brauk toward its fanged maw. The spider army piled over one another, skittering closer and shooting threads that filled the sky. The silk landed on Rahkki and his brother, sticking to their skin and clothes.

Rahkki tried to break the silk that connected his brother to the black magna. If the spider got close enough, he'd spin Brauk into a webbed cocoon. Then he'd inject him with venom, but not the killing kind.

Black magna venom was the strongest healing medicine in the Realm. The serum entered the blood and immediately healed disease, killed infection, and knitted damaged bone and tissue. It was difficult to collect, but Sandwen Borlas kept doses of the rare venom on hand for their queens. The venom could heal just about anything. But the spiders used it on their victims for a darker purpose. Diseased or damaged food would be rejected by their spiderlings. So after binding their prey in silk, they injected the serum to ensure a healthy, disease-free meal.

"Get behind me!" Brauk screamed.

And then dark hooves came crashing down, pounding the magna into the mud—it was Drael! He'd rallied enough to fight.

The spider rolled over, spitting silk from its belly.

Drael stomped its head, and pale-blue blood squirted

across Rahkki's nightdress. He stared up at the stallion between flashes of lightning. The beautiful bay was sweat frothed and rain soaked, and the splintered piece of wood still jutted out from his chest. Drael wheezed for breath; he didn't have much fight left in him, but maybe just enough. . . .

Brauk snatched Rahkki's hand, and they fled from the spider army while their mother's stallion battled for them, slamming spider after spider with his hooves.

The silk threads flew.

The boys ran.

The last time Rahkki looked back, Drael's legs were trapped in sticky silk, and he had fallen onto his side. The black magnas swarmed him, spinning their threads.

After that, Rahkki just ran, mindful only of his brother's slapping heels. They jogged for miles, heading away from the spider army. Finally Brauk came to rest at the base of huge kapok tree with a hollowed-out trunk. After poking around with his stick and finding nothing living, Brauk ordered Rahkki inside.

Both boys scooted into the tree, and Rahkki curled into a ball. Brauk yanked the arrow out of his shoulder and wrapped the wound with cloth he tore from his nightdress. The brothers sat in silence for a long, long time.

Then Rahkki slumped over. "Dee Dee, Dee Dee, Dee Dee," he chanted.

Brauk said nothing. He just sat and sharpened his wet stick on a stone.

The brothers spent ten long days surviving in the jungle. They fed on figs and grubs, and hid from panthers and territorial chimpanzees. They were stung by insects and attacked by jungle rats. Rahkki had his first run-in with a carnivorous plant. It snapped its leaves around him and would have eaten him if Brauk hadn't snapped the creature's stem, killing it. That's when Brauk decided they couldn't live in the jungle alone forever, but they also couldn't go home. Their mother was gone. And now Lilliam was the new queen and the boys were her enemies.

Rahkki had denied it. "No, Momma jumped through the fireplace. She's alive."

"If she's alive, then why is Fort Prowl flying the black banner?" The boys had climbed a tree the day before and spotted the black flag waving. It meant that the sitting queen was dead. It would remain black for a full moon cycle, and then the red flag would return. Brauk laughed, his tone bitter and cold. "Time to grow up, Rahkki."

And Rahkki had fought hard to grow up, to be brave, to accept Brauk's truth; but to do so, he had to deny what he'd witnessed: his mother's seemingly magical disappearance. Over time, a veil had dropped onto Rahkki's memories, covering them like snow.

The rest, Rahkki had always known. After ten days in the jungle, Brauk had made a decision. "We have to go to Uncle." The brothers had avoided this, fearing the queen would kill Darthan too, but Brauk was just old enough to know that he needed help and just young enough to ask for it. "Maybe he can hide us."

When the boys reached Darthan, they were weak, starving, and exhausted. Uncle had run outside to meet them, looking as dirt streaked and bramble-torn as they. "I knew you were alive," he'd cried, embracing them. "The new queen announced you weren't, but I didn't believe it. I've been searching and searching."

A few days later, their uncle had struck a bargain with Lilliam, promising his harvests to the Fifth Clan army and receiving a mere tenth for himself. He became her indentured servant, but in return, the new queen promised to allow Rahkki and Brauk back into the clan and grant them their inheritance, which Brauk had quickly squandered gambling. But before they lost everything, Brauk had

purchased Kol, joined the Sky Guard, and risen rapidly
through the ranks. And Rahkki had become his groom.

Now, in his sleep, Rahkki groaned. The black magnas
turned into leopard spiders, Drael morphed into a piece
of fish. Rahkki tossed and tried to turn over, but a terrible weight crushed his chest. He cried out, struggling to
breathe. He clawed at his blankets, but they covered his
head. Someone was sitting on him. Then something long
and smooth slid down his leg. He heard a serpent hissing.

"Help!" he rasped.

A pillow slammed onto Rahkki's head. He tried to
shove it aside, but the person pressed it into his face, cutting off his air. Meanwhile, the serpent bumped against
his thigh.

Rahkki's mind screamed one word: *Assassin!*

31

ASSASSIN

RAHKKI THRASHED INSIDE HIS BLANKETS AS THE wool pillow filled his mouth.

Footsteps barreled toward him, and then someone slammed into the first person, shoving him off of Rahkki's chest. He heard them wrestling in the dirt. He rolled away and finally whipped his legs out of his blankets and freed his head.

Torchlight came, bobbing in the hands of a soldier. "Ay, what goes?" he cried.

The light illuminated two figures—Rahkki saw Harak Nightseer and a small hooded person holding a gleaming dagger.

Harak lunged at the assassin, who dodged him and

then raced into the jungle. "Who are you?" Harak shouted at the retreating figure, and then, to the soldier carrying the torch, "Seize him!"

The rumpled soldier, who'd probably just woken from sleep, lumbered into an awkward chase.

Harak shoved Rahkki aside, took up a loose branch, and thrashed the bedroll. The long shape of a serpent flailed beneath the covers, hissing furiously. "Stay back!" Harak shouted. "It's a blood viper." He beat the creature and then dragged the limp body out of the bedding by its tail. Rahkki spied the red-scaled bands that warned of the serpent's deadly venom. This snake was one of the deadliest in the Sandwen Realm.

"Land to skies," Rahkki breathed.

Harak narrowed his green eyes, nodding toward the dark forest where the mysterious figure had disappeared. "Someone tried to kill you, little Rider. They trapped you in your blankets with a blood viper. Did it bite you?"

"The assassin or the snake?"

"*Mushka*," Harak snarled. "The snake, yeah."

Rahkki examined his exposed skin. "I don't think so." Then he stared up at Harak. A thin line of blood had appeared on the Headwind's arm where the dagger had cut him. "You saved me," Rahkki said, incredulous.

Harak sneered at him. "You're lucky I was near." He inspected the cut on his arm. "Bloody rain," he growled. "You owe me for this." Harak strode away, flinging the snake's body into the brush.

Rahkki glanced around him. Where was Sula? Where were Mut and his protectors? He pulled on his trousers, slipped a small torch out of his supply bag, and tiptoed toward his team's bedrolls. They were empty. Around the encampment, soldiers snored and patrols guarded the perimeter. Rahkki's hairs stood on end. This was the second attempt on his life in four days. His thoughts turned to General Tsun; maybe the general knew something about the assassin.

Rahkki slunk toward the general's tent but saw it was well guarded and dark. He decided to speak to the general in the morning, and then he returned to his mangled blankets and walked in a spiral around them, hunting for Sula's hoofprints. When Rahkki spotted her tracks, he followed them, but abruptly, they disappeared.

For a long moment, Rahkki was perplexed. How had his mare just vanished? Then he noticed a few purple feathers trapped in the branches overhead. Of course, he chided himself. She'd lifted off to fly, and he had no way to track a winged mare.

Rahkki tread into the clearing by the lake, scanning the star-laden sky. The hiss of an alligator startled him. His gaze swept lakeward and located the reptile, crouched on the shoreline in the distance, watching him. Its parted jaws revealed sharp teeth. "What are you looking at?" he groused, feeling unsettled.

The black alligator hissed again and whipped its tail. Rahkki realized he hadn't grabbed a weapon, more proof of his overall incompetence. He turned and trudged back to his bedding. Lifting it, he saw the viper's blood splattered against the wool. The smell would attract predators, which was the last thing he needed tonight. He bundled the mess, tucked it on the western side of a bushy fig tree, and lit it on fire where the flames were shielded from view.

He returned to his lime tree, spread out his rain cloak, and lay upon it, curling for warmth. Moments later, Sula floated down and landed beside him.

"Where have you been?" he whispered, relief filling him.

She nickered and sniffed him. Then alarm rounded her eyes. Traces of blood still darkened the soil—the snake's and Harak's—and she'd caught wind of it. Sula pressed her muzzle against Rahkki's face, exchanging breath with him. It was a Kihlara greeting but also an expression of affection. "I'm all right," he said, stroking her petal-soft muzzle. "I'm just fine."

Sula buckled her knees and lay beside his cloak, seeming to offer her larger body for warmth. Rahkki nestled close, pressing his cheek against her sleek silver hide. Perhaps she'd gone for a drink at the lake, or off to graze. All that mattered was that she'd returned to him and they were both unharmed.

His mind shifted to Drael. If the stallion had escaped the magnas, he would have found Reyella and flown her across Cinder Bay. Rahkki's heart swelled as he snuggled closer to Sula. Perhaps his mother and her stallion had both survived. He shut out the nagging question—*where had they gone*—and turned his eyes toward the stars.

Morning arrived, quick and loud and shrouded in mist. Rahkki woke and snacked on Darthan's spiced rice cakes, and then he and Sula strode toward the general's command tent. Koko, Mut, Tam, and Jul were still absent. The calls of birds and monkeys ricocheted throughout the canopy overhead, and the deep rumbling of orangutans filled his ears. Upon arriving at General Tsun's tent, Rahkki begged entrance.

"Ay, Stormrunner," the general greeted, biting into his flatbread. Harak, Meela, and Tuni squatted nearby. Before Rahkki could complain about the assassin, the general spoke. "I heard there was trouble last night."

"Yes, sir. Someone tried to kill me," Rahkki answered.

Tuni swore under her breath.

The general flinched. "You sure it wasn't a prank?"

"I don't think so, General. It was a blood viper. Harak saw it. And whoever put it in my bedroll was armed with a dagger. He cut Harak with it." Rahkki guessed the dagger was a backup weapon in case the snake had failed to strike. Rahkki exhaled, realizing how close he'd come to death—again.

"You're right," General Tsun agreed. "That doesn't sound like soldiers messing around. What did this assassin look like?"

"He was cloaked," Rahkki said. "I didn't see his face."

The general addressed Meela. "Headwind Swift, dispatch a patrol into the woods at once. Find this cloaked assassin!"

She nodded briskly and exited the tent. Satisfied, the

general changed the subject. "I have a mission for you, Stormrunner."

Rahkki brightened. "Yes, General."

"Take your team up to Mount Crim and scout for the wild herd. We need to know *exactly* where the giants are keeping them."

"Just me and my team?" Rahkki asked, surprised. "But—"

Tuni, who had tied back her dark-red hair, interrupted. "He might be our Battle Mage, but he has no experience, General."

"I think the boy will be safer *outside* of camp," the general said pointedly, and Tuni nodded in reluctant agreement.

Rahkki imagined his new friends: Mut Finn, Jul Ranger, Tam Woodson, and Koko Dale. What did any of them know about scouting giants? "When? How?" Rahkki asked.

"You're the Commander of Dragons. Use your powers," Harak teased.

General Tsun shouldered past Harak. "Let your mare guide you. She found them once; she can find them again. Take your daggers, but not your swords or armor. You are kids exploring, got it? If you're caught, the giants will never suspect you're part of an army. Once you locate the wild herd, fly back and tell us where they are. I expect you to return by high sun tomorrow. It's not complicated."

"But giants eat kids."

"Not the little ones," Harak said, laughing, and Tuni knocked him in the shoulder.

General Tsun flashed Rahkki a sympathetic look. "It's a simple exercise, Rahkki."

Rahkki nodded to the general and strode away, a chill settling in his gut. He doubted any of this was going to be simple.

32

THE TEAM

"COME ON, SULA," RAHKKI SAID AS THEY returned from the general's tent. "Let's get our camping gear and find the team."

Echofrost followed him, guilt rolling through her in waves for leaving him last night. She'd only done it because she'd wanted to scout the area on her own, to search for clues of her friends, but she'd found nothing.

Rahkki slipped the bridle over her ears and buckled it to her head, but he didn't bother with the saddle. Instead, he loaded bags onto her as if she were a pack buffalo: a sack of grain, his satchel, and his extra clothing. *What now?* she wondered.

Next he removed the barbed beads from her tail and

plaited her mane to keep it from tangling. She wondered why he was leaving most of his weapons and their armor stacked tidily on the ground.

"Ay, Stormrunner," called a voice. It was the tall red-haired Landwalker named Mut, followed by Koko, Jul, and Tam. Echofrost had learned their names during their four-day journey to this encampment.

Rahkki took Echofrost's reins and led her to Mut. "Where were you all last night?" Rahkki asked the teen, his jaw muscles fluttering.

"Having some fun," Mut said, winking slyly at Jul. The two burst into laughter.

"Fun?" Rahkki repeated, narrowing his eyes.

"Yeah, the kind that's not funny to anyone else," Jul added, choking on a giggle.

Mut twisted his lips. "But pretty bloody funny to us."

Rahkki glanced from one to the other. The boys covered their mouths, laughing harder. "The look on that soldier's face," Mut said, his humor exploding.

"And that hairy tarantula, the biggest I've seen," Jul added. He used his hands to indicate a spider as wide as his chest, then he forced a frown. "Yeah, we might have chosen a smaller one."

Mut clutched his belly. "The soldier screamed like a

monkey when he put his boots on . . . remember? *Ooh, ooh, ah, ah!*"

Jul bent over, wheezing, and Mut leaned on him.

"Fools," Koko muttered, but her mouth curved into a half smile.

Tam shook his head. "It wasn't *that* funny."

Echofrost listened; understanding that the Landwalkers thought something was hilarious.

"Well, if I'd known he was General Tsun's third cousin, maybe I wouldn't a done it," said Mut. "Anyway, we didn't hurt the kid."

"Kid?" Rahkki asked, crossing his arms.

"Ah, don't look so spiced, Rahkki; he's sixteen, and he whined all the way here. Figured I'd give him something to really cry about."

Rahkki's boot tapped faster and faster. "But you never came back."

His team exchanged guilty glances. "About that," Jul said. "Meela Swift was telling stories at her tent, and by Granak, she knows how to tell a story. We all fell asleep there."

"You ditched me for a story?"

"An' chocolate," Koko added, her eyes dreamy.

"Yeah, she had a pot of it, all melted from the sun." Jul

licked his lips. "We were going to come back for you," he added quickly.

"Oh yeah?" Rahkki asked, his voice flat. "Well, while you four were listening to bedtime stories and eating chocolate, someone put a blood viper in my blankets."

His friends' laughter skittered to a halt. "As a joke?" Jul asked.

Rahkki rolled his eyes. "Why does everyone think that a viper in my blankets is funny? Someone tried to *kill* me."

His friends shut their mouths.

"You know you're supposed to be *protecting* me, right?"

"Yeah, from the giants," Mut said with a weak smile. All five of them spit on the ground when Mut said *giants*.

Rahkki lowered his voice. "Well, now you need to protect me from *assassins* too. And we have new orders from General Tsun. He's sending us to scout the hordes for the wild herd. The army needs their exact coordinates before we fight."

"Just us?" Tam asked, raising his thick black eyebrows.

"Just us." Rahkki circled his finger, pointing at each of them.

"Nice!" Jul said.

"Not nice," Rahkki countered. "I'm sure Harak is hoping we're spotted and tossed into the soup."

"But that would alert the giants that they're under attack."

"Oh no, it gets better," Rahkki said. "We have to scout them *without* armor or large weapons. We're just stupid Sandwen kids out exploring, so they'll never suspect we're military."

"Yuh can say tha' again," Koko drawled.

Rahkki shook his head. "Let's not think about it too much. Just pack up and move out."

The team scattered to gather their satchels and rejoin Rahkki. When they were all ready, the cub clucked to Echofrost, and she trotted by his side as the group walked to the lake to fill their waterskins. Overhead, the Sky Guard circled, and Echofrost whinnied to them. "What's happening now? Why are we the only ones going out?"

Rizah nickered down to her. "I don't know, but keep your nose to the wind, Sula. The sooner one of us finds your herd, the sooner this will be over."

I hope so, Echofrost thought.

The golden pinto mare banked and flew away, guided by Tuni. The patrol cruised between the trees, scanning the encampment for giants, predators, and game to hunt.

Rahkki tugged gently on Echofrost's reins, urging her forward. She remembered playing with him last night in

259

the lake. They'd come far since she'd vowed to kill Rahkki on her first day of captivity.

Her cub stood on his tiptoes and whispered into her ear. "It's almost over." Then he clucked at her with his tongue, which she'd learned meant he wanted her to increase her pace. She did, and the team marched toward the misty ranges ahead. When the wind kicked up, it tore out some of Echofrost's plumage, and Jul ran behind her, collecting it. She flexed her hocks, wanting to kick him but knowing she'd better not.

"She doesn't like you behind her," Rahkki grumbled.

Jul pocketed the purple feathers. "Tonight I'll make charms for each of us, for luck."

Koko snorted. "Nay, don' make me one," she said. "Tha' wildin' mare ain' lucky."

Soon they reached the jungle lands at the base of the mountain. The group entered the rain forest, where the air was instantly cooler and the sunlight muted, and they stopped talking. They'd entered the territory of the Gorlan hordes.

Echofrost flared her nostrils, drinking in the scent of rot, flowers, and predators. The leaf canopy screeched overhead: insects, primates, and birds—the usual noise-makers of the jungle—chirped and bellowed. Her ears swiveled, listening for the grunts and heavy footfalls of Gorlanders.

Rahkki used hand gestures to signal his friends, and sometimes this made them giggle. Echofrost's heart sank. Why would the armies send these weanling kids instead of experienced warriors?

She rattled her feathers, suddenly understanding.

No one cared if these cubs lived or died.

∼33∼

SCOUTING

AS RAHKKI AND HIS TEAM CLIMBED THE BASE OF
Mount Crim, the early-morning steam evaporated, and
the sun heated Rahkki's black hair, making him sweat.
Tam, who was built like a bear, lumbered along, breathing in a loud lulling rhythm, and the others glided with
efficient grace.

Hours passed, the heat cloyed their skin, and the air
grew static. A storm brewed over the northern ocean,
heading toward them. The Sandwens moved quickly
through the jungle, as comfortable in the woods as animals. Shifting their eyes constantly from the treetops to
the dark depths around them, they stepped over trails
of poisonous ants, dodged spiny toxic plants, and ducked

beneath spiderwebs large enough to entrap them.

In one of the trees, Rahkki spotted a rare white jaguar. It stared back at him, and his gut knotted; but every Sandwen knew it was the jaguars you didn't see that attacked you.

"Keep walking," Tam whispered. He drew his dagger and pointed it at the jaguar as if daring it to pounce.

Sula trotted beside Rahkki's team, as careful and as silent as they. Having never lived wild, tame Kihlari crashed through the trees like stampeding elephants, but Sula trod softly. Uncle was right, the Fifth Clan Fliers could learn much from the wild herd.

"Hold up," Mut said, raising a fist. The group froze.

Ahead of them, branches crashed and swayed. Jul opened his mouth to say something, but Koko seized his arm and pressed her finger against her lips. Jul squirmed until he saw them too.

There were giants on the trail ahead.

Sula pricked her ears and inhaled. It was a small group of four Gorlan males. They carried two woven nets on their backs: one full of melons, the other heavy with nuts. Their bare feet thudded the soil, sending vibrations that Rahkki felt through his boots. They gestured with their hands but made few other noises. Their scent carried on the breeze, a mixture of sweat, animal hides, and goat's milk. Rahkki spied full waterskins attached to their belts and noticed the dried white liquid rimming the tops. Legends said that giants loved milk, but until now, Rahkki hadn't actually *believed* it.

He waited for the Gorlanders to walk farther ahead of them before giving his team the signal to follow. Sula was careful, placing each hoof softly in front of the other. The teens hunched, creeping along the path.

Rahkki studied the giants. They walked far ahead of his team, shoving small trees aside as they traveled. The blue-eyed, flame-haired Gorlanders were the complete opposites of Rahkki's slender, sun-darkened clansfolk. Thick muscles shaped their chests, crisscrossed their arms, and bulged from their legs. A Sandwen was a twig next to a giant.

He also noticed that the thudding giants scared away all the animals in the area, and he wondered how they hunted meat for their soup. Granak the dragon was also too big to tread quietly through the rain forest, so he hid and ambushed his prey. Rahkki imagined the giants did the same.

The tallest Gorlander reached up, scratching his head, and Rahkki gasped. Tied to his wrist was a feathered bracelet. The color of the stolen plumage was jade green, the exact color of the buckskin stallion's feathers. Rahkki wondered if Sula had noticed it too, and when his mare rattled her wings, a sign of anger or distress, he guessed she had.

"Calm down," he whispered, stroking her silver hide. The others held their breath, watching his wild mare react.

Sula flattened her ears and flashed the deep pink within her nostrils, but she knew better than to make noise.

Rahkki exhaled and turned his attention back to the giants, wondering what the feather meant to the Gorlander. Was it a kill trophy? Or was it like a Sandwen charm, a decoration? The team paused as the giants drew farther away. Then Sula shoved Rahkki hard with her muzzle, urging him forward. He nodded, and the group resumed their creeping, avoiding the path the giants had taken.

At midday, Rahkki's team paused to rest, and Sula glared at them, seeming annoyed by their slow progress. Jul leaned against a fig tree, guzzling from his waterskin.

"Sun and stars, it's hot."

"Why don't you fly ahead of us?" Mut suggested to Rahkki. "We won't reach the peaks until nightfall at the pace we're climbing, but you and Sula can scout the hordes and get back quick."

"I was starting to think the same thing," Rahkki answered. "But what if we're spotted?"

"Giants are lazy," Koko huffed. "Nuthin' hunts 'em, so they don' patrol their territories like we do."

"And they have terrible distance vision," Jul added. "If you just fly up and circle round a bit, maybe you'll find the wild herd, and we can head back for the army."

You're the lazy ones, Rahkki thought, but they were also correct; it would be faster to fly. "All right, Sula and I will scope out the peaks, but you all keep moving. If I can't find the herd, we may have to go in on foot. If I'm not back by dark, set up a camp at that first ridge and wait for me." He pointed to a jagged peak, guessing they could reach it by nightfall, and the team agreed.

Rahkki mounted Sula, and his anxious mare kicked off the path with such power that Rahkki slid toward her tail. He clutched the base of her wings and scrambled back into place. But as she soared higher, his belly trilled—not with fear but with joy!

Stunned, Rahkki held on to Sula's reins with one hand, as if he'd been flying his entire life. His dread of heights had evaporated! Rahkki let out a happy breath. Now that he'd finally remembered more things about the night his mother had disappeared, he also remembered that he *did* love to fly—always had! It was Drael's death that had changed him. Since that night, flying had made him sick. But the horrible queasiness and fear had nothing to do with the heights and everything to do with the horror of Drael's last flight.

This is good, he thought. There was enough to fear in the coming battle without worrying about falling off Sula's back.

34

HIGHLAND HORDE

ECHOFROST GLIDED UP THE SLOPES OF MOUNT Crim. The trees thinned as she and Rahkki reached the upper peaks. Her soaring body cast a large shadow that rippled across the swaying sea of green leaves below. But as she flew closer to the top of Mount Crim, she realized its monstrous size. The mountain peaks expanded as far east as she could see. She flared her nostrils, filtering the moist air for scents of pegasi.

Soon, Echofrost spied tendrils of smoke and heard the trumpeting of elephants. Rahkki urged her to fly lower, and she dipped into the jungle and soared between the trees, avoiding the dangerous hanging vines that threatened to ensnare her. With unexpected pleasure, she noticed that Rahkki rode her with new confidence. *What changed?* she wondered.

Ahead, she detected the edge of the Gorlan horde encampment. She soared around a sharp outcropping of boulders and gasped. Rahkki sucked in his breath. Across a deep ravine, they spied a huge plateau of dirt, stone, and shredded meadow. Several hundred elephant-hide tents flapped in the breeze, and fenced pens full of mountain goats and small sheep had been erected along the outskirts of the camp. The giants had sawed large tree stumps into tables and chairs. Reed dolls and carved toys were strewn throughout.

Hundreds of Gorlanders worked and played on the plateau while their elephants dozed in the meadow. Echofrost guessed this was Highland Horde, since Rizah said that only they kept elephants. Great Cave Horde kept saber cats, and Fire Horde kept burners, though they sometimes lent their beasts to the other hordes. Echofrost landed in the woods, peeking at them through the heavy-leafed branches that provided cover.

In the center of everything rested a huge black cauldron of bubbling broth. A large blackwood frame secured the pot over a pit of red-hot coals and steaming logs. This was the "soup" that the Kihlari had warned her about. If the giants had eaten any of Echofrost's friends, they would be in that soup. She shuddered as the scent reached her, but to her surprise, it was not unpleasant.

But what troubled Echofrost the most was what she *didn't* see: Storm Herd. The sprawling camp was busy, full of adults moving about or resting in the shade. The pups sat on their rumps or played with one another, their thick lips agape and their sharp baby teeth glinting in the sun. Like their parents, they were pale as clouds, with small blue eyes and shades of red hair. Being younger, their faces were smooth and unmarked by the perpetual scowls of the adults, but she spotted no pegasi.

"I don't see your friends," Rahkki whispered. Just then a bull elephant became alarmed. Its trumpeting cry echoed between the mist-strewn peaks of Mount Crim.

Echofrost and Rahkki were hiding some distance away, but she wondered if the elephant had caught her scent. The adult giants gestured to one another and scanned the surrounding peaks.

Rahkki tugged on Echofrost's reins, urging her away. Since Storm Herd wasn't there, she followed his direction, and they cantered away from the camp and deeper into the mountains. Rahkki stroked her neck, seeming to sense her stress. The sight of so many giants had unnerved them both.

When they'd reached a safer distance away from the encampment, Rahkki peered skyward and tugged up on her reins, the signal to fly, and suddenly she understood the benefit of reins—they enabled a Rider to communicate with his or her Flier without words, which was good when a Pair was scouting their enemy. Echofrost spread her wings and galloped off the ground, enjoying the pleasant drop in her belly as she rose.

She and Rahkki coasted the mountaintops as the sun sloped toward the west, and the golden light retracted into shadows. Rahkki pulled her into a slow hover. "We should head back soon," he whispered.

She flicked her ears, not understanding but sensing her Rider was ready to quit for the day. He can't see well in the dark, she surmised, or maybe he's hungry. But she wasn't ready to quit. That's when the scent hit her, drifting on the evening breeze, enveloping her in feelings of home—Storm Herd! She gripped the bit in her teeth, flattened her neck, and soared toward the scent. "Hazelwind," she nickered, and her throat tightened.

"Whoa," Rahkki whispered. He tugged uselessly on

her reins and then gave up.

They crested a small ridge, and then a huge valley opened up before their eyes. In the settling light, three lakes glimmered across a wide expanse of succulent plants and massive shade trees. High cliffs spanned three sides of the valley, and the fourth end opened to the jungle. It was a deep, wide basin, but huge, and well hidden. Surveying the shadows of the valley, Echofrost encountered a joyous shock. Over a hundred pegasi stood fanning their wings—staked to the ground. She'd found Storm Herd!

"Look!" she nickered, forgetting that Rahkki couldn't understand her. Echofrost scanned the pegasi—there was proud and angry Redfire and stoic Graystone. She hunted for jade feathers, growing anxious.

And then, gnawing on his tether, she spotted Hazelwind, and her eyes sharpened as she focused on him. Three of his legs had been loosely bound together by rope that was tied to a heavy boulder. He could hobble in a small circle, but he couldn't run or fly. Hazelwind appeared healthy other than his dull coat and crushed feathers, and each Storm Herd steed was trapped in a similar fashion. "He's alive," Echofrost nickered, her body quivering. Tears soaked her cheeks.

Next her eyes found Dewberry, and Echofrost began to tremble. The mare's belly, heavy with twins, had dropped lower—Redfire was correct, she was very close to foaling. But Dewberry couldn't give birth *here*, in this awful valley, trapped by giants! And the pinto's face was gaunt, her shoulders and rump thin from stress.

Rahkki tugged on Echofrost's mane. "Your friends are okay," he whispered, pointing toward Storm Herd.

Not seeing any giants in the area, Echofrost flattened her ears. "By the Ancestors," she hissed. "We can free them *now*!" She swooped across the trees, skimming toward the valley and whinnying to her friends.

"No!" Rahkki yanked on her mane. "Wait!"

Hazelwind threw up his head, scanning the sky. "Echofrost!" He reared, but his tethers kept him from flying. "Watch out!"

On the side of the mountain, a small band of twenty Gorlanders marched along a narrow trail. They'd been invisible to Echofrost on the ridge, but now she spotted them—and they spotted her. They roared an alarm.

The silver mare retreated from the valley, too late. A small tree spiraled up from the Gorlan party, thrown like a spear. It struck her square between the eyes.

Rahkki's sharp scream assailed her as her vision blackened and she tumbled across the sky, hoof over wing. Rahkki slid off her back. Then her muscles went limp, and the Pair dropped down, down, down.

Straight toward the hard jungle floor.

35

SILVERBACK

"SULA!" RAHKKI AND HIS SILVER FLIER PLUM-meted toward the tree canopy. Was his mare dead?

They crashed into the trees, and the thick flexible branches slowed their fall. Rahkki slipped through first and smacked onto the sloped terrain. The landing knocked the breath out of him. His arms pinwheeled as he somersaulted down the thick-brushed slope. He clamped his jaws shut and tried to protect his head as he bounced over bushes and slid through the scrub, his limbs twisting. His own foot kicked him in the head, and his ear scraped against a tree trunk. The pain burned like fire. But the heavy brush also slowed his momentum.

Rahkki dug his fingers into the soil and slid to a halt.

He didn't know where Sula had landed. He lay still a moment with his tunic shoved up beneath his chin and his belly scraped pink and raw, catching his breath.

Hot blood trickled from Rahkki's hairline. He ran his hands along his body, checking for injuries; but other than his raw skin, a few cuts, his throbbing ear, and a pulled muscle in his thigh, he was undamaged. He grabbed the nearest tree branch and heaved himself to his feet.

Drawing his shining dagger, Rahkki crept through the tangle of foliage, hunting for Sula. He'd noticed one of the largest giants charging toward his mare after she fell—where was he now?

Rahkki sprinted down an animal path. "Sula," he hissed, hoping she'd hear and nicker to him. He'd vowed to protect his mare with his life, and he'd fallen off her like a greenfoot.

Anger iced Rahkki's veins. He swiped jungle vines and branches out of his way, his fear and fury at the giants mounting. Sula trusted him more than anyone, and he'd let her down. Hot tears burned down his cheeks. "Sula! Where are you?"

***

A small creature dashed across Echofrost's right leg. She opened her eyes in time to see a sparkling blue-scaled lizard disappear into the corded vines that wove throughout the underbrush. She blinked, disoriented. Pain radiated from her left wing to her shoulder. She lifted her head and rolled sideways, releasing her weight off the feathered limb. The hard landing had stung her muscles, but the wing was unbroken.

She stood and shook herself from her ears to her tail. Where was Rahkki? Then she remembered that she'd found Storm Herd—and they were all alive, but guarded. She needed to find her Rider and alert the Sandwen armies, right away!

Swiveling her ears, Echofrost filtered the surrounding noises—flapping bird wings, chattering insects, rustling leaves—and began trotting, placing each hoof quietly in front of the other. The muscles of her left wing were too stunned to carry her, not yet; but she needed to keep moving.

The last rays of daylight filtered between the leaves, illuminating her path, and in the distance, one of the three volcanoes rumbled and burped. Overhead, the monkeys studied Echofrost with round unblinking eyes, the moist jungle floor squelched beneath her hooves, and insects scurried out of her path.

A thundering noise reached her ears, and Echofrost halted and crouched. She fanned her wings, testing the injured one for flight readiness.

Suddenly, a rock struck her flank and she whirled around.

Fifty winglengths down the animal path lurked an adult Gorlan male, squatting and facing her. His lips curled back, and a low rumble emitted from his throat.

She flapped hard, lifting above the trail, but then sharp pain streaked through her weakened limb and she sank back down.

The giant rose and thumped toward her, gaining speed. His pounding footfalls rattled her teeth. She turned and bolted, galloping like a horse, all four hooves striking the soil at once. The Gorlander smashed through the trees. Echofrost's left wing throbbed and dragged on the ground, the feathers ripped on thorns. Excited, the monkeys swung from branch to branch, rattling the leaves.

The giant leaped. Echofrost knew it by the double smack of his feet and then the sudden silence as he flew, powered by his massive muscles. She kicked off the soil, aiming for the clouds, but the giant reached her and wrapped his thick arms around her flanks.

"Let go!" she whinnied.

He dragged her to his chest, and they crashed onto the animal trail together. The shock of their heavy landing shook the trees.

She pummeled his skin with her hooves, thrashing like a trapped wolverine. He slid his fists around her tail and lifted her by its base, hanging her upside down.

Snared tight, Echofrost twisted her neck to face him, blinking at the brightness of his copper hair and small blue eyes. He grunted at her, flashing his double set of tusks. He smelled of milk, roots, and spearmint. He freed one hand to pull leaves out of his hair, and his bare arm was so wrapped with muscle that he reminded her of a silverback gorilla, except this Gorlander was mostly hairless, straight backed, and pale skinned. He lowered her to the ground but did not let go of her tail.

She strained for release, digging her hooves into the dirt and lunging, but he held her easily.

Reaching into a bag strapped to his back, the giant threaded out a long rope. At the sight of it, Echofrost pinned her ears.

He caught her, tugged hard, and rolled her onto her side. She landed on her left wing again, and sparkles of pain dotted her vision. The monkeys went silent and stared at her, chewing on figs. The giant leaned over Echofrost, his scent spiced with aggression. He dragged her closer, like a puma drawing its prey toward its mouth.

She kicked the giant heartily in the chest. He snatched her legs and wound the rope around them. Unable to fly or kick now, she panted in furious defeat.

Once the giant was satisfied she was bound tight, he sat down next to her, opened a waterskin jug, and took a long swig. Again Echofrost smelled milk as the white liquid dribbled down his chin. He wiped his face and closed the waterskin, and she noticed that his thick, clawed fingers were almost as agile as a Sandwen's.

The Gorlander reached down and touched her back. She flinched, but his huge hand was gentle, as though he was trying to relax her. Next he drew a reed pipe out of his pack and blew on it, creating a sound that was high, piercing, and far traveling, like a breeze. She guessed he was calling his warriors. His eyes drifted often to the surrounding foliage as though he expected them to arrive at any moment.

Echofrost lowered her head to the dirt path, resting while she could. By the giant's relaxed posture, she assumed that he was not going to kill her or eat her at this moment. Perhaps he'd take her to Storm Herd.

She imagined Hazelwind's round jaw, large eyes, and dusty black mane blowing in the wind, and her heart pounded faster. She'd missed him so much! She glanced up. In Anok, her herd would appear and rescue her—but this was not Anok. The expanse above was endless and blue.

And empty.

36

THE GORLAN PRINCE

A HIGH-PITCHED PIPING NOISE REACHED RAHKKI'S ears. Glancing at the nearest tree, he leaped onto a low, thick branch and swung himself up, traveling monkey-style toward the unusual sound. A family of agitated gibbons screamed at him, and their horrible racket masked his progress.

He leaped from one tree to the next, using the vines to swing himself when the distances were too wide. He almost missed a branch, and as he wrestled for a stronger hold, he spotted a lone Gorlander through an opening in the leaves.

And he had Sula!

The massive giant was kneeling beside Rahkki's mare,

playing a reed pipe. He'd tied her silver legs together and laid her out on her side, but Rahkki glimpsed the rise and fall of her rib cage—she was alive.

He crept closer and halted on a wide branch directly above them.

The Gorlander paused for a swig of goat's milk, humming contentedly. Muscles like boulders framed his neck and bulged from his arms. He wore only a loincloth, revealing a flat, tight stomach and corded legs. His curly red hair was long and tied back with a string of leather; his pale face seemed creased into a permanent frown. He held Sula down with one thick hand, and Rahkki noted the half wreath of ivory around his neck. This was the Highland Horde prince he'd seen at the parlay.

A loud crack resounded as Rahkki's branch suddenly broke. He tumbled out of the tree and landed with a soft thud at the giant's bare feet.

The beast curled back his wet lips, showing his double set of tusks, and Sula loosed a shrill whinny.

"Hi . . . uh, hello," Rahkki said, his eyes trailing up the giant's muscular body.

The prince roared, and his breath assaulted Rahkki like a hot wind.

Rahkki swallowed. This wouldn't do; he needed to be

fierce, not nice. *Pretend you're Brauk.* He threw himself onto the balls of his feet, drew his dagger, and bobbed, dancing and weaving toward the prince.

The beast made a noise that sounded like laughter.

Sula rolled from side to side, trying to stand.

The trees shook behind the prince, making the Gorlander turn around, and Rahkki heard more giants coming. Desperate, he sliced the prince's arm with his dagger. "*Meh wan sa kinwahnni*," he shouted, which meant "Glory to the winner" in Talu.

Sula whinnied sharply, as if encouraging Rahkki, and a thin line of blood appeared on the giant's forearm. The prince turned back in muted surprise.

Without thinking, Rahkki gestured in Gorlish. "*Mine.*" He pointed at Sula. Giants could hear well enough, but their short flat tongues could not form language, which was why they spoke with their hands. "*Mine,*" he repeated.

The giant snorted, and his quick exhale blew Rahkki over. Then he answered back, his fingers flying, and Rahkki understood three words: "*Winged horse*" and "*Mine.*"

"*No!*" Rahkki shook his head.

The prince made to lunge, but then he froze in place.

His beady eyes widened in fear, and sweat erupted on his brow.

Just then the Highland prince's hordemates burst into the clearing, and among them was the largest Gorlander Rahkki had ever seen. He wore a full wreath of ivory, which meant he was the Highland Horde king, the sire of the prince. The king and his envoy also came to a fearful sliding halt, and the rain forest went as still as death.

Bumps erupted down Rahkki's arms. What in the jungle could frighten a giant?

37

HELP

THE GORLAN PRINCE BACKED AWAY FROM RAH-
kki, his body trembling.

*Have I channeled Brauk so well that the Highland
prince is afraid of me?* Rahkki wondered. Shrugging,
he pressed his advantage and pointed his dagger at the
prince's head.

That's when he noticed a reflection in the Gorlander's
blue eyes—the triangular head of a massive python, hovering right behind Rahkki.

A faint tremor rolled down the serpent's scales. Rahkki threw himself to the ground just as the monster shot
over his head, its body unfurling like a heavy ribbon. Dirt
from its shiny belly splattered onto his head.

But the Gorlan prince was the prey, and when the python reached him, it sank its teeth into his short neck.

The giant roared and toppled onto his back, and the snake's great weight pinned him. The beast ground the prince into the soil, and then its long body, at least forty lengths, began to coil around him. The giant beat the scales with his fists and tried to unwind the snake, but he was no match for this python, who was probably the Mother of Serpents herself. Its emotionless black eyes remained open, as blank as a starless sky.

The prince's sire and hordemates charged forward to help, but the python's muscular tail whipped out, knocking them down like saplings.

When the tail came at Rahkki, he braced, and it swept him across the jungle floor. His new boots skidded through the underbrush. He clutched the snake's cool, smooth scales and climbed onto its back. The forest rushed by him in a blur as he rode the beast.

If the python noticed its tiny passenger, it ignored him, instead pressing its weight against the Gorlan prince. His pale face bulged, turning dark red. A quick glance at the giant told Rahkki that he was in dire trouble.

Sula whinnied again, sharp and clear, drawing Rahkki's attention to her. But then quick movement caught his eye. The giant prince had let go of the snake with one hand to speak to Rahkki in Gorlish. It was just one word, but Rahkki recognized it. "*Help!*"

Help? What could Rahkki do against a giant python?

The prince pleaded again. "*Help me.*" His eyelids fluttered shut.

Without thinking, Rahkki raced up the body of the snake as fast as he could.

The python had quieted to focus all its energy on squeezing the life out of the Gorlan prince. Occasional tremors rippled through the length of its body, and each time the giant let out his breath the python tightened its grip.

The prince's horde had paused, just for a breath, but now they charged forward.

Rahkki was faster. He reached the base of the python's skull and drew his dagger. "Granak protect me!" he whispered. Then he tightened his fists around the pommel and drove the sharp blade straight into the python's brain.

The serpent bucked, but Rahkki held tight to his weapon. He wiggled the blade deeper into its skull, hoping to end the snake's pain quickly.

Meanwhile, Sula had managed to loosen her ropes, untangle herself, and roll to her hooves, panting.

Rahkki held his pommel firm until the snake's jaw went slack, its coils loosened, and the Gorlan prince gave a huge sputtering cough.

Only then did Rahkki yank his blade out of the python's skull. It was slick with fluid, and he wiped it across his thigh.

The Gorlan horde surrounded them, grunting and signing. Their prince slid his hands to the dirt to steady himself while his hordemates yanked on the heavy snake, trying to uncoil it.

The Highland king bypassed his son, marched to Rahkki, and squatted in front of him. The boy froze and peered up, his belly fluttering. The king grunted and stared at Rahkki for a moment, then dipped his head, his massive collar of ivory clattering around his neck. Then he stood so fast that Rahkki felt dizzy watching him rise.

The jungle, which had seemed to be holding its breath, roared back to life. Sula flew to Rahkki's side and whinnied, her voice strident.

"Let's get out of here," Rahkki whispered, tucking his dagger back into its sheath.

The giants rumbled as they worked on uncoiling the dead snake and freeing their prince.

Killing the python had seemed to happen in slow

motion, but now Rahkki's blood whooshed through him. He heard the parrots cawing, smelled the sweet pineapple plants, and felt the hot sun on his black hair. Sweat ran into his eyes.

Sula nuzzled him urgently, her wings flapping. He leaped onto her back and wrapped his hands in her tangled mane. "Go!" he cried.

She twisted away from the Highland Horde and the dead snake and flapped desperately toward the clouds. The giants carried long spears and slingshots, but they didn't use them. They watched Rahkki fly away, their spears pointed down, and then they turned toward their home.

Rahkki glanced back, surprised. Giants usually didn't show mercy. They could communicate and make tools, but they were beasts nonetheless—like jaguars or snakes or sea dragons. And no jungle beast walked away from an easy meal, so why had the Gorlanders?

His brain began to ache—everything he believed about giants conflicted with what he'd witnessed today. *Help me*, the giant had signed to Rahkki. Those were not the words of a beast. But if Gorlanders weren't beasts and weren't people, then what were they? Rahkki felt unsettled, but grateful that he'd boiled the toxins out of the dragon drool.

He'd be darting the Gorlanders with sleep medicine during the coming war, not killing them. And he was curious. Perhaps his mother had been right about befriending the hordes. Perhaps giants *could* be reasonable.

38

INTRUDER

AS RAHKKI AND SULA SOARED DOWN THE MOUN-
tainside, Rahkki stroked his Flier's neck, inspecting her
as best he could from his position on her back. The tree
branches had scraped her glossy silver hide, drawing
blood, but none of the scratches appeared deep or severe.

Her beautiful purple feathers, however, were bent and
crushed on her left wing, and Rahkki noticed that she
strained to flap her limbs in unison. Also, the bandage
had come off her other shoulder, revealing her healing
brand. *How it must ache*, he thought. His matching injury
still occasionally throbbed.

He glanced around them. In the distant north, over the
Dark Water, lightning sparkled between smoky clouds. It

was evening by the time he and Sula arrived at the jagged peak where he'd told his team to wait. Sula stumbled upon landing, and her left wing hung to the ground. Rahkki's new friends rushed him.

"Did yuh fly 'er or crash 'er?" Koko asked.

"Both," he answered.

"You smell like death," Mut said.

Rahkki glanced at the night sky. "It's too dark to return to General Tsun tonight, and Sula needs to rest her wing. Let's finish making camp," Rahkki said. "And then I'll tell you everything."

As his team rustled about, Sula's large eyes rolled toward him, and she flicked her tail in frustration. "Come here," he whispered to her.

His mare lowered her muzzle, and Rahkki exhaled toward her nostrils. She sucked up his scent with a deep whuffing noise, and then Rahkki pressed his forehead against hers. He'd seen her do this with her wild friends, and he knew it calmed her.

Slowly, she relaxed.

Then Rahkki pulled away and stared into his mare's dark eyes. "We'll free your herd tomorrow. I promise you."

Rahkki sighed, wishing for a nearby lake or a stream so he could bathe his tortured skin. "No fire tonight," he whispered to his team. "And keep your daggers close." They'd rolled out their beds, and Rahkki spread out his rain cloak since he'd burned his bedroll.

"Tell us what happened," Jul urged.

While Koko tended Sula's injuries, Rahkki recounted his adventures, beginning with the location of the wild herd and ending with the python attack.

"A snake big enough to attack a Gorlan prince—I don't believe it," Jul said.

"He ain' lyin'," Koko mumbled.

"How do you know?" Jul asked.

"Cuz Rahkki's a terrible liar. Can't pull nothin' on no one." The four peered intently at Rahkki.

"I can lie," he said, and they all busted out laughing.

"But we *know* he talks to dragons," Mut said, his face afire with admiration. "So I suppose he can kill a giant serpent too."

And since no one argued against that, the team settled for the evening. Rahkki wished his brother were with him, but thoughts of Brauk saddened him. Was his brother truly paralyzed—forever? Rahkki couldn't believe it.

"We'll set up a watch, so you and Sula can sleep," Mut offered.

"Thanks," he said, yawning. Koko had rubbed a salve

of chamomile and mint on Sula's sore muscles and fed her willow bark for her pain. Rahkki now rubbed the same salve on his aching thigh and bruises. Just as he reached into his pack for dinner, a small figure shifted in the dark, moving toward them.

"Ay, who goes?" Mut hissed, pointing at the hooded shape.

Koko, who had just lain down, flipped onto her feet before the rest of them could react. She charged the intruder, knocked him down, and rolled him into a choke hold.

"Wait," wheezed the stranger.

Koko dragged her prisoner into the center of their small encampment.

Rahkki's heart stuttered when he recognized the stranger's cloak. "It's the assassin who put the blood viper in my blankets!" he cried.

With a guttural snarl, Koko ripped off the stranger's heavy cape.

They each gasped as a long, sun-soaked braid rolled down the assassin's back.

∽39∾

THINK

"I'LENNA?" RAHKKI RECOILED, STUNNED AT THE identity of his attacker.

Koko wrenched the girl's arms behind her back, making her whimper in pain. A familiar dagger hung from I'Lenna's belt, and Rahkki remembered her holding it over him last night. "You tried to kill me."

I'Lenna stared back at Rahkki, her cheeks flushed, her chin defiant. "Is *that* what you think?"

His eyes drifted from her dirt-smudged face to her sheathed blade. "You weren't?"

The crown princess wrestled with Koko. "Let me go!"

Rahkki nodded to the head groom, and Koko released the princess, but remained close to her. "Who sent yuh ta kill Rahkki?" Koko asked. "Yur mum?"

I'Lenna flinched. "I'm *not* an assassin."

Confusion choked Rahkki, sending his mind spinning.

"If she was a killer, would she admit it?" Tam asked, genuinely curious.

"Prob'ly nah," Koko said, ready to leap if I'Lenna tried to escape.

I'Lenna addressed the group. "May I camp with you tonight?"

"Land to skies," Rahkki sputtered. "You can't just show up here like nothing happened."

She stared at him, unblinking.

Rahkki dropped his face into his hands, shaking his head. The soil beneath him felt unstable, the world shifting. Last night's assassin was I'Lenna's size, wearing the exact same cloak and holding the exact same dagger. Could he be wrong? Was I'Lenna's outfit just a coincidence? Frustration roiled his stomach. "Tell us why you're here. Right now."

"I can't."

"Bloody rain." Rahkki wrung his hands. "You can trust us. We're not part of the uprising against your mother."

"I know you aren't, but don't pretend you're *for* her either."

Rahkki held I'Lenna's gaze. No one on his team supported I'Lenna's mother—and the princess knew it. How did that make her feel? But being against her mother didn't make his team against I'Lenna. Or did it? *Were* they on opposite sides?

He tugged at his hair and peered into her dark eyes, looking for answers. She smiled at him, one cheek dimpling.

"Don' fall fo' tha' smile," Koko warned him.

Rahkki shut Koko out. For all he knew, I'Lenna was everything bad—an assassin and a liar—but he had no proof. What he did know was that she was his friend. Or at least had been. *That* wasn't a lie. It didn't *feel* like a lie. "You can camp here," he said to I'Lenna.

"Rahkki!" Koko gasped.

"You can't trust a Whitehall," Mut groused, annoyed.

I'Lenna kept her eyes on Rahkki. "Thank you," she mouthed. Then she removed her torn cloak and her ill-fitting soldier's armor. Beneath it, she wore the thick dark-leather outfit she'd worn the night Rahkki had filled his waterskin with dragon drool. "Much better," she said, stretching her arms.

A moment later, muffled wing beats startled them all, and Firo floated down between the trees, landing next to the princess. I'Lenna flashed her pet a brilliant smile. "Firo and I left the Fifth Clan territory yesterday to catch up to the army," she explained.

Mut, Jul, and Tam stared at the wild roan mare with blatant envy.

Firo trotted to Sula's side, and the two Kihlari exchanged breath, nickering happily. Still baffled, Rahkki withdrew a smoked fish from his satchel and tucked into his dinner. Seeing this, his friends settled: Koko smoothed her bedroll, Mut tugged jungle debris out of his hair, Tam cut into a pineapple, and Jul made charms out of Sula's shed feathers.

All was quiet until Jul spoke, his eyes on the wilding mares. "My parents are going to buy me a Kihlara Flier next summer. I just have to apprentice for a year, in case I change my mind. But I won't. I want to be a Rider."

Mut nodded, his eyes dreaming. "Maybe the queen will let us have a few of those wild steeds after we rescue them. We can train them like Rahkki trained Sula."

Koko nodded, and Tam grunted with longing.

Rahkki interrupted. "We have to set them free."

I'Lenna turned her sharp eyes to Rahkki, but it was Jul who spoke first. "How? General Tsun's orders are to bring them home."

"I don't know how," Rahkki said. "But it's wrong to keep them and wrong to sell them. They were born wild."

"But the clan needs to sell those steeds to pay for this war," Jul said. "I was at the same meeting you were, Rahkki."

Mut tossed back a handful of seeds, crunching noisily as he spoke. "If Lilliam didn't waste all the clan's money on herself and her kids, we wouldn't need to sell them." His eyes cut to I'Lenna, taking in her fine-stitched leather clothing.

The princess frowned and looked away.

"Isn't it against Clan Law to sell Kihlari to the empire?" Jul asked.

"Technically, but my mother planned—" I'Lenna stopped herself abruptly and then continued. "I mean, my mother *plans* to sell them to a zoological society. The wild Kihlari would be held in trust for our people and placed on exhibit in the empire. The seven clans would receive a cut of the entrance fees."

"It's wrong," Rahkki repeated, dismissing the subject.

The princess had unbraided her hair, and it curled down around her shoulders, reaching her waist. "Let's not forget that we have to *free* the wild herd first," she said sullenly.

"We?" Rahkki asked.

"You," she corrected.

"We will," he said. "Tomorrow morning I'll give the coordinates to General Tsun." Rahkki imagined his water-skin bag of boiled dragon drool. "We won't lose this war."

I'Lenna smiled. "You're confident."

"I have a plan." He shrugged. "Let's get some sleep, everyone."

Rahkki's team dispersed to satisfy their evening needs. While he ate his fish, Rahkki watched I'Lenna press chunks of hard cheese inside her folded flatbread and then devour it. Eventually she left her blankets to sit next to him. She placed her hand in his, and a jolt of heat shot through his body.

"Do you trust me?" I'Lenna asked, her brown eyes huge in the darkness.

Rahkki considered all her odd behavior: sneaking around Fort Prowl, standing over him with a dagger, following him into the jungle, and refusing to explain herself. His answer popped out before he'd finished thinking about it. "I trust you," he said, and then a ridiculous grin spread across his face. "I have no reason to, but I do."

Mut was near, and he shook his head at Rahkki like one does at a trusting animal about to be slaughtered.

I'Lenna grinned back, her unease with him erased. "Good." Then her gaze shifted toward her gleaming dagger. "You *know* who the real assassin is, Rahkki."

He laughed. "I do?"

She tapped her head. "You have a brain, but you're not using it. *Think*." Then she crawled into her bedroll. "Good night."

Rahkki leaned back to do as she asked. One by one, his friends each slunk beneath their covers.

Sleep came with I'Lenna's challenge swirling in Rahkki's mind. Three people were involved in the moments surrounding the assassination attempt: I'Lenna, Harak, and the rumpled soldier who'd chased the assassin into the woods.

If, for the sake of her argument, he ruled out I'Lenna, that left Harak and the solider. The soldier had appeared after the incident and carried no weapon. He was yawning and confused, so either a very good actor or he really had just woken from sleep.

That left Harak, but he had tussled with the assassin and taken a blow from the dagger—all to save Rahkki.

And none of this changed the fact that I'Lenna was the only one with a weapon. Rahkki rubbed his eyes. *Think*, he said to himself. *She says you know the truth. Find it!*

Rahkki drifted off to sleep, and when morning dawned, so did the truth. "Mut, Koko," he whispered. "Jul, Tam, wake up."

Koko rolled over, her blond hair stuck to her head. "Kill the gator," she yelped, still dreaming.

"I know who the assassin is." But no one was listening to Rahkki. He leaped out from under his covers and crawled through the early-morning mist toward the princess. "I'Lenna," he whispered. "I know it wasn't you." But when he arrived at her sleeping spot, all her things were gone, including her and her wildling mare.

His eyes found footprints. I'Lenna had walked away on foot, leading Firo behind her.

Rahkki woke his team with a strangled shriek. "I'Lenna is missing!"

40

CHARMED

"DO YOU THINK GIANTS TOOK HER?" TAM WON-dered aloud.

"Stinkin' giants!" Mut growled, spitting. For all their mistrust of I'Lenna, she *was* the crown princess of their clan and they were obligated to protect her. Koko drew her dagger. Her lips tightened, and her fingers clutched the grip so hard they turned white.

"No, I don't think so," Rahkki said. He scanned the area again. There was no sign of Gorlan footprints or broken foliage. "We would have heard them."

"Maybe a predator?" Jul suggested.

Rahkki's scalp tingled. "No. Her gear is gone too." He paced, thinking. Her footsteps led straight toward the

Highland Horde encampment. Was her business in the east with the Gorlanders? The giants wouldn't welcome I'Lenna, not after her mother refused the soup. "Land to skies! Break camp. We have to find her."

Quickly, Rahkki bridled Sula, and his team buried their camping supplies, marking the spot with a pile of stones. Jul gave each person a Kihlara charm bracelet—a thin leather strap twined with beads and feathers, which they tied around their wrists. Koko declined hers. "I'm tellin' yuh, tha' mare ain' lucky."

Rahkki stroked the amulet Ossi had made for him, which contained Kol's bright feathers, and he accepted Jul's charm—he'd take all the luck he could get! Rahkki pointed at I'Lenna's small boot prints and motioned for all of them to track her on foot.

Mut Finn was the best tracker, and as the tallest person in the Fifth Clan, he could also see the farthest. Mut took the lead, and the others dropped in line behind him.

Mut stepped carefully, his eyes down, inspecting the surrounding foliage. Koko watched for danger overhead while Tam, Jul, and Rahkki guarded Mut's sides and rear.

"No way." Mut halted and straightened.

Rahkki edged past the others. "What is it?"

Mut pointed. Straight ahead was an abandoned Gorlan

campsite. The fire was out but still smoldering, and the giants were gone. "Her footprints have joined theirs. She's traveling *with* the giants."

Chills rippled down Rahkki's spine.

"They didn' kill 'er?" Koko asked.

"Not yet." He circled the camp, studying the bushes, the footprints, and the moist soil. "There's no sign of struggle or force either."

Koko swiped her shiny blond hair off her forehead, her sweat making her face glow, and she narrowed her eyes. "Could I'Lenna be a spy?"

"For us, or for the giants?" Rahkki sputtered.

Koko shrugged. "Could be either."

"Koko's right," Jul said. "I'Lenna's a Whitehall; anything's possible." He cut his eyes toward Rahkki. "But you know that."

"You're wrong," Rahkki snapped. "I mean, *I* was wrong. It was Harak who tried to kill me, not her."

"She told you this?" Mut asked, eyebrows raised. "The princess has charmed you, Rahkki."

Rahkki shook his head. "No, I figured it out. Harak knew what kind of snake was in my bedroll *before* he saw it. He said, *'Stay back! It's a blood viper!'* But he said it while the snake was still hidden beneath my blankets!"

His team stared at him, blinking.

"Don't you see? It had to be him who put it there. The princess tried to *save* me."

Rahkki explained his new view of his attack. After Harak slid the snake into his bedroll, he'd sat on Rahkki's chest and covered his face with a pillow, waiting for the snake to bite. Rahkki's death would have appeared as an accident, as an unfortunate run-in with a viper. But the princess had charged Harak and knocked him away. They'd tussled, and she'd cut the Headwind with her dagger.

When the sleepy soldier arrived to help, she'd sprinted into the woods. Since Harak was the only witness, he'd spun the attack in his favor, playing the victim and the hero. But now it was all clear—so clear that Rahkki felt ridiculously stupid for thinking otherwise.

Jul smiled at Rahkki the way one does at a dreaming child. "Sure, whatever you say."

The team exchanged looks, and Rahkki's anger ignited. "I'm not . . ." He trailed off. He wasn't what—charmed by her like Mut claimed? And then another truth slammed him—he *was* charmed. *Land to skies!*

"Yuh like 'er," Koko said, smirking. "It happens."

"I—" Rahkki felt his face turn hot. He didn't know what to say.

"Your eyes forge your path," Jul added, and everyone except Rahkki chuckled.

Jul must have learned that Riders' saying from Meela. It meant that a Rider flies toward whatever he or she focuses on—it was a warning to keep your eyes fixed on the safest path. Was it so obvious to everyone that Rahkki was flying straight toward I'Lenna? Did *she* know it? "I'Lenna wouldn't hurt me," Rahkki insisted.

Mut patted Rahkki's back, sympathy shining in his eyes.

Koko nodded toward I'Lenna's boot prints. "Point is, tha' girl snuck off ta meet wit' the giants. Why?"

Rahkki grunted, having no good answer. "I don't know, but it was her choice. They didn't steal her." Rahkki's heart squeezed at the sight of her tiny boot tracks beside the giants' massive bare footprints. "Whatever she's up to, it doesn't change our plan," he said. "We have to attack now, before the giants move the wild herd, or worse, kill them."

He leaped onto Sula's back, noticing that her left wing no longer dragged on the ground. Sula pranced beneath him, her muscles tensed to bursting. "It'll be fastest if

Sula and I retrieve the army on our own," he said to his team. "Wait here for us. Stay hidden."

Sula lifted off as soon as Rahkki leaned forward. They sailed between the trees, flying low so that any lurking giants wouldn't spot them. Rahkki grinned, delighted to be flying. His quick, agile mare responded to his lightest touch with heart-thrumming power, leaving Rahkki breathless. Looking at them now, no one would guess that just a few days ago, he'd been afraid of heights. Gliding fast and true, they soared back to the Sky Guard and General Tsun.

41

TO WAR

ECHOFROST SOARED TOWARD THE WAITING Sandwen armies, her blood on fire. It was happening! She could feel it in Rahkki's excited muscles, his aggressive posture. Today they would fight to free Storm Herd. She flexed her sore wing. Koko's treatment last night had helped it immensely.

Tuni and General Tsun met them when they landed. "Where's the rest of your patrol?" Tuni asked Rahkki, glancing around.

"Waiting on the mountain," he answered. "We found the wild herd."

"I knew the viper could do it." Harak reached out to clap Echofrost on the shoulder.

She beat her wings in his face, pushing him back, and Harak shot her a furious glare.

"What is the location?" General Tsun asked.

"They're tethered in a huge valley . . . deep within the ridges of Mount Crim. They're alive." Rahkki sucked in a deep breath. "We can rescue the herd today, right now."

But General Tsun frowned. "How many giants are guarding them?"

"Just a small group."

Harak shook his head. "The hordes have shared soup, yeah. Fire and Great Cave Hordes could be close by."

Tuni spoke. "My Riders spotted Fire Horde earlier today. They're scavenging on the north side of the mountains. If we're quick, perhaps we can contain this battle to just one horde."

"Let's go then," Rahkki said, and Echofrost, feeling his urgency, rattled her feathers. She'd forced herself to behave, and she'd endured the humiliation of captivity—it was almost unbearable to wait another moment.

General Tsun turned to the Headwinds. "Take the Sky Guard and fly ahead, but don't engage the giants unless you're forced to. Wait for my ground forces; we'll be right behind you. Then we'll attack from land and sky. Rahkki, I want you to go with the Sky Guard."

"He can't. He's the Battle Mage, yeah," Harak said.

General Tsun thrust out his chest. "And I'm the general. Our Mage has served his purpose. He led the march to Mount Crim and located the enemy. Now I need *all* winged warriors in the sky . . . where they belong," he added.

"You're opposing a direct order from the queen," Harak said, his face reddening.

"We're about to engage in battle, Headwind Nightseer, and the queen is not here. Full authority of the armies has transferred to me."

Echofrost's eyes shifted from Harak's twitching jaw to the general's commanding expression.

"You won't get away with this," Harak warned.

"Watch me," the general replied. He dismissed Harak and the others with a final directive. "Let's make this quick and clean. Yes?"

Headwinds Hightower and Swift dipped their heads. "Yes, General."

Harak snarled. "Let's kill some bloody giants, yeah!"

The four leaders spat on the ground and then dispersed to collect their forces.

"Armor up and follow me," Tuni called to Rahkki over her shoulder.

He nudged Echofrost with his heels. She'd grown to understand his leg commands and flew to the lime tree where Rahkki had left his things. He quickly buckled on their armor, grabbed his skin of dragon drool and his blow darts, and bagged up his team's weapons too. Then the Pair flew to Tuni and Rizah, who were hovering just a winglength off the ground.

"Mount up!" Tuni called to Dusk Patrol, her division of the Sky Guard army. Upon hearing her voice, her warriors leaped to their boots. Armor straps were checked, saddle girths tightened, and weapons donned, and then the Riders were ready.

Echofrost watched the Fliers prance and flare their vibrant feathers as the Riders dressed them for war. Rizah swooped closer, her golden hide and silver armor gleaming in the sunshine. Sharp beads had been woven throughout her flaxen tail, but her hooves were rounded and dull.

"You don't sharpen your hooves for battle?" Echofrost asked the palomino pinto.

She blinked her large eyes. "No. Our Riders have arrows," she explained. "We fly above the battle while they shoot."

Echofrost gaped at her. "You mean Kihlari don't fight?"

Rizah bristled. "Of course we fight! But only when

necessary." She glanced at Echofrost's hooves. "Is that why yours look so strange, because you sharpen them? How do you do it?"

"We scrape the edges on rough boulders until the sides are sharp enough to cut through hides. My friend Redfire taught me how to do it when we were in Anok."

The gold-and-white pinto pricked her ears. "Can you teach me?"

"Yes, but there's no time now."

Rizah nodded. "Keep Rahkki up high. He's good with his darts, but he can't swing a sword well. Not yet."

The silver mare dipped her head. "I'll try."

Tuni leaned over her mare's wing and motioned for Rahkki and Echofrost to follow her. They soared to a private spot away from the other Riders. "About that blood viper attack," Tuni said.

"It wasn't a prank," Rahkki insisted. "Harak put it there to bite me."

"Harak?" she asked, seeming unsurprised. "Look, Rahkki, that's what I want to talk to you about. The giants are the least of your worries today. Some of your own people— warriors like Harak who support the queen—want to kill you. They're afraid of the Stormrunner name, that your family will rally the villagers against Queen Lilliam." Her eyes darted toward the armies. "Watch your back." She donned her helmet, made a fist, and then pointed four fingers down.

"You're a rebel too?" Rahkki whispered. "Why? You're sworn to protect our queen, whoever she might be."

Tuni grimaced. "And she's sworn to protect the clan and its interests before her own. But she doesn't, does she? She's bleeding the Fifth dry, Rahkki. She's dangerous." Tuni's flat tone was final, decisive. With a curt nod, she sailed off aboard Rizah and commanded her patrol, "Riders up!"

The Dusk Patrol steeds galloped forward, flapping their multicolored wings. One by one, they climbed into the sky and joined the other two patrols, soaring up and out of the jungle. Echofrost muscled her way into the sky. The four-day march to Mount Crim had helped acclimate her to the weight of the armor, and the longing to free Storm Herd lent her fresh energy.

As she rose higher and higher, Rahkki released her mane and spread out his arms, riding with no hands.

Rizah nickered. "Look at your Rider; he's not afraid."

Pride swelled within Echofrost as if Rahkki were her own colt.

Harak glared at the boy. "Stormrunner! Take up your

reins and pay attention."

Echofrost felt Rahkki clutch the leathers with one hand and check his blow darts and waterskin with the other. Then he urged Echofrost into formation.

Almost four hundred Kihlari buzzed their feathers in excitement. Below them, the Land Guard army—four hundred and fifty foot soldiers, archers, and battle horse riders commanded by General Tsun—marched up the base of Mount Crim, toward Storm Herd.

42

SUSPICION

ECHOFROST IMAGINED HER ENEMIES—THE RED-topped, pale-skinned Gorlan beasts—and she couldn't wait to soar into the valley, slaughter the giants, and slash the bindings that tethered her friends to the ground. Pegasi sought to live in peace, but they were born for war. It was a paradox that plagued Echofrost's kind in good times and bad.

Rahkki wrapped her mane in one hand and her reins in the other, holding them loose so as not to tug on the bit that rested in her mouth. He'd donned leather gloves to protect his palms. Holding on to her during battle would be difficult, but her cub had good balance and thankfully, his fear of flying had vanished.

Echofrost loathed the hard bit resting on her tongue but shook off her anger. This flying army was her herd today. The Kihlari steeds—Rizah, Ilan, and Meela's gold dun named Jax—they were her captains. And while they irritated her by flying in inefficient formations, she needed them, and so she conformed to their ways.

A fast wind fled from the northern storm clouds and whipped through her tail. Echofrost shivered with anticipation. Beside her, Tuni's golden pinto spoke as they coasted up the mountain slopes. "You found the wild herd?" Rizah nickered.

"Yes, in a deep canyon valley."

Rizah nodded. "Good. Perhaps this will be over quickly." They flew so low that Echofrost had to tuck up her legs to prevent her hooves from snagging on treetops. The armor, while heavy, was designed not to impede her movement; and she cruised efficiently, saving her strength for battle.

Soon they reached the ridge where Rahkki had left Mut, Koko, Tam, and Jul in hiding. The Sky Guard landed to wait for the Land Guard to catch up. Echofrost touched down on an animal path next to Rizah. The Kihlari steeds spread across the jungle, folding their wings.

"Giants could be anywhere," Tuni warned the Sky

Guard. "Draw your weapons, be ready."

Mut and the others surrounded Rahkki as he distributed their weapons. "Have you seen any giants?" Rahkki asked.

"No. It's been quiet here," Mut answered.

Rahkki dismounted, and Echofrost watched him pour Granak's boiled drool into each of the quivers that carried his scored darts, soaking the tips in poison. Two quivers were attached to Echofrost's sides and one to Rahkki's back. They carried hundreds of darts each.

She glanced from the darts to Rahkki's face. A light sheen of sweat brightened his tan skin, and the pupils of his golden eyes had shrunk, making the yellow orbs look as huge and bright as suns. He placed a dart in his blowgun, his expression serious, and she nickered softly, noticing that his pulse hammered in his throat. She doubted her cub had killed before. This day would change him forever.

Harak passed by. "You're going into battle with a *toy*?" he asked, laughing at the blowgun.

Echofrost snapped her wings at him, and Harak veered away from her, shaking his head.

The sun rose higher, and then the Land Guard army arrived. The Headwinds and Riders gathered around General Tsun, who looked pale. "We passed a dead python just over there," he said, pointing north. "A monster, forty lengths or so, killed by a knife." He appraised the group. "Giants don't hunt with knives, so who did it?"

After a weighted pause, Rahkki stepped forward. "I did it."

Someone laughed, but Meela's words shushed him. "Pythons are the guardian mascots for the Second Clan, and that one was big enough to be the Mother of Serpents. Why did you do it, Rahkki? *How* did you do it?" she added. All eyes shifted to the cub.

Harak leaped off Ilan's back and shoved the boy. "The Second is Queen Lilliam's birth clan. Is this a message, Rider? Are you against the queen?"

Tuni scoffed. "Let's not get paranoid, Harak."

Rahkki worked his jaw. "I— No, it's not a message. The snake attacked me."

Echofrost snapped her head toward Rahkki, noticing the sour tang of his sweat. He's hiding something from his people, she thought, and she wondered if their senses were acute enough to notice.

"A snake that size, and you survived?" Meela asked, eyebrows arched.

Mut stepped beside Rahkki, crossed his arms, and raised his chin. "Our guardian mascot wouldn't harm him either, remember?" he reminded everyone. "If Rahkki commands dragons, why not snakes?"

A hush fell over the Sky Guard as all eyes shifted toward Rahkki, some full of fear, others bright with awe. Tuni's eyes darkened with concern.

"We'll sort this later," General Tsun said, shoving between Harak and Rahkki. "We're more than halfway up the mountain. We need to attack now, before we're spotted—if we haven't already been spotted."

"My patrol will rescue the wild steeds," Tuni said. "We'll halter the wildlings and unlash the tethers Rahkki described." She addressed Dusk Patrol. "Whatever happens, hold on to the wild steeds. Don't let them go."

Meela nodded. "My patrol will scout the cliffs. If this is a trap and the giants plan to drop boulders on you, we'll stop them."

"I'll set up a perimeter," Harak added, "in case any wild Kihlari escape, yeah."

"And we'll guard the pass," stated General Tsun.

The leaders slapped hands, and then the Fliers lifted off, the foot soldiers donned their helmets, the saddle soldiers mounted their warhorses, and everyone drew their weapons. Mut, Koko, Tam, and Jul raced to Rahkki's side. "This is it," Jul said, grinning.

"Gonna kill some giants," Koko drawled, and then spat.

"You all should stay hidden," Rahkki advised.

Mut frowned. "And let you have all the fun?"

Rahkki blanched. "Fun?"

Koko shrugged. "We're soldiers, Rahkki."

"That's right," Jul added.

The boy nodded. "All right, but be careful." Rahkki clasped his blowgun in one hand and Echofrost's reins in the other, and he leaped aboard her back. Perching forward, their eyes met. "Ready?" he asked her.

Echofrost nuzzled him, grateful he'd made her fight his fight. But what would this war cost her cub? She blinked hard. *Don't think about it.* All that mattered was freeing Storm Herd. But her heart tightened as she realized that was no longer true. Rahkki also mattered, more than she'd ever believed possible. As his thin arms encircled her neck, she made a silent vow to protect him, wondering at the same time what that promise might cost *her*.

43

BATTLE

GENERAL TSUN SIGNALED BOTH ARMIES FOR-
ward, and Echofrost thrilled at the bite of the wind, the
rattling of feathers, and the challenging brays of the
Kihlari army as they soared toward Storm Herd. With
no giants yet in sight, it was possible her friends would
be free in a matter of moments! Finally, she'd fulfill her
promise to Storm Herd.

The Sky Guard army reached the canyon valley first.
They crested the edge of the high cliffs and dived straight
down. The riders whooped and hollered, their hair flapping from beneath their helmets.

Below, the Storm Herd steeds threw up their heads,
and Echofrost's heart squeezed. There was Dewberry with

her huge swaying belly and Hazelwind, proud and defiant. Anok wasn't home, this blasted continent wasn't home—Storm Herd was home; Hazelwind was home! Echofrost would never leave him again. She whinnied to her herd, full of joy.

They whinnied warnings back to her, and Hazelwind flung back his long forelock. "Stop!" he brayed. "It's a trap!"

"No, I have two armies with me," Echofrost whinnied back.

Hazelwind stomped his front hooves. "Get out of here!"

Echofrost's mood curdled. Something was very wrong. Dusk Patrol touched down in the valley, and Echofrost galloped to Hazelwind's side, drinking up his scent in a huge breath.

Rahkki slid off her back and unlashed the bindings that secured Hazelwind's legs to a heavy boulder. "Halter that stallion," Tuni screamed at him.

Rahkki refused to look at Tuni. Instead, he ran to another pegasus and freed her too. But all around him, Sandwen Riders were slapping halters onto Echofrost's friends.

"Please let the wildlings go!" Rahkki cried.

When Dewberry reared, her leather halter snapped in half. She stomped the Rider who had slid the contraption over her head, wheezing with the effort. "This is no res-cue!" she neighed.

"Stay calm," Echofrost blared at the pregnant mare, but she was confused. Rahkki was trying to free the herd, but his people were not.

Then came the roar of the giants.

Echofrost spun a circle, wings flared, and Hazelwind rattled his feathers.

Chaos erupted as a heavy net, a hundred winglengths long, dropped from the cliffs overhead. It thudded upon Echofrost and Storm Herd and the Sandwens, ensnaring all of them.

Next, the sky filled with burners. The colorful little dragons swarmed the valley's egress, shooting hot-blue flames. Fire roared across the grass, blocking the Land Guard from entering the valley to help.

Then the screeching of cats filled Echofrost's ears. She swung her netted head toward the far end of the valley. There, tucked in the shadows, she spied the mouth of a cave that was so recessed it had been invisible from the ridge. From it poured a battalion of massive fanged felines ridden by young giants. The cats charged toward her, jaws hinged wide open.

Echofrost gasped, swallowing air. This *was* a trap,

a horrible trap! She flared her wings, becoming further entangled in the nets, and she trumpeted a furious battle cry, blasting her frustration across the valley. Hazelwind's voice joined hers.

Rahkki's pulse whooshed between his ears, pushing out all other noises. He whipped out his sawa sword and hacked at the heavy netting with mad fervor while the tan-striped saber cats galloped across the grass toward him, their long fangs exposed.

The Great Cave Horde teens carried sharp spears in one hand and held the reins of their vicious felines in the other. The cats wore soft leather saddles and bitless bridles. They galloped in huge leaps, their muscular legs swallowing the meadow as they charged toward the nets.

"Stop them!" Harak screamed. He rallied his patrol, and they rocketed to meet the saber cats.

Overhead, Meela's Riders shot arrows into the giants who'd tossed the huge nets. Several Gorlanders toppled off the cliff.

Screams and shouts and smoke filled the valley. Rahkki's legs shook, and his thoughts vanished. From the ground, he hacked at the Gorlan netting with mindless speed. It fell easily apart against the sharpness of his blade. A taller Rider spied the opening he'd made, grasped its edges, and ripped the gap open wider for the Sandwens and Kihlari to escape.

"Tuni, we can't hold on to the wild herd *and* fight the giants!" a Rider screamed.

"Forget it. Cut 'em loose!" she screamed back. "Retreat!"

Harak whipped around. "No, hold on to them!" Then he turned away to fight the cats.

More holes appeared as Riders cut additional slits in the netting. It began to unravel. Uncertain what to do, some Sandwens tried to halter the wild Kihlari while others abandoned them.

Meanwhile, Sula and her buckskin friend struggled out from beneath the net. Using their wings, they held it aloft so their friends could also escape.

Rahkki sheathed his sword and took up his blowgun. The first dart was already inserted; the others waited in his quiver. It was time to see if the boiled dragon drool had the desired effect on his enemy.

He lifted the long pipe to his mouth and huffed. The dart fell short of his target—a rampaging saber cat. He needed to calm his breathing to get a good puff.

But when Rahkki inhaled, the rising smoke choked

him. He glanced at the open end of the valley where the tiny dragons swarmed, their colorful scales flashing. They switched their flames to red, which were hot, but not as hot as the blue, and they stoked the fire higher. Steam burped from their mouths as they chirped in excitement.

Several Land Guard soldiers rolled across the grass, trying to snuff out their burning tunics. Others swiped at the burners with their sawa blades, cutting them out of the sky. This made the little dragons angry, and they chortled in deadly harmony.

Meela Swift and her patrol attacked the giants who had been hiding on the upper cliffs.

Meanwhile, the first saber cat reached the captured wild herd, and its long fangs punctured a mare's throat, severing the vein.

Rahkki bent over and vomited.

Sula whinnied sharply at him, and her familiar voice jarred Rahkki back into action. He raised his blowgun, steadied himself, and blew a drool-soaked dart at the fanged cat that had killed the mare. It pierced the feline's striped hide, and she collapsed with a snarl, not dead, but sleeping! *It's working,* he thought.

"Sula, here!" he called to his Flier.

She glided to his side, and Rahkki leaped onto her

saddle. "Hah!" he shouted. His fearless mare hurtled off the grass and carried him toward the charging cats. Her winged friends glided beside Rahkki, their legs coiled back to strike.

"Look," Rahkki shouted to Tuni. "The wild herd is helping us!"

Behind Rahkki, fire blasted toward the sky, like a geyser exploding. The giants had painted the grass with torch oil to escalate the fires set by the burners, thus keeping the Land Guard army trapped on the other side of the flames, unable to help. Rahkki had not expected such cunning from the Gorlanders.

The saber cats roared, and the giants sent fast commands with their fingers.

Harak and his Riders glided over the cats and dived upon their riders like hawks, striking and plunging their swords. The tan-striped cats twisted and hissed. One giant guided his cat into a leap, and they snagged a Rider and Flier out of the sky.

Rahkki aimed and shot a dart, striking the cat, and it fell over.

He reloaded and shot again, this time striking a young giant.

He reloaded again.

And again.

And again.

Sula sensed Rahkki's intentions, and she flew and hovered right where he needed her. His treated darts whistled through the sky, instantly felling giants and saber cats in swift numbers. Harak gaped at him, and Rahkki grinned. A ferocious Gorlander charged the distracted Headwind, and Rahkki blew a dart straight into the giant's neck. The giant thudded onto the grass, instantly asleep.

Harak blinked, looking furious and grateful at the same time. Rahkki had just saved his life.

Rahkki soon ran out of darts, but he had two more quivers full of them. He unhooked the empty tube, let it fall, and snatched a new one. He strapped it to his back and refilled his blowgun. He could only shoot one dart at a time, but could reload and take aim faster than the archers.

The afternoon breeze gusted harder, and the clouds thickened, swallowing the sun. "Land to skies," he muttered. The wind would make shooting straight more difficult.

Pausing for breath, Rahkki surveyed the valley. The pale bodies of his victims littered the brush, appearing dead. His plan was working better than he'd expected, but more saber cats were coming. Meela's patrol had driven off the giants atop the cliff, but there hadn't been many up there to begin with. Sula's wild friends circled the valley like vultures, dropping down to slice at the giants with their knife-sharp hooves.

Fire Horde giants had dragged several Kihlari out of the sky, and these fought with tooth and hoof for their lives. Sula's buckskin stallion galloped into the fray and head-butted a Gorlander, toppling him. Then Rahkki heard the trumpeting of elephants—where were they coming from?

Sula faltered when a spasm gripped her still-healing left wing. "Land," Rahkki called, guiding her to the valley floor.

His mare touched down with a hard jolt. Rahkki dismounted to help her recover, but as soon as his weight was lifted, she reared up, her eyes white rimmed. She whinnied a warning, her loudness shocking his ears.

"Rahkki, behind you!" Tuni screamed. She and her patrol were trying to free the last few wild steeds. Tuni screamed again. "Watch out!"

44

BETRAYAL

HIS PULSE SPEEDING, RAHKKI TURNED AND FACED
the fangs of a charging saber cat. It galloped at him, tail
lashing, jaws wide. Sula snatched Rahkki by his belt and
threw him out of the cat's way just as it pounced. The cat
snarled and lunged at Sula. She flared her wings with
such a loud snap that the feline recoiled.

The wild buckskin stallion blasted across the valley
and slammed into the cat, knocking it onto its back. Hissing and spitting, the cat struck out with its huge paws.
The buckskin lifted off and twirled out of its way.

Rahkki reached for his blowgun, and realized he'd
dropped it. He grabbed his sawa sword instead. The cat
turned on him, muscles rippling, lips curled back in a

snarl, whiskers bristling. It prowled forward, its yellow gaze on Rahkki.

The elephants trumpeted again, and from the corner of his eye, Rahkki watched them burst out of a wide waterfall. They'd been hiding behind it, waiting. This valley was full of tricks and traps! At least fifty elephants emerged from the hidden cave and swam across the watering hole. They were lead by the biggest giant of all: the Highland Horde king. The elephants paddled toward land. Ferocious adult Gorlanders sat astride them, carrying long spears in their palms.

Rahkki's heart walloped.

The hissing feline edged closer as the clouds shivered and dropped a torrent of warm rain on the valley. The fanged cat growled at the sky, its expression offended. Then it sprinted toward the boy. Rahkki charged it. *Use all your might*, he told himself. *All your might!* He slammed his sawa blade into the cat's chest and pushed. It hissed and bucked. Sula flew down and kicked the cat in the head, knocking it out. It tumbled onto Rahkki, pinning him to the ground. The valley floor spun around and around. He couldn't breathe.

"Help!" Rahkki tried to push the cat off him.

A pregnant pinto mare and a huge hairy white stallion

flew to Rahkki's aid. They kicked the cat off him. The emerald-feathered mare cocked her head, nickered, then flew away to battle more giants.

"Th-thanks," he whispered. *Land to skies, she looked right at me*, Rahkki thought. He yanked his blade out of the cat, feeling sorry for killing it. Then he retrieved his blowgun off the grass, loaded it with fresh darts, and whistled for Sula.

She and her handsome buckskin friend glided across the grass and landed. Sula lowered her wing, and Rahkki climbed aboard, guiding her toward Harak Nightseer for orders. Sula's buckskin followed them, whinnying piercing whistles at the rest of the wild herd. When they reached Harak, Rahkki spoke, catching his breath. "They're too many giants!"

Harak's exposed arms were slick with sweat; his green eyes glowed. He twirled his blade and grinned. "Nah, Rahkki. Look."

Following Harak's gaze, Rahkki sighed in relief. The rain had doused the fire that was blocking the pass, dwindling it to embers. General Tsun raised his fist and issued a war cry, and the Land Guard army crossed the fuel-soaked grass as the fire gasped.

Harak hollered for his patrol to regroup, Headwind Swift's Riders flew down from the cliffs, looking fresh, and Rahkki snatched another breath. His team of protectors raced to join him, coughing on the smoke. "About time you got here," Rahkki whispered, smiling weakly.

"Who killed all those giants?" Mut asked, astonished.

Rahkki shrugged, not yet ready to reveal the secret about his treated darts.

Harak sent fifty warriors to help Tuni capture the wild Kihlari who remained trapped and then shouted the order to attack the elephant army. The pounding rain had agitated the remaining saber cats to the point that they'd become difficult for the giants to control.

Rahkki aimed his blowgun and kicked Sula forward. The more giants he shot, the more lives he'd save and the quicker this would be over. At this moment, that was all that mattered to him.

Then a flash of green material fluttered down from the cliff overhead. He watched it, transfixed, as he realized it was a Sandwen cape.

His eyes trailed up, and there he saw I'Lenna—walking to the cliff's edge surrounded by a respectful entourage of red-haired, soot-smudged giants. Fire Horde. I'Lenna's winged roan, Firo, trotted by her side. The princess caught Rahkki's eye, her expression triumphant, and his entire body felt suddenly cold.

I'Lenna was *friends* with the giants. Had she betrayed the clan?

45

QUEEN OF THE FIFTH

I'LENNA'S GREEN CAPE HAD RIPPED LOOSE IN THE wind and was dropping fast, pushed down by the rain. The oddness of it—a plummeting cape embroidered in gold silk—drew all eyes, even the saber cats' and elephants' eyes, toward it. A quiet pause drifted onto the battlefield, the fighting momentarily forgotten as the cape twirled to the ground.

I'Lenna had reached the edge of the sheer rock wall above the valley. Her body teetered, and a waterfall of stones tumbled down the cliff's face. Firo dipped her head and nickered to the wild herd.

Rahkki's heart stalled: What was I'Lenna doing? Her unbound hair stuck flat against her head, drenched, and her dark-leather vest was so soaked with rain that it appeared black. Behind her, the clouds massed and roiled like living things. Her dark eyes scanned the valley and settled on Harak Nightseer. She lifted her hands, preparing to speak.

The quiet grew quieter.

I'Lenna signed in Gorlish and spoke in Sandwen. "Cease fighting, Fifth Clan." Her voice echoed down to them, sounding both tiny and huge at the same time. The soldiers and giants fidgeted.

I'Lenna continued. "I've parlayed with the hordes and reached terms with all three. A peaceful bargain has been struck."

Peaceful? That sounded good. Rahkki let out his breath.

"What terms!" Harak shouted, his expression savage. "And on whose authority?"

General Tsun lifted his sword. "Let her speak."

I'Lenna gazed at them both. "I've traded the Fifth Clan fallows in exchange for the release of the wild herd."

The Sandwen soldiers broke into angry grumbles; others clenched their swords tighter. Rahkki fidgeted. So this was why I'Lenna had snuck off with the giants last night—to parlay for her mother.

"No!" Harak spat, signing his words for the giants. "Our queen would never allow that."

The Highland Horde king urged his elephant forward, his fingers signing to Harak. *"This girl says she is the Queen of the Fifth."*

Jul Ranger, who'd been studying Gorlish as part of his Rider's apprenticeship, translated for Rahkki's team. "The giants say that I'Lenna *is* our queen. Did she lie to them?" he wondered.

"Of course she lied," Mut said.

"Can' trust a Whitehall," Koko added, nodding her head like she'd just tallied a huge hay order without a mistake.

"Shh," Rahkki admonished.

From her place on the cliff, I'Lenna glared at Harak, and anger shot between them in spite of the great distance they stood apart. Then she reassured the giants. "I told you, I don't need the queen's permission—I *am* the queen."

Her words hit Rahkki like a punch to the gut. Had I'Lenna usurped her mother? Had she been leading the uprising *all along*?

Harak shouted in Sandwen and signed in Gorlish to the three hordes. "Nay! She lies! She's not the Queen of the Fifth."

The Highland king knit his brows over his small blue eyes. His pale skin reddened. *"Answer to this charge,"* he signed to I'Lenna. *"Who are you?"*

I'Lenna opened her satchel and produced a crown. It was forged of iron and dragons' teeth. A giant black dragon scale sat ensconced in the center. It was Queen Lilliam's crown, a replica of Reyella's original. I'Lenna lowered it onto her head. "I am the *new* Queen of the Fifth." And then she made the sign of the rebellion: a closed fist and then four fingers pointed down.

Uproar from the Sandwen warriors filled the valley. The queen's crown was kept in a chest with three locks. Lilliam, her Borla, and General Tsun each possessed a key; and all three keys were needed to open the chest. Lilliam and the Borla would never willingly give up their keys, which meant that I'Lenna had secured the crown by force. It also meant that the princess was telling the truth—she *was* the new Queen of the Fifth.

Rahkki clenched his jaw, his thoughts swirling. *But how? When?* Lilliam had retreated to birth her child, only six days past. Had I'Lenna assassinated or banished her mother while she was helpless?

His brain throbbed as he tried to piece it together. General Tsun was here, which meant he must have given

I'Lenna his key before he'd left. And the general had already admitted he was against the queen. Rahkki had assumed that General Tsun was the leader of the rebels, but no—it was I'Lenna. He remembered the table full of parchments in the secret tunnels. That's where she met with the rebels, he guessed.

I don't want the throne, she'd claimed.

This is an inside job, Brauk had insisted.

I'Lenna had lied to him twice!

Her gaze met Rahkki's across the span of cliff and valley that separated them. Her expression was sad, maybe even regretful, but unashamed. She'd supplanted her mother, and there was no turning back. Rahkki couldn't believe it. *Can't trust a Whitehall,* Koko and Mut had said more than once. *The princess has charmed you, Rahkki,* Mut had accused. Were they all correct? Had I'Lenna misled him so soundly?

Harak's sun-dark face paled, and he screamed at I'Lenna. *"Lilliam isn't dead!"* He bent over, hiding furious tears.

"I didn't kill my mother, Headwind Nightseer," I'Lenna said calmly. "She abdicated her throne to me. I ordered her banishment from the Realm, and the Borla coronated me four days ago." I'Lenna let the word *banishment* settle on the Sandwen armies. "As soon as my mother and her new prince are fit to travel, my forces will escort her to Daakur. She'll live comfortably there with her children— in *exile*." She tossed a smile to General Tsun.

"Prince?" Harak rasped. "The baby is a boy?"

I'Lenna ignored his query as tension filled the space between the soldiers loyal to Lilliam and the soldiers who were not. Eyes shifted, and swords clanged against boots. Who was a loyalist? Who was a rebel? The confusion soon turned to suspicion.

Rahkki tried to piece together the timing. I'Lenna must have ousted her mother right after the armies marched to Mount Crim—that meant the palace guards were on her side. It was all clear now, as if the clouds had parted. If I'Lenna had *failed* to overthrow her mother, all her associates would have been punished for treason: General Tsun, the palace guards, and Rahkki, if he'd known she was involved and had chosen to join her. He realized I'Lenna had lied about her part in the rebellion to *protect* him.

Cold relief swept through Rahkki—reminding him of the time when he was six years old and Brauk had caught him playing with a scorpion. One bite from the insect would have stopped Rahkki's heart forever. Now the boy stared at I'Lenna—her matted hair, proud eyes, stick-straight back, and heavy crown—and his body shuddered. He'd had no idea he was playing with such a dangerous girl.

I'Lenna turned to the Highland king and projected her voice so that every Sandwen could hear. "All fighting must cease. I am the rightful Queen of the Fifth, and tonight I will seal my treaty with the Gorlan hordes over soup. You will return home now. The battle is over." She pointed west. "Go. I command you."

Harak lifted his fist and roared, *"Never under the bloody skies!"* He drew an arrow and aimed it straight at I'Lenna. General Tsun blasted across the field to stop him. Harak whirled, facing the general. "Traitor!" Harak loosed the arrow, and the shaft plunged straight through Tsun's throat.

His breath cut short, the general collapsed and his life force pooled atop soil that was too wet to inhale another ounce of moisture.

Thunder cracked, and Harak hollered to the Sandwen armies. "You heard the princess; her mother lives and breathes on Fifth Clan soil!" Then to the giants he signed, *"I'Lenna cannot bargain with you. She's a false queen!"*

The three Gorlan kings rumbled at I'Lenna, signing

angrily. Rahkki recognized one word. *"Liar."* I'Lenna screamed when the Fire Horde giants swarmed her.

"Kill her and all who follow her!" Harak bellowed. Then he led a charge to battle—not against the giants, but against his fellow Sandwens.

The Fifth Clan's unrest ignited as clansmen charged clansmen.

46

CHOICES

ECHOFROST REARED AS THE SANDWENS SPLIT
into two groups and charged each other. "This isn't good,"
she whinnied to Hazelwind.

"Stick together," the stallion neighed. They pressed
their foreheads together, and tears sprang to Echofrost's
eyes, but there was no time to talk.

Harak leaped onto his stallion and flew Ilan at the line
of Sandwen rebels, his sawa blade raised as he attacked
his own people.

"Harak, no!" Tuni screamed.

Rahkki leaned over Echofrost's neck, ducking to avoid
the cast of arrows flying all around them. His breath came
loud and fast; his muscles flexed against her hide.

Shysong leaped off the cliff and soared down its face. "Now's our chance to free the last of the trapped pegasi!"

Echofrost's blood thrummed as she and Hazelwind followed Shysong to the net where several steeds struggled, still encaged by the heavy ropes. Rahkki tried to steer her toward the princess, but she flouted him, choosing her own path.

The valley dissolved into chaos as the Highland Horde king directed his fighters to resume their attack against the clans.

I'Lenna's voice rang out from the cliff's edge. "STOP! I command you!"

"Don't listen to her," Harak shouted.

Echofrost threw her gaze skyward and watched the Fire Horde king snatch the princess off her feet. I'Lenna fought him; furious tears streaming down her face. Her beautiful green riding cloak lay mud-trampled far below.

"I'Lenna!" Rahkki cried, and Echofrost felt his tension ratchet higher.

Several Land Guard soldiers dipped their arrows into the remains of the oil-fueled fire and shot flaming missiles at the elephant-riding giants. The Great Cave Horde warriors rushed toward Hazelwind, their spears lifted high. Their saber cats had deserted them, seeking shelter from the pouring rain.

Rahkki's legs tightened around Echofrost's ribs. "The giants think I'Lenna lied to them!" he screamed at Tuni. "Help her!" But Tuni was fending off her own attackers.

Hearing the princess's name, Echofrost glanced up again. I'Lenna had been made to stand at the very edge of the high shelf. The angry giants were scouring the flat mesa, picking up rocks.

"They're going to hurt her," Rahkki shouted, yanking harder on Echofrost's reins and kicking her sides. The metal bit chafed her tongue and clanked against her teeth. Echofrost bucked hard, and Rahkki flew off her back. Her hooves tore the grass, her nostrils flared. Rahkki wanted to help the princess, but *she* wanted to free the rest of her trapped friends.

The cub rolled over, his eyes pleading with her. "Save I'Lenna, please." He pointed at the princess on the high cliff.

"Watch out," Hazelwind neighed.

A spear shot toward them. Echofrost reared onto her back heels, and the whittled tree-spear whooshed past her. Then more spears flew in their direction. Blast it!

She galloped to Rahkki, snatched his collar, and tossed him onto her back. Then she and Hazelwind powered off the grass and glided toward Shysong and the netting. "Hazelwind and I will free the rest of the herd," Echofrost neighed to Shysong. "Go help your princess."

Shysong nodded and darted away.

Echofrost and Hazelwind joined Storm Herd in unraveling the massive net. Dewberry stood near, trying to loosen a stubborn knot. The mare was drenched in sweat.

"Stop," Echofrost whinnied to her. "It's almost your time."

The pinto whirled. "I won't leave anyone behind." Her once-glossy white-and-bay coat had dulled, and dry flakes dusted her emerald feathers. Her round flanks had hollowed, exposing sharp hip bones.

A sob caught in Echofrost's throat. "You must rest. Please."

Dewberry pressed her forehead, quick and fast, against Echofrost's. "I'm fine," she said, clasping her wings around her belly. "I won't let anything happen to these foals." Then the mare cantered away to disentangle the final few pegasi. With Echofrost and Hazelwind helping, they lifted the frayed net with their wings, freeing steed after steed in frenzied motion.

Lightning crackled, and static filled the cloud-dark sky. Moments later, the final Storm Herd steed was loose. Echofrost's herd was united, though some had died in the battle.

Hazelwind arched his neck. "Let's go!" He glanced at the melee around them. "This isn't our fight."

"Wait! What about Rahkki?" Echofrost nodded at the boy on her back.

"Shrug him off!" Dewberry neighed.

"I can't leave him in the middle of this." Echofrost leaped out of the way as a lone bull elephant thundered past, trumpeting in grief for his slain keeper.

Hazelwind reared, and his long wind-tangled mane blew in the breeze. He was bug bitten and filthy, and her heart soared with love for him. But she couldn't just *leave*. "Rahkki brought this army to free Storm Herd," she reminded her friends.

"Then let's honor the cub by going!" Hazelwind neighed.

Echofrost glanced at the battle—Sandwen against Sandwen, giants against Sandwen. The Fifth Clan armies would not survive this day. Sorrow gripped her.

Hazelwind pinned his ears. "We're losing time! We crossed the Dark Water to start a new herd. Now let's fly!"

"But—"

"Have you forgotten Star and Nightwing, and all we've endured?" Frustration lifted Hazelwind's tail.

The front line of elephants trampled through a formation of Sandwen soldiers. Then spears flew down from the cliffs, thrown by the Fire Horde warriors. Dozens of Sandwens fell where they stood, and Echofrost's gut twisted.

Shysong descended, huffing. "I can't save I'Lenna by myself. I can't get past the giants," she cried.

Hazelwind tossed his mane, his patience gone. "They're Landwalkers! What are you two waiting for? Just leave them." He trumpeted the call to retreat, and the Storm Herd steeds collected.

Echofrost twirled, shedding purple feathers in the center of the valley. Rizah was kicking at a giant with her back hooves, Ilan bled from a spear strike, and Jax had his powerful jaws locked on a teenage giant's arm. Koko, Mut, Tam, and Jul backed themselves into a circle and fought against the Gorlanders together. *This wasn't Storm Herd's fight, or was it?* Echofrost thought.

She nodded toward Rahkki. "I won't leave him in this mess," she sputtered. Tears erupted and striped her muddy cheeks.

"What about *me*?" Hazelwind neighed, his eyes hot

with anguish. "*I'm* your future, not that cub." He dodged a spear that flew toward him, but kept his eyes trained on Echofrost. Behind him, an elephant tossed a warrior across the valley; giants screamed as molten arrows pierced their skin, and the boldest saber cats deserted their shelters and galloped across the grass, fangs flashing.

"I'll catch up," Echofrost neighed to Hazelwind. "Get Dewberry out of here. Please."

He recoiled from her, his jaw gaping.

She knew she was making the wrong choice, knew it to the core of her soul, and yet she did it anyway. *I'll never learn*, her mind bellowed. She gazed wistfully at Hazelwind, Dewberry, Graystone, and Redfire. They were her herd, but Rahkki—he was her friend. "I'll catch up," she repeated.

Frustrated, the buckskin arched his proud neck. "No," he breathed. "I won't leave you, Echofrost." Then Hazelwind whinnied to Storm Herd. "Take Dewberry to the tree nests we built earlier. I'm staying to fight."

"So am I," Redfire bugled.

"And I," Graystone echoed.

"The rest of you, go," Hazelwind commanded. "Protect Dewberry. Wait for us."

The pegasi refugees from Anok rose out of the valley, a blur of vibrant colors with Dewberry at their center— like a living heart—and they soared together through the untamed sky. Watching them go, Echofrost's soul felt renewed.

Storm Herd was free, and Hazelwind had chosen to fight beside her.

Then a sharp nicker reached her ears. Echofrost whipped her head around to see Shysong bolting toward her, her eyes round. "I'm with you too, Echofrost!" Upon those words, the five friends rallied together.

"Yes!" Rahkki cried. He reloaded his blowgun and shouted up to Fire Horde, signing with his hands in Gorl-ish. *"That's my princess!"* Then he aimed his weapon and fired.

Reloaded.

And fired again.

He shot his treated darts, and all around him, giants smacked onto the grass. Awed stares followed Rahkki. He smiled and reloaded.

47

MAGIC

RAHKKI TIGHTENED HIS LEGS AROUND SULA AS he shot his darts at the Gorlanders. The Fire Horde giants were preparing to knock I'Lenna off the cliff. Liar or charmer—it didn't matter anymore—he couldn't let I'Lenna *die*. And he knew how to save her and his people. He'd show the Gorlanders the full measure of his power.

Just because you don't understand something doesn't make it magical, I'Lenna had said, but she was wrong. Lack of understanding was *exactly* what made something magical, and Rahkki was going to prove it.

The Sandwens had ceased fighting one another, for now, as the giants pressed harder against them, forcing them to unite. Rahkki and Sula blasted across the valley, his blowgun to his lips. His drool-soaked darts only needed to graze a Gorlander's skin to fell the beast—the sleep medicine was that powerful—and he had hundreds of darts left. Firo, the buckskin stallion, the tall copper-colored steed, and a thick-bodied white stallion followed him and Sula into battle.

His silver mare tucked her wings and cruised toward the elephant-riding giants, speeding like an arrow. The buckskin soared beside her. Firo and the other three spread around them. Rahkki sat tall on Sula's back, adjusting his weight as she rocketed toward the front line of Highland Horde warriors, flying almost sideways. Years of riding young, untrained horses helped him balance and anticipate her movements.

As Sula's wings brushed the sides of the charging elephants, Rahkki shot his darts in rapid order, zapping Gorlanders in their exposed necks, calves, and arms. They tumbled off their elephants in droves.

The Land Guard and Sky Guard warriors rallied. "Rahkki the Giant Slayer!" Tuni hollered, grinning in relief and surprise.

Rahkki spotted Mut, Koko, Jul, and Tam. They raised their fists in victory. Firo peeled off, returning to hover along the cliff wall, near I'Lenna, as though calculating how to save I'Lenna. The rest of the wild herd was gone; they'd flown out of sight, and this relieved Rahkki's mind. He no longer had to worry about Lilliam selling them to Daakur. But why had Sula and these others stayed behind? His heart fluttered. Had the silver mare grown to like him *that much*?

A bludgeon swung toward his head. Sula dipped so fast that Rahkki floated off her back. Snatching her mane, he pulled himself back into the saddle, and the bludgeon just missed striking him. Rahkki twisted and blew a dart into the giant's neck, and the Gorlander tumbled off his elephant.

Sula and her buckskin stallion dived, feinted, and attacked, their movements fluid and their timing perfect, like a long-practiced dance. Rahkki complimented their efforts with hard puffs into his blowgun. The length and special dynamics of the long pipe caused his darts to launch farther and faster than he could have shot arrows. The rain and wind might have interfered, but years of hunting slippery fish in the River Tsallan had made Rahkki mighty accurate in spite of the breeze.

Then the Highland Horde prince rushed toward them aboard his massive ivory-tusked bull. His gaze met Rahkki's. The wound left by the python still marred his neck.

The prince snorted at the boy but left him alone, perhaps because Rahkki had saved his life. His warriors followed the prince along the valley, stealing weapons off felled soldiers.

Meanwhile, the Highland king's fingers sent rapid orders to his horde, and he rumbled at Rahkki like an angry tiger. Sula darted up and out of the elephant brigade, hovering a moment to catch her breath. Rahkki stroked her sweating neck, suddenly grateful for his slight weight. His mare, unused to carrying armor, let alone a person, would not last much longer.

Then Harak soared beside them, distracting Rahkki. The Headwind's blond hair was matted with dirt, his eyes bloodshot. "How are you doing that?" he asked, pointing at the battlefield.

Hundreds of Gorlanders were strewn across the valley—their eyes closed, their bodies still—and Rahkki knew that no warrior in Sandwen history could claim such a death toll. Sure he could tell Harak the truth, that he'd sent them into a deep sleep; but in this case, it was much more enjoyable to lie. "It's magic," he said.

Harak flinched, and, just like that, Rahkki's legend sprouted a new flower. Satisfaction welled within the orphan prince.

Tuni, who was gliding across the valley aboard Rizah, banked her mare toward them. Then Meela shot across the sky, and the four of them hovered, facing one another, tension zipping between them.

"This will be over soon," Tuni said. Her eyes shifted to Rahkki, her expression wondrous. "Our new Rider has decimated two Gorlan hordes by himself."

"*Magicker*," Harak mouthed at Rahkki.

Tuni kicked her mare toward the blond Headwind, and Rizah's chest pushed against Ilan's. "Victory is at hand, Harak, but whose: Lilliam's or I'Lenna's?" She lifted her chin, and her wet red hair curled around her shoulders. "We don't have to fight each other. The clan can unite behind the new queen."

Harak swiped his drenched hair. "You're all traitors, yeah. If you take orders from I'Lenna, I'll arrest you."

They each stared at the princess on the cliff, including Rahkki. I'Lenna's agile fingers blurred as she argued with the Fire Horde king. She stomped her boots and beat her fists like a horde-born Gorlander.

The Fire Horde king silenced everyone by blowing through a carved-out tusk, creating a bellowing noise that filled the canyon valley. Rahkki glanced around him, startled. His quick darts had swung the advantage back to his clan—the giants were now outnumbered. The Fire Horde king signed to the Highland king and the Great Cave king, and then he addressed the Sandwens.

Tuni flew Rizah closer to translate his words in her most booming voice. "The giants say they will release I'Lenna Whitehall if we leave the valley now."

The Sandwens who were loyal to the princess cheered. The others shouted in protest.

Harak addressed the armies. "Look around, we've won this battle, yeah." He laughed, motioning toward the fallen giants. "Let's finish off these beasts and bring victory home to our true queen and her new princeling son! *You can keep the princess,*" he signed to Fire Horde.

A Fire Horde warrior approached I'Lenna, looking furious and betrayed.

"Don't!" She leaned away from him, and one foot slipped off the cliff. The giant yanked her back onto two feet and slid a hood over her head, covering her face.

Rahkki's gut flipped at the sight of his princess—hooded like a falcon.

The soot-smudged Gorlan warrior pushed I'Lenna to the very edge of the cliff, quickly binding her hands and feet in twine. Ten giants formed a line facing her. Each held a handful of rocks. They were going to strike her off the cliff, but it wouldn't be the fall that killed her. It would be the first volley of stones hurled by giants. I'Lenna would be dead before her body hit the ground.

Conflicting images clashed in Rahkki's mind: the laughing girl who snuck into his bedroom, the ambitious princess who usurped her mother, the fierce idealist who stood up to Harak, and the generous friend who shared her candy. Which I'Lenna was real? Could she be all of them?

He jabbed his heels into Sula's sides. "Yah, Sula!" His mare sprang off the grass and rocketed straight up the side of the cliff, leaving Rahkki's gut floating behind him. He leaned over her neck, squinting against the wind. Firo glided near, whinnying in distress. Rahkki met the roan's ice-blue eyes, and a reckless idea formed in his mind.

Then he and Sula cleared the top of the cliff.

The princess swayed, alone and blind, her body trembling, the breeze pressing the heavy hood against her face.

Sula swooped low over the plateau, and Rahkki leaped off her back, falling several lengths. He landed in a squat, then quickly stood. The Fire Horde king challenged him, and Rahkki signed in Gorlish, using his limited vocabulary. "*Mine*," he said, pointing at I'Lenna. Then he ripped off her hood, his dagger in hand.

I'Lenna froze at the sight of Rahkki's blade inches from her face. Her skin was pale, her eyes dark and wide. Blood and dirt caked her fingernails.

The horde backed away from the small Sandwen boy who'd single-handedly slain hundreds of Gorlanders.

Rahkki sliced the bindings around I'Lenna's wrists. She exhaled hard. "Rahkki, I—"

The king roared at the sight of I'Lenna being cut free, and the line of ten giants loosed their stones at the princess. Rahkki clutched her close, blocking her body with his. The rocks struck his armored back and legs. It was like being rammed by water buffalo. He stumbled forward, almost knocking her off the cliff. Pain seared his thoughts.

I'Lenna screamed at the giants. "Don't hurt him!" But they didn't understand Sandwen.

Next, Rahkki's mare charged the Gorlanders, kicking their outstretched arms. They drove her off with spears and then hurled another round of stones at Rahkki.

The rocks dented his new armor, but the metal protected him. One stone, however, slammed into his anklebone and he heard it crack. Another stone struck his helmet. He released I'Lenna and crumpled to his knees, his ears ringing. I'Lenna crouched beside him, and he pushed the handle of his dagger into her palm. "Cut your legs free," he said, gasping.

She sliced off her ankle bindings. "There!"

Rahkki heaved himself onto one leg and yanked her upright. The wind whistled around them, and the raindrops rolled down her cheeks like tears. She wriggled, panting. "I'm sorry, Rahkki." Her control broke, and her lips trembled. "I never meant to drag you into this—"

Another stone crashed into the boy, striking the back of his leg. Pounding footsteps filled his ears as the giants ran toward them.

I'Lenna stared over his shoulder, and panic bloomed in her eyes. "They're coming!"

Sula circled overhead, braying louder. Firo hovered below the cliff's edge, piercing the air with sharp whinnies. The giants rumbled, and I'Lenna's tearful gaze met his. In a burst of clarity, Rahkki's earlier confusion about her shattered and he was sure of one thing; he trusted her. He leaned forward and kissed her lips. She tasted sweet, like peppermints.

Her eyes widened. "Oh," she gasped.

Then Rahkki twirled I'Lenna around and shoved her off the cliff.

48

FRIENDS

"CATCH HER AND ARREST HER!" HARAK HOL-
lered, pointing at the falling princess. His Riders rushed
toward her.

I'Lenna's scream ripped through all other noises in the
canyon valley. Above Echofrost, a third volley of stones
struck Rahkki. Her cub collapsed while shouting, "Firo!
Fetch I'Lenna!"

But Shysong was already in action. She'd pinned her
wings, dived after the flailing girl, and swooped beneath
her. I'Lenna crashed onto the mare's back. She wrapped
her hands in Shysong's slick mane and pulled her legs
tight under her wings. I'Lenna's sides heaved as she wiped
away her tears.

Harak kicked Ilan into action, and they hurtled toward I'Lenna with five Riders following.

"Stop them," Hazelwind whinnied. He, Echofrost, Graystone, and Redfire charged toward Harak and his Fliers.

Ilan saw them coming and flattened his ears. "Incoming!" he neighed to the others.

Harak and two Pairs peeled off and dived toward the Kihlari steeds. "What do we do?" a Rider asked the blond Headwind.

"Kill the wildlings!" he shouted. "You others, arrest the princess, take her home, and lock her in the Eighth Tower."

Hazelwind neighed to Shysong. "Fly that girl back to her village. Then meet us at the nests. Hurry! It's time for us to go."

Harak nocked an arrow and loosed it at them.

"Scatter," Echofrost whinnied. The pegasi darted in four different directions, and the arrow missed all of them. They circled back on their attackers, diving in and striking the Riders.

Ilan whirled around and struck Graystone with his beaded tail. Thin scratches appeared on the white stallion. Graystone startled. "How did he do that?"

"Avoid their tails," Echofrost warned.

The pegasi ducked beneath the clumsy Kihlari, rearing and clubbing them with sharpened hooves as they passed overhead. Redfire opened a long gash across the flank of a chestnut mare.

"We don't want to hurt you," Echofrost whinnied to the Fliers.

Ilan snorted as each of their three Riders drew their swords. "Come closer and tell us that," he nickered, his blue eyes glinting.

Hazelwind soared straight up, flapping his wings in Ilan's face and kicking him square in the neck. Redfire struck the Flier's chest, and the spotted stallion lost his breath.

Meanwhile, Shysong and I'Lenna had disappeared into a massive dark cloud. Two of Harak's Riders had bolted in behind her. The clashing of hooves against bone reached Echofrost's sensitive ears. She powered toward the fight, panicked. "These Kihlari are just distracting us! Shysong needs our help!"

Black-edged blue feathers drifted down from the cloud mass as Echofrost neared the smoke-dark mist, ears cocked. Hazelwind and the others abandoned the fight with Harak and joined her.

"Listen," Echofrost nickered.

The wind rushed and the clouds shifted, but otherwise, silence.

"What happened to them?" Hazelwind wondered aloud. The four friends entered the rolling puff, instantly blinded. Echofrost swam through it, her wings creating holes that revealed the green valley below. She found emptiness. Where had they gone?

Harak and his Riders flew back toward the fighting in the valley. But where were Shysong and the princess? Echofrost brayed, but there was no answer. Had the two Riders captured them? Echofrost hoped that Shysong and the princess had escaped—that would explain the silence. The roan mare wouldn't want to give up her position by whinnying back to Echofrost.

Below, Harak pulled up next to Tuni and Rizah, and a heated argument erupted between the two Headwinds.

Echofrost whipped her eyes back to Rahkki on the cliff. He lay in a heap, surrounded by Fire Horde giants. She exhaled in frustration. He'd tried to save his princess, but now *he* was in trouble!

Hovering beside her friends, Echofrost listened to the wind rushing in the heights with her eyes locked on her cub. He'd saved her life more than once. She hadn't known that a pegasus and a person could be friends, but *he* had known. And he'd asked for nothing in return. She wanted to be free but realized she was helplessly bound—to Rah-kki. Not because of the Pairing ceremony or because he fed her—but because she cared about him.

Echofrost bent her wings and dived toward her Rider. The giants saw her coming and swarmed the boy. Rage shot through her. "Don't touch him!" she neighed. *He belongs to me.*

49

MUTINY

THE CLIFF SHOOK BENEATH RAHKKI'S BODY AS the giants thumped toward him. Sprawled on his back, he let out his breath. Sharp pain radiated outward from his ankle. His armor had saved his life, but he suspected that his bone had been fractured. He wondered about I'Lenna. She and Firo had entered the clouds, followed by two of Harak's warriors, and then they'd all seemed to vanish. Had they arrested I'Lenna, or were they still trying to catch her?

His silver mare shot down from the sky, her friends on her tail. They swooped to rescue him, but the Fire Horde king called his burners. The tiny little dragons collected, swarmed, and warded off the wild Kihlari with flames and steam. The wildlings retreated to the nearest ridge to watch, and the burners returned to Fire Horde, perching on the Gorlanders' arms and shoulders. Sula reared in frustration.

Meanwhile, the Fire Horde Gorlanders yanked Rahkki upright as the Highland Horde king climbed toward him, guiding his elephant up a steep mountain trail. The Highland prince followed. Even though Rahkki had saved the prince from the python, he didn't expect mercy. At least not until he revealed his latest trick—that he'd killed no giants.

Harak circled over the clan armies, grinning. "The princess is arrested."

Rahkki's blood pulsed between his ears. Had I'Lenna been captured that quickly?

"You all have a choice, yeah?" Harak said, facing the divided Sandwen armies below. "I won't seek remedies against you traitors if you pledge yourselves to Queen Lilliam right now. You hear me? I'll seek *no* remedies."

Tuni leaned forward. "You have no more power than I do, Harak. We'll decide as a group who is queen."

Harak kicked his stallion toward her. "Are you siding *against* me?" His Riders flew closer, menacing Tuni and Rizah. Around them, the rebel soldiers whispered in confusion and lowered their weapons. Both their leaders, General Tsun and Princess I'Lenna, were gone.

Tuni's eyes darted helplessly around her. Finally, she lowered her shoulders. "I'm not against you, Harak. I'll follow the rightful queen, whoever that may turn out to be."

Harak nodded to Tuni. "Good."

Rahkki stared up at the layered sky. The rain had stopped, and the clouds began to break apart, leaving no clue as to what had happened to I'Lenna or Firo.

Rahkki spotted his mare, Sula, still armored and looking exhausted. Unable to get past the giants, she and her wild friends had flown to an empty ridge and landed. Sula shuffled from hoof to hoof, watching him anxiously. She was free, so why didn't she fly away, he wondered.

Just then the Highland Horde king and his prince reached the top of the mountain dais. They dismounted their elephants with a resounding thud. The king strode toward Rahkki, speaking rapid Gorlish. The Fire Horde giants trudged back, making room for him. All eyes turned up.

Rahkki shouted to Tuni. "What's he saying?"

Tuni flew closer and watched the king's hands, translating word by word. "He's saying, '*When you saved my son from the python, we repaid you. We let you go.'"* Rahkki watched the king's fingers make a walking motion. *"'But you came back, and you destroyed Highland Horde.'"* The king exhaled, his breath rippling through Rahkki's hair.

Harak clutched his reins, his fists turning white. "You told us the snake attacked *you*, yeah. But you slaughtered it to save our *enemy*?"

Rahkki pretended not to hear Harak, training his eyes on the Highland king instead. The giant stared back at Rahkki, his eyes full of grief. In the valley below, his warriors' bodies littered the grass.

But Rahkki had *not* destroyed Highland Horde. "Translate for me, Tuni!" he shouted. "I'm not a giant slayer!" His voice cracked, rising higher when he said *slayer*.

The Gorlanders and the Sandwens stilled. Some laughed, and others shouted in retort.

Rahkki swallowed, sweating and tense. His eyes shot to the bodies he'd darted with his blowgun. He needed just a few more minutes, and then he would show them. He lifted his hands, stalling for time.

More grumbling arose from the Sandwen armies. Rahkki's gaze swept over his people—no one wanted war, did they? "We can have peace between our people and the giants," he declared.

"Why?" Harak asked. "We've defeated them, yeah."

"No." Rahkki shook his head. "We haven't."

"He's stalling," Harak shouted, then he hollered for his supporters. "Finish the hordes!"

"No!" Rahkki's voice ricocheted across the battlefield. Then he saw what he was waiting for, and he couldn't help it—he smiled. "Hold back and watch."

Harak gathered his soldiers, readying to massacre the remaining Gorlanders.

Tuni flew toward him. "Hear Rahkki out!" she ordered.

The Highland Horde king stomped toward the boy.

"Wait!" Rahkki threw up his hands. Just then the clouds parted, and a burst of sunshine stretched toward the trampled grass. Every warrior present squinted up at him.

What good timing, Rahkki thought. He limped to the edge of the cliff and spoke as Tuni returned to translating. "Giants!" he shouted. "Saber cats! Elephants! *Rise up!*"

"Rahkki, what are you doing?" Tuni cried.

He opened his palms. "Just a little magic."

50

DEATHLIFTER

"DID HE SAY MAGIC?" HARAK ASKED.

Tuni whipped her head around. The bodies strewn across the valley floor had begun to twitch. A fallen Gorlander near Tuni groaned. She guided Rizah away from it. Then another body moved. One lifted its head.

On the next ridge, Sula and her friends pricked their ears.

The watching hordes stared, their tusked mouths agape.

All around Rahkki, the giants, elephants, and saber cats that he'd nicked or pierced with his treated darts rose up and stood, shaking their heads and looking groggy.

Rahkki's huge grin widened as hundreds of creatures

seemed to come back to life magically. His plan had worked, and now the creatures he'd put to sleep were waking!

Rahkki lifted his arms higher as more sunshine lit the valley, drying the rain. A shocked growl rose in the throats of the giants.

A Sandwen warrior screamed and pointed at Rahkki. "Deathlifter!"

The Highland prince smiled, showing his yellowed tusks. *"You helped the hordes?"* the prince signed in Gorlish.

Rahkki nodded. *"Yes, I helped."*

Harak Nightseer, surrounded by waking enemies, urged his stallion off the ground. "Traitor! Giant lover!" He hurtled up the cliff face toward Rahkki. Flying no handed, he drew an arrow, his green eyes fixed on the boy.

"Don't, Harak!" Tuni chased the Headwind aboard Rizah.

Rahkki tried to run, but white-hot pain shot through his ankle and up his leg. Then a sharp neigh resounded from the ridge, and a flash of silver caught Rahkki's eye as Sula plunged headfirst toward him. Wings tucked, she raced Harak, who was flying up from the valley floor.

Ilan crested the cliff wall and hovered so Harak could nock his arrow, drawing a bead on Rahkki's neck. Harak meant to kill him—another Rider—in plain view of the armies! Unable to run, Rahkki threw up his hands to cover his face. The Highland prince roared. Tuni screamed.

Harak released the arrow.

Rahkki heard the twang, watched the missile slice toward him, and knew Harak would not miss. But then Sula's agile body darted between the arrow and Rahkki's neck. It slid between her armor and into her rib cage.

Rahkki jolted. "No!"

His mare gasped and swept past. The buckskin joined her, and they attacked Harak and Ilan.

But the Headwind was ready with another arrow, and another. He loosed them, striking the two magnificent steeds. Some arrows pinged off Sula's armor, others found their mark.

Rahkki lurched to his knees, tears blurring his vision. "SULA!" He drew his dagger and hurled it at Harak. It bounced off the man's armor and twirled back toward Rahkki, landing on the hard stone.

Sula faltered, wheezing for breath. The wild stallions gathered around her as she swam through the sky like a drowning horse. They supported her wings and lifted her back toward the ridge. The buckskin was injured too, but not as badly as Sula.

Fury sloshed through Rahkki's veins, blurring his vision. He crawled to the edge of the cliff and screamed at Harak, who had descended back toward the valley. "You shot my Flier!" The rocks crumbled around Rahkki, and he began to slide off the high cliff.

The Highland prince plucked Rahkki into his arms. Then the prince roared at the Sandwen armies, his voice shaking birds loose from the surrounding trees. His resurrected forces aimed their weapons.

Tuni pleaded with the Highland prince, speaking rapid Gorlish. She balked at his response. "He says he won't let you go, Rahkki."

Below them, the baffled and disorganized Fifth Clan soldiers and Riders gathered together. The sight of the revived Gorlan army had knocked the stuffing out of the Sandwens. Besides all that, the prize—the wild herd—had escaped. There was no profit left in staying and fighting.

"Leave Rahkki the Giant Lover here, yeah," Harak commanded. "That's an order."

At first, no one moved.

"Retreat," Harak repeated.

The Sky Guard and Land Guard armies turned and marched past the body of General Tsun. The fact that their leader remained dead when their enemies had come back to life stung the defeated rebels all the more because they didn't understand Rahkki's trick. The Sandwen soldiers turned frightened stares toward Rahkki the Deathlifter, the Commander of Dragons, and Lover of Giants. The small boy now lay folded in the arms of a Gorlan prince.

The prince motioned to his elephant, and the bull stomped across the dais and knelt. It regarded Rahkki with small, intelligent eyes.

The prince boarded his mount and spread Rahkki gently on top of its head. The bull's wrinkled skin was warm, his short hairs prickly. Rahkki tried to stand, but his ankle screamed in rebellion. Saliva filled his mouth, and the world tilted as waves of pain rolled through him. The prince held Rahkki still and urged his mount down the cliff path, heading back to the valley.

Tuni glided after them. Far below, Mut, Koko, Jul, and Tam hunched near a tree, weapons drawn, ready for anything.

"Where are you taking him?" Tuni signed to the king.

The prince flashed his terrifying Gorlish grin. *"To the soup."*

Tuni blanched. "He's taking you to his camp, Rahkki, to the *soup!*"

"Land to skies," Rahkki hissed. Everyone knew that Gorlanders ate Sandwens! Was the prince taking Rahkki to rescue him or to eat him? Suddenly he wasn't sure. "Help me, Tuni!"

She dived closer, but the king's warriors drove her easily away. "Meela!" she called for help.

"I said, leave him here," Harak warned Meela.

Tuni hovered aboard Rizah, her body shaking. Dusk Patrol surrounded their Headwind, awaiting her orders. "Rahkki!" Tuni screamed.

The boy turned, saw her anguish. "Tuni, go! Find I'Lenna," he cried. "Protect her."

Harak and his Riders surrounded Tuni. "Order your patrol home," Harak commanded.

She spat in Harak's face. "No."

Rahkki blanched as Harak and his Riders yanked Tuni off Rizah's back. She punched and kicked, but she was outnumbered. Harak flew her down to the Land Guard soldiers.

Rizah followed, whinnying sharp peals of alarm. All the Kihlari rattled their feathers in distress. Harak threw Tuni off his mount and she landed on the grass with a hard thud. "Tie the traitor up," he commanded.

Diving fast, Rizah attacked the Land Guard soldiers who grabbed Tuni. She clamped her jaws around a man's arm.

"Rizah, don't fight!" Tuni shouted.

Her mare tossed the man across the field and then kicked another.

A soldier, not more than a teen, shot an arrow at the angry pinto. It was a casual shot, meant to scare her off. But his aim was poor. The arrow lodged deep in Rizah's neck. The boy blanched and dropped his quiver.

"What have you done?" Tuni screamed.

The golden mare pinwheeled toward land and struck the grass. She toppled over, wheezing.

"March on!" Harak ordered.

"Sa jin, you heartless dragons." Tuni kicked and punched her captors.

"Put that Kihlara out of her misery," Harak ordered the teen soldier. "Finish what you started."

Heart racing, Rahkki watched the army depart from his vantage on top of the elephant. Tuni's stricken face and tangled red hair soon disappeared from view. The boy stood over Rizah, a new arrow nocked. Tears rolled down his cheeks.

But he couldn't shoot the mare. Instead, the young

soldier waited until the army was out of sight, and then he left the field. Rizah lurched to her hooves, choking and coughing. She limped slowly out of the valley and disappeared into the jungle. Between the scent of blood and her injuries, Rahkki doubted she'd survive the day.

Overhead, the Fire Horde giants retreated. The Great Cave Gorlanders whistled for their saber cats, and then disappeared into the shadowy caves from which they'd come. Soon the valley was vacant and only the truly dead remained.

And Sula.

Rahkki's silver Flier stood on the ridge, shedding her beautiful purple feathers, flanked by her friends. Their eyes locked across the distance.

"You're free," Rahkki called up to her. His lips curved into a weak smile at the word *free*. "Leave with your herd," he mouthed. Then Rahkki turned his back on her, hoping that whatever she did next, she did it for herself and not for him.

51

TOGETHER

ECHOFROST WHINNIED, A MOURNFUL, ANGUISHED cry. Rahkki was captured, Tuni was in the clutches of angry Sandwens, Rizah was wounded, and she didn't know what had happened to Shysong or the princess. But the Landwalkers were gone, and she took a deep, sobering breath.

Wing beats drew her attention skyward as Shysong fluttered down from the clouds, panting hard. "The Sandwens ripped I'Lenna right off my back." Tears slid from her ice-blue eyes. "I failed her."

"Rahkki is gone too," Echofrost lamented, and the two mares pressed their foreheads together, shocked by the day's events.

"You're hurt," Shysong cried, noticing the arrows that quivered from Echofrost's flesh.

"It's nothing," she lied.

Hazelwind, who also wore several arrows scattered across his body, danced on the rough stone. "We need a medicine mare."

"Dewberry's the closest we have," Redfire nickered. "Her mother was a medicine mare and taught her much." The five pegasi stared at one another, aghast at their failure to bring a practiced healer across the Dark Water with them.

"Dewberry can't help me; she needs to focus on her coming foals." Echofrost drew shallow breaths, and her legs trembled to hold her body upright. "At least we're free," she nickered, but the victory suddenly felt hollow and lonely.

Hazelwind flared his wings. "Let's get to the nests, where Dewberry and the others are waiting."

"Can she fly?" Shysong asked. Harak's arrow had pierced Echofrost's lung. They all heard the air whistling out of her.

Hazelwind peered at Echofrost from beneath his long, black forelock. Then he nuzzled her as tears filled his eyes. "You were right. You were always right, Echofrost. What sort of herd are we if we abandon each other? I'm sorry I deserted Shysong when she was first captured."

Echofrost gulped a breath. "Shh," she said, "It doesn't matter now."

"It does matter. When we fail one, we fail all."

He exhaled, and she smelled Dawn Meadow: sweet grass, a flowered breeze, and the feathers of her family— home. And it struck her that she'd always been free. She'd chosen to let the Sandwens capture her—twice. She'd chosen to bind herself to Rahkki Stormrunner. She'd chosen to cross the Dark Water. Freedom was about having choices, and she had them still, even as she leaned against Hazelwind, dying. "Save Rahkki for me, please, if I can't."

A great sob choked the stallion. "Don't—don't talk like that. I'm with you, Echofrost. I'm with you forever."

She sighed, and more air rushed from her deflating lung.

Shysong threw up her head. "Wait! We do have a healer," she whinnied. "Brim Carver—she's a Sandwen healer."

"A Landwalker?" Redfire neighed.

"Yes," the roan answered. "We must get Echofrost back to the Fifth Clan village, quickly. Brim will save her."

"What about the others waiting at the nests?" Gray-stone asked.

Hazelwind lashed his black tail. "We'll collect them on the way. From now on, we stick together. All of us!"

"What are we waiting for, let's go," Redfire whinnied. Graystone and Hazelwind gripped the roots of Echofrost's wings, and Redfire gripped the base of her tail in his teeth. The three stallions lifted her, and they flew west.

Echofrost groaned softly, her thoughts tumbling.

As they flew across the peaks of Mount Crim, they passed the Highland Horde encampment. The giants had kidnapped her cub, and she didn't know why. She peered between the drifting clouds, trying to catch sight of the boy.

Here she was again, in need of an army to free a friend. How had her quest for freedom across the Dark Water led to so much captivity? Fresh misery stormed through her and Echofrost's thoughts drifted to Dewberry. The foals were coming soon, what awful timing! She glanced down at herself. Harak's arrow wobbled from her rib cage; it had sliced between two plates of armor. The pain hadn't fully registered—not yet.

But Echofrost was done making promises she couldn't keep. If she survived, she would return to save Rahkki.

He was not a pegasus, but he was her Rider and she was his Flier; and suddenly, without him, she felt like a Half.

She glanced at Hazelwind. "Don't let me die, not yet."

Grief closed his throat. "You won't," he rasped. "Remember what I said? From now on, we stick together. *All* of us."

His words filled her heart. Whatever happened next, she wouldn't suffer it alone. Comforted, Echofrost felt her body relax. And then the world blackened as her eyelids closed.

↪ACKNOWLEDGMENTS↩

THANK YOU FOR READING *THROUGH THE UNTAMED Sky*! Authors write alone, but we don't publish alone. I'm grateful for enthusiastic support from a team of highly talented people at HarperCollins Children's Books. Executive editor Karen Chaplin is my first point of contact, and she oversees every aspect of production for The Guardian Herd and the Riders of the Realm series. It is my goal to write a book as worthy as possible for Karen, for the team, and for the readers. I hope you enjoyed the result!

I also want to thank the first two publishing professionals who believed in me—my agent, Jacqueline Flynn at Delbourgo Associates, and HarperCollins Editorial Director Rosemary Brosnan. I remain forever thankful. We all need someone to hear us on our tiny speck of dust.

Extra special thanks to the interior artist, David McClellan, and the cover illustrator, Vivienne To. You bring imaginations to life with your brilliant minds and clever hands. I'm ever in awe.

Lastly, I'm grateful to the books' fans. I receive hundreds of pegasi drawings and fan emails and letters each year. I love hearing about your pets, viewing your artwork, and knowing that kids around the world—from Singapore, to Australia, to Denmark, to North Pole (a little town in Alaska)—are meeting Star, Morningleaf, Rahkki, and I'Lenna. Your letters and comments encourage me.

To join in the fun, please visit theguardianherd.com. There you can play herd games, take book quizzes, view the series' maps, see fan art, fan pets, and read interviews with some of the team. If you want to know more about the supernatural black stallion named Star, begin with book one of The Guardian Herd series: *Starfire*.

Your author, Jennifer Lynn Alvarez

Turn the page for a sneak peek
at the final action-packed novel in
the RIDERS OF THE REALM trilogy

1

THE SOUP

"LET ME GO," RAHKKI SIGNED. HIS MOTHER HAD taught him the silent language of the giants when he was a toddler, and he was grateful for it now. The Highland prince had captured him and was taking Rahkki to his soup cauldron—whether to feed him or eat him, Rahkki wasn't sure.

The prince ignored Rahkki's plea as they traversed a weed-strewn plateau aboard an elephant. Rahkki peered over the bull's head. Jagged peaks sawed the skyline that surrounded the Highland encampment, which was a flat mesa sliced across otherwise rugged terrain. Beyond the camp, tame elephants foraged in a trampled clearing and

3

the sky spanned overhead, a smear of blue between the mountains.

"I saved your life," Rahkki mumbled. The giants didn't understand his Sandwen language, but just yesterday Rahkki had saved this Gorlan prince from being eaten by a snake. *He* should be grateful!

The prince's blue eyes narrowed. His breath whooshed in a rumbling snarl.

Highland Horde had just returned from war with Rahkki's clan over the release of the wild Kihlari steeds. Queen Lilliam had dispatched the Fifth Clan armies to rescue the rare animals so she could sell them. However, the wild herd had escaped during the battle and flown away. Rahkki was glad about this. His Flier, Sula, was finally free.

But the wild herd's freedom was the only good thing that had come from that battle. In the middle of it, civil war had erupted between the Sandwens loyal to Queen Lilliam and the rebels who were loyal to her eldest daughter, Princess I'Lenna. I'Lenna's side had lost and Harak had arrested her after killing her most loyal supporter, General Tsun.

Rahkki sighed. Everything had gone wrong and he had to get home. He turned his golden eyes toward the

Highland prince. *"Let me go,"* he repeated. *"Please."*

The prince chuffed, sounding to Rahkki like a jungle tiger. They entered the Highland camp and giants approached from every direction when they spied their prince. They beat the mossy stone and roared like thunderclouds, gesturing to one another in rapid Gorlish.

Rahkki flinched, and sparkling pain shot through his injured ankle. Fire Horde giants had fractured it when he'd tried to protect I'Lenna from them, and Sula had been injured too. She'd taken an arrow meant for Rahkki. Truly, nothing had gone as he'd expected.

He scanned the patchy blue skies, hoping Sula's injury wouldn't prevent her from leaving the Realm with her wild herd. His belly tightened with worry.

Trailing behind Rahkki and the prince were wounded Highland warriors and their elephants, straggling into camp. Several giants ran to help their hordemates while the prince continued on with Rahkki. Soon they arrived at the massive cauldron of soup that simmered over a low flame. A huge shade structure loomed above it, protecting the broth from rain and sun.

"Daanath! Daanath!" the giants signed in Gorlish. Rahkki didn't know what the word meant, but understood that it was the Highland prince's name or title, or both.

Daanath curled his lips, showing the full length of his yellowed tusks. His horde gathered closer, growing silent and expectant. Some drooled, others licked their lips. Rahkki, who had been raised on Fifth Clan warnings, feared the worst.

Be home by dark or the giants will eat you.

Take your bath or the giants will smell you.

Go to sleep or the giants will hear you.

Next, the Highland king emerged from his tent and a hush fell over the encampment. Rahkki knew from listening to his brother, Brauk, that Gorlan princes led raids and commanded warriors under the watchful eyes of their kings. Kings also enforced horde laws.

Prince Daanath dipped his head toward his gigantic sire, and Rahkki's eyes drifted up the king's wide girth and thick chest, to his graying red hair. He plodded across the flat mesa, tusks bared, and sank his heavy body onto a seat that had been carved from a great boulder. He turned his attention to the soup.

Bubbles popped on the surface of the broth, releasing a scent that, surprisingly, wasn't awful. *How will it taste with me in it*, Rahkki wondered. A light breeze ruffled his hair, carrying the faint scent of rain.

The horde passed stacks of empty bowls to one another,

forming a circle around the cauldron. The toddlers, some as tall as Rahkki, leaped up and down, rumbling happily and clutching their bowls to their chests.

They're excited to eat me, Rahkki thought. Fresh pain erupted from his fractured ankle and crackled up his leg. He flopped over and vomited all over the prince's callused fingers.

The Gorlander swapped Rahkki to his cleaner hand and wiped the dirty one on his loincloth. But he continued stomping toward the soup.

"*Stop*," Rahkki gestured.

They reached the rim of the pot. The chuffing and roaring ceased.

"*Help me*," Rahkki signed, throwing the same words at the prince that the prince had used when the python had attacked him.

Daanath didn't respond.

Land to skies! Rahkki had saved countless lives—both human and giant—during the day's battle. He'd shot the giants using darts treated with powerful medicine. He'd fooled everyone into thinking he was a mighty warrior by putting Gorlan warriors temporarily to sleep. This had prevented much bloodshed, and when the quick-acting sedative wore off, the giants had risen, unharmed.

But, as usual, Rahkki's plans seemed to have back-fired. His clan had called him a *Deathlifter*, the most terrifying type of sorcerer, and they'd abandoned him. And now this horde wanted to eat him. It didn't seem fair, honestly. *Don't wish for life to be fair, Rahkki*—this was one of his uncle's favorite sayings, and Rahkki sighed because he couldn't stop wishing it.

The youngest giants grew restless and began slapping their hands against the bottoms of their carved wooden soup bowls, creating a unique and complicated rhythm. The beat swelled as each member of the horde drummed, adding to the song until it culminated in a deafening cre-scendo that abruptly ended. The giants plopped down all at once.

Just get it over with and toss me into the soup, Rahkki wanted to shout. Large logs glowed red beneath the caul-dron and the steady heat warmed his face.

Prince Daanath finally set Rahkki down. Rahkki peeked at the rain forest that surrounded the mesa. If his ankle weren't busted, he'd run for it.

Six lanky Gorlanders approached the cauldron, wield-ing ladles. They dipped them into the soup and then trod around the circle, filling the bowls.

Rahkki stared at his human-sized serving, exhaling in

relief and horror. They weren't going to eat him; they were going to feed him. Neither option was ideal. Green and brown lumps floated on the surface of the yellow broth. Rahkki couldn't make out if the lumps were flesh, roots, vegetables, or all of that. What if there were Sandwens in this soup? His belly shrank, but his mouth watered. He'd missed lunch, after all, and the soup's scent was surprisingly good.

The prince motioned toward his mouth, and Rahkki recognized the Gorlish word *eat*. His mother had used it often when Rahkki was young.

He shook his head. "*No, thank you.*" Perhaps if he refused it, they'd offer him something else. Something less . . . disgusting.

The prince snarled at Rahkki so loudly that the boy covered his ears. "*Eat,*" he repeated.

Rahkki's blood drained toward his toes. Suddenly he understood why Queen Lilliam had refused to eat it when the Gorlanders had come to parlay for their ancient farmland. Maybe it *wasn't* because Lilliam didn't speak Gorlish, maybe it was because the soup was bloody disgusting and she didn't want to be a cannibal! "*No eat,*" he signed, wishing he knew their language better.

The prince slammed the mesa with both fists. The

black cauldron rocked and the horde screeched. Rahkki scooted away from Daanath, crawling like a three-legged crab.

Signing fluidly, the prince spoke to him while the horde waited. Rahkki stared at the prince's fingers, trying to understand. Around him stomachs grumbled and drool seeped, but not one Gorlander touched the soup. It dawned on him that the horde would not eat until he did. *They're trying to honor me*, he realized.

Rahkki knew his mother, Reyella Stormrunner, the past Queen of the Fifth, would never refuse this honor. He inched closer to his bowl, glancing up at Prince Daanath. The beast curled his lips again, showing the full length of his sharp tusks. Was he smiling or snarling? *Did it matter?* If Rahkki didn't eat the soup, the horde would only get hungrier waiting on him. They might change their minds and toss him into the pot after all.

"Okay," he said, breathing through his mouth. He lifted the bowl to his lips, and the entire horde leaned closer and excited grumbling buzzed around the circle.

Warm soup flowed toward Rahkki's throat. He slurped a mouthful, chewed the lumps, and swallowed. He'd expected to vomit, but instead wonderful flavors burst across his tongue, making him gasp.

The horde exhaled in a collective sigh of satisfaction.

Rahkki drank more. Delicate seasonings spiced the savory broth and it slid smoothly down his gullet, causing his eyes to roll with pleasure. Never in his life had he tasted anything so good, so comforting.

All around him the giants roared their approval and tipped their bowls to their mouths.

The more Rahkki drank, the more he wanted, and his entire body hummed as the nutrition flooded his bloodstream and raced through his limbs. The pain in his ankle subsided and contentment filled him. He finished the entire bowl and then licked the side. When he was finished, he reclined on the stone, lost in a stupor of satisfaction.

The horde also finished and then broke their circle to return to their camp duties. The children gathered around Rahkki, breathing loudly. He recognized the prince's flame-haired daughter. She and her brothers had attended the Sandwen parlay with their sire. That peace negotiation had failed as miserably as I'Lenna's more recent one.

Rahkki shifted his attention back to the prince. *"I go home now?"* he signed.

The giant shook his head. *"The three hordes are meeting to discuss your clan. You will attend the meeting."*

Rahkki didn't catch every word, but he understood well enough and melted into the stone. *"Why? When?"*

"Soon," the prince answered without further elaboration.

"But I can't wait."

The prince slammed down his fist. *"You can wait."*

Rahkki narrowed his eyes. Why did the hordes want to meet with *him*? He had no power, nothing to say.

Daanath's clawed hand swept toward him and, moments later, he deposited Rahkki into what appeared to be a Gorlish healing tent. Everything inside was Gorlan sized—the tools, the containers, the cabinets, and the wooden cots. Rahkki recognized special herbs hanging from the ceiling and rolled bandages, supplies similar to those used by Brim Carver, the Fifth Clan's healer. Wounded warriors lay strewn on cots and across the floor. They grunted at Rahkki, not quite as accepting of the Sandwen boy as their unscathed hordemates.

The healers, two old Gorlanders, one male and one female, nodded receipt of Rahkki, and Prince Daanath exited the tent, leaving him alone with them. The male giant scooped Rahkki onto a huge gurney, felt his fractured bone, and then gathered cloth wraps from a bin, cutting them into boy-sized pieces.

Rahkki sat up, confused and curious. It seemed the giants were going to treat his wounds. But why? So far, their behavior was shocking and unexpected—it went against everything he had been taught about giants. Rahkki still wasn't sure he could trust their kindness but saw no profit in rejecting it. Through an open tent flap, he watched the sun drop fast in the western sky, casting the clouds in scorching hues of orange and pink. Outside, the Gorlanders went about their evening business, grunting and stomping and playing reed pipes.

As the healer splinted and wrapped Rahkki's ankle, Rahkki remembered Sula's bravery when she'd taken Harak's arrow to protect him. She'd been using Rahkki to save her friends from the hordes—he knew that—but he'd never guessed she truly *cared*. She'd proved she did when she risked her life for his. Rahkki clenched his fists, hoping she was safe.

The Gorlan giant had just finished casting Rahkki's ankle when a ruckus outside startled all of them. Giants beat the ground and rumbled. Rahkki's medical cot shook. *This is it*, he thought. *They're coming to kill me.* He tensed, waiting.

Another flap swept open and two giants carried a feathered creature into the massive tent. Fresh claw marks raked her gold-and-white flank and an arrow jutted from her throat.

"Rizah!" Rahkki scrambled out of his cot and crawled toward the Kihlara mare. This was his friend Tuni Hightower's Flier. A young Sandwen soldier had shot Rizah after Harak ordered Tuni arrested during the Sandwen uprising. The boy had been trying to scare Rizah off, but his aim was poor and his arrow had pierced her throat.

Rahkki stroked the golden pinto's forelock. "Shh, Rizah," he whispered to the mare. Her green eyes, glassy with pain, met his and brightened with recognition. She tried to nicker and her throat rattled. "Shh," he repeated.

He studied the claw marks in her flank and exhaled dizzily. A jaguar had attacked her, drawn by her weakness, no doubt. The giants must have found her and carried her to their camp. More unexpected kindness! Everything Rahkki thought he knew about the giants swirled in his mind, a confusing jumble when compared to what he was witnessing firsthand. He couldn't wait to tell his uncle and his brother, Brauk, about it.

The female healer prepped an awl and sinew and set about removing Rizah's arrow and treating the wound. The male healer cleaned the claw marks on her flank and dressed them in salve. Rizah's eyelids flickered as she lost consciousness. When they'd finished treating her, the healers layered a bed of furs on the floor and gently placed the golden pinto on top of them.

Rahkki curled beside her. "You're going to be okay," he whispered. Her breathing was shallow and marked by wheezing. He doubted she would have survived another moment alone in the jungle. Rahkki's heart swelled, overcome with gratitude. He grunted to draw all the healers' attention. "*Thank you*," he signed, and they nodded.

But Rahkki remained suspicious. *Was* this kindness, or were the giants healing him and Rizah for a darker purpose? His mother had believed that the hordes could be allies, and maybe she was right, but his mother was gone.

Rahkki rolled onto his back, feeling drowsy. All the Fifth Clan's troubles had begun eight years ago when Lilliam had attempted to assassinate Reyella and failed. His mother had reached the docks of Daakur, very pregnant with her third child and traveling with two Sandwen guards, but there her trail had gone cold. No one knew where she was now, or if her unborn child had survived.

Eyes watering, Rahkki turned his thoughts toward Sula. He and his mount had Paired and now she was gone. As glad as he was for her new freedom, the pain of it stabbed his heart, sharper than any arrow. He imagined her soft gray muzzle, her dark eyes, and her powerful wings. They'd worked hard to understand each other. She'd accepted a bit and armor and let him ride on her back. She'd reminded him that he did love to fly! Rahkki could feel the pleasant looping sensation in his belly as he remembered her sharpened hooves pushing off the grass, her nose angled toward the clouds, and her agile purple wings shaping the wind. Sula—his Flier, his protector.

From the first moment he'd spotted her wild herd flying above his territory, hopes and dreams had blossomed within him. Clan elders had taught him that no wild Kihlari existed anymore, but they'd been wrong, and maybe they were wrong about the giants too.

As the Gorlanders rumbled and chuffed around him, and the crickets launched into their evening chorus, Rahkki snuggled tight against Rizah. He dreamed of his own mount, wondering where Sula was and if she missed him half as much as he missed her.

2

THE FIFTH CLAN

HAZELWIND, REDFIRE, AND GRAYSTONE CARRIED
Echofrost by her wings and tail, flying her just above the
treetops. The Storm Herd steeds glided beside her, casting nervous glances at their silver friend. Harak's arrow
had slid neatly between a gap in Echofrost's armor and
pierced her lung. Beside her, pregnant Dewberry panted
hard. The round weight of her belly drew down her hind-
quarters, causing her to fly at an almost upright angle.

Echofrost moaned. "What happened to Rahkki?" she
whinnied.

"Don't speak," Dewberry nickered. "We're far from
your Landwalker friend."

Echofrost's eyes slid toward the pinto mare's stretched

17

belly and pinched expression, and she guessed Dewberry
had entered the early stages of labor. She glanced back
toward Mount Crim, the home of the Gorlan giants. The
massive ranges reached toward the clouds, forming a bar-
rier around its plateaus and valleys.

Her Rider, Rahkki Stormrunner, was trapped somewhere in those mountains. She imagined his golden eyes
and gentle hands, his chattering voice. Rahkki's people
had abandoned him to their enemies, the giants. Her
heart walloped with familiar fury and disappointment.
How could they leave such a young cub behind? She tossed
her mane. Actually, she *did* know how they could do it.

When she was a weanling in Anok—her homeland
across the Dark Water ocean—she'd been abandoned too.
A foreign herd had stolen her and another colt because
they'd trespassed. Her herd had decided not to risk a war
to rescue them. Eventually, the foreign steeds had let her
go, but Echofrost had suffered horrific bullying from their
yearlings.

And after crossing the Dark Water and landing on
this continent, the Fifth Clan people had captured the
roan mare named Shysong. Hazelwind and the others had
decided not to risk Storm Herd in order to save her, so
Echofrost had gone back to rescue Shysong on her own.

She didn't understand the point of a herd or a clan if they didn't fight to save each member. One might as well live alone! But now Hazelwind had promised that they would stick together, all of them. She gasped for air; afraid she'd pass out again in the heights.

Below her dangling hooves, the palm trees swayed and the jungle creatures quieted as the winged shadows of Storm Herd passed over them. The static-filled sky had darkened, the clouds once again piling high and threatening rain.

Still dressed in the Sandwen armor Rahkki had given her, Echofrost knew her body was heavy. "We're almost there," she nickered, encouraging the friends who supported her.

"There it is," Hazelwind whinnied through a mouthful of feathers.

Ahead, the Fifth Clan village rolled into view. Small torches brightened the Sandwen settlement like fallen stars. The Landwalkers had carved the chaotic jungle into organized pathways, built stone dens, corralled animals, grown food in perfectly aligned rows, and tamed an ancient herd of pegasi, turning them into flying warhorses.

"Are they going to attack us?" Graystone asked,

glancing nervously at her and Hazelwind's wounds. Harak's arrows had punctured each of them.

"I don't think they'll hurt us," Echofrost answered, "but they might try to catch us."

"What's the difference?" Dewberry huffed.

"You're right, we'll land in the jungle," Echofrost decided. "Brim will have to come to me."

Her friends were carrying Echofrost to Brim Carver, the Fifth Clan's healer. It was Shysong's idea. The roan mare had lived with the Sandwens long enough to know that Brim was a talented and gentle healer, and she was one of the few Landwalkers Echofrost and Shysong had learned to trust. Storm Herd had quickly agreed, hoping Brim could repair the hole in Echofrost's lung.

"I'll fetch her," Shysong nickered. "Brim knows me."

The pegasi quickly descended and landed outside the settlement. Beneath the wind-brushed jungle canopy, singing insects, calling parrots, and hooting primates performed their daily chorus. Hazelwind, Redfire, and Graystone lowered Echofrost as gently to the soft soil as possible. Still, she grunted on impact.

"Sorry," Hazelwind nickered. He anxiously swiveled his ears, and Echofrost leaned against her best friend.